THE NOVEL AS AMERICAN SOCIAL HISTORY

RICHARD LOWITT, GENERAL EDITOR

THE CIRCUIT RIDER

THE CIRCUIT RIDER

A TALE OF THE HEROIC AGE

BY

EDWARD EGGLESTON

INTRODUCTION BY

HOLMAN HAMILTON

THE UNIVERSITY PRESS OF KENTUCKY

LEXINGTON 1970

INTRODUCTION

by Holman Hamilton

Edward Eggleston was born in Vevay, Switzerland County, Indiana, on December 10, 1837. Like so many Hoosier literary figures, he had southern antecedents, his father being a Virginian and his mother's family Kentuckian. Principally because of ill health, Eggleston never went to college. But he did attend school for a number of years in several counties of southern Indiana and for some months in Virginia.

At least as important as his formal schooling, from the standpoint of his subsequent career, was Eggleston's familiarity with backwoods life and dialect, dating from a period of his youth when he lived in rustic Decatur County, Indiana. Other details of frontier life and education came from a younger brother who taught school at Ryker's Ridge. These first- and second-hand experiences supplied many of the raw materials that went into Eggleston's first and most famous book. Written in 1871 when he was thirty-three years old, *The Hoosier School-Master* had a generally favorable reception. It was largely responsible for establishing its author as one of America's leading local colorists and early realists in the field of fiction. A second novel, *The End of the World,* was written in 1872; a third, *The Mystery of Metropolisville,* in 1872-1873; and a fourth, *The Circuit Rider,* in 1873.[1] By the standards of the day, all were successful.

Thus far, this account makes Eggleston's literary progress

sound wonderfully easy and uncomplicated. Actually, it was nothing of the sort. To be sure, he believed and later acknowledged that his basic "desire for literary production must have been innate."[2] But problems and convictions of a religious nature also affected Edward's outlook in numerous ways. Stepson of a Methodist minister whom he greatly admired, the adolescent passed through a series of cycles of intensive soul-searching and exaltation. "Two manner of men were in me," and young Eggleston found himself beset by "fits of moral ardor in which my literary pursuits seemed a sort of idolatry."[3] All this before he was nineteen.

As if the mental and spiritual tug-of-war were not challenging enough, Eggleston suffered in his teens from at least three ailments—malaria, an almost constant cough, and insomnia. He either had tuberculosis or was on the edge of it. At eighteen, he was feared to be dying. Pale and desperate, Eggleston headed for Minnesota in hope that the climate would prove salubrious. For a time, the experiment worked wonders; he returned home "sun-browned and well," and took a crucial step in his life by becoming a Methodist minister. Yet he was not well enough to bear up under the strain of six months as a circuit rider in Dearborn County, Indiana. Again "I was . . . a candidate for the grave." And again he went out to Minnesota, partly for the sake of his health and partly to continue his Methodist ministry in a place where he thought he could serve God effectively—"doing the hardest task I could find."[4]

This time, Eggleston stayed in Minnesota nine years, but he did not enjoy robust health then or at any time thereafter. Every so often, in need of rest, he would be

---

[1] William P. Randel, *Edward Eggleston* (New York, 1946), pp. 3-13, 121-44.
[2] Edward Eggleston, "Formative Influences," *The Forum* 10 (November 1890): 281.
[3] Ibid., p. 285.
[4] Ibid., pp. 288-89.

compelled to give up pastoral and other duties. Yet overall his activity was prodigious. Preaching in the lake-dotted Minnesota countryside and in the villages and growing towns, Eggleston also worked as a Bible salesman, manufactured soap, sold insurance, ran a library, and exhibited photographic transparencies. Some of his vocational endeavors were motivated by the need for money to support the wife he married in Minnesota and their growing family.

During these years, Eggleston read poetry, history, plays, and fiction with enthusiasm and absorption, and found himself increasingly propelled by the creative literary drives of his youth. The early "innate . . . desire for literary production" gradually reasserted itself and eventually became dominant. As early as 1865, the twenty-seven-year-old Eggleston's "Round Table Stories" for children began appearing in *The Little Corporal*, a Chicago juvenile publication. The next year, he made a break from pastoral to editorial work. Moving to Evanston, Illinois, he was at first employed by the *Corporal* as a contributor-editor. Then his religious and literary interests fused when he made a fine record for several years as editor of the *Sunday School Teacher*. At length, he moved to the New York area, joining the editorial staff of *The Independent* before being invited to take charge of another periodical, *Hearth and Home*.

In the brief span of the next twenty-seven months, Eggleston contributed over a hundred stories, articles, poems, and editorials to *Hearth and Home*. The same period also saw three of his novels published in serial form in the magazine.[5] Eggleston's pen was never more facile. When the decision was made to bring out *The Hoosier School-Master* in book form, he had doubts as to its probable success; however, within half a year over 10,000 copies were

[5] Randel, *Edward Eggleston,* pp. 42-121, 284-92.

sold. Although the praise accorded the slender volume was not without reservations, *Harper's, Scribner's* and the *Christian Union* had favorable things to say. "Mr. Eggleston," declared William Dean Howells in the *Atlantic Monthly*, "is the first to touch in fiction the kind of life he has represented, and we imagine that future observers will hardly touch it at more points." While the plot and characters might not be fully developed, Howells continued, such criticism was less germane than emphasis on Eggleston's achievement in presenting "a picture of manners hitherto strange to literature."[6]

While southern Indiana supplied the background for his first two novels, Eggleston constructed *The Mystery of Metropolisville* in and around a Minnesota boom town with numerous place names thinly veiled and—as in *School-Master*—some localities and people not veiled at all. In the aggregate, critics received *Metropolisville* less enthusiastically than its predecessors. Its raggedness contrasted with the freshness of *School-Master* and what Howells termed the "poetic elements" of *The End of the World*. Nevertheless, there is a deep vein of meaning in the *Metropolisville* preface. "I have wished," the author wrote, "to make my stories of value as a contribution to the history of civilization in America."[7] As the admiring Meredith Nicholson pointed out in the year of Eggleston's death, 1902, when Eggleston's novels "cease to entertain as fiction they will [still] teach as history."[8]

In the context of American fiction's relationship to social history, few studies are as fascinating or revealing as Eggleston's *The Circuit Rider*, which was first serialized in the *Christian Union* and then published as a book in 1874.

[6] *Atlantic Monthly* 29 (March 1872): 363-64.
[7] Edward Eggleston, *The Mystery of Metropolisville* (New York, 1873), p. 7.
[8] Meredith Nicholson, "Edward Eggleston," *Atlantic Monthly* 90 (December 1902): 804.

A résumé of characters and plot barely begins to suggest the book's significance. Its hero, Morton Goodwin, is a young man who at first scoffs at the Methodist Church, drinks, gambles, nearly loses his life, is converted to Methodism, and thereafter is an exemplary minister and circuit rider. The heroine, Patty Lumsden, is the charming Episcopalian daughter of the southern Ohio locale's largest landowner and meanest man. Her young cousin, Hezekiah ("Kike") Lumsden, is at once the volume's most vivid character and a lad who comprehends Methodist joys and glories long before the light dawns for Mort.

The life of a nineteenth-century circuit rider was hard. Men assigned to such ministries were expected to make physical and financial sacrifices virtually beyond the comprehension of Sunday-only Christians in eastern urban centers. For weeks at a stretch they rode into the wilderness, facing dangers and privations, threatened by criminals, ridiculed by the scornful, rarely finding rest on successive nights in the same cabin or on the same pallet. The steadfast faith of those zealous preachers, the joy they found in converting fellow mortals, their courage, their moral fiber, their weatherbeaten faces, their clothes, horses, saddlebags, language, manners, and customs—all are graphically set forth in *The Circuit Rider*. The book contains much else— a bit of symbolism, the element of twice-mistaken identity, humor personalized in an Irish pedagogue, drama, pathos, an attractive female sinner, ruffians, vigilantes, and of course the emotion-charged camp meetings where so many conversions took place. But it is in the depiction of something approaching the totality of the frontier minister's life and his day-to-day surroundings that the real strength of Eggleston's contribution lies.

Affected by the adverse criticism in the reviews of *Metropolisville*, Eggleston devoted more time to *The Circuit Rider* and composed it with greater care than his earlier

X   INTRODUCTION

books.[9] With faithfulness to fact he describes a corn-shucking at Cap'n Lumsden's, refers to "carding and spinning,
winding and weaving, cutting and sewing to get a new
linsey dress," and attires his hero in a "picturesque coon-
skin cap," buckskin breeches, and rawhide boots. From
memory he recreates a "wide old log-kitchen, with its loom
in one corner, its vast fireplace . . . [and] bark-covered
joists overhead, from which are festooned strings of drying
pumpkins." In the backwoods, the author asks, "Did you
ever observe the stillness, the solitude, the softness of sunshine, the gentleness of wind, the chip-chip-chlurr-r-r of
great flocks of blackbirds getting ready for migration? . . .
the lazy cawing of crows? . . . the half-laughing bark of
cunning squirrel, nibbling his prism-shaped beech-nut. . .?"[10]

A present-day reader of *The Circuit Rider* may wonder
about the values critics then found in Eggleston's use of
dialect, details of clothing, or descriptions of woods and
kitchens, so familiar to moderns through later literature and
recorded history as well as through movies and television.
The fact is that, as the *Nation* pointed out, such scenes
were then "almost entirely new to the Eastern reader and
the new generation of Westerners." According to Nicholson,
"But for Eggleston's tales there would be no trustworthy
record of the period" in the region he described.[11]

For Eggleston's depiction of Methodism on the southern
Ohio frontier before the War of 1812, commentators have
made much of his reliance on and use of the Reverend
Jacob Young's *Autobiography of a Pioneer*.[12] It is true that,

[9] Randel, *Edward Eggleston*, pp. 141-42.
[10] Edward Eggleston, *The Circuit Rider: A Tale of the Heroic Age*
(New York, 1874), pp. 10-19, 33.
[11] *Nation* 19 (24 September 1874): 207; Nicholson, "Edward
Eggleston," p. 807.
[12] Randel, *Edward Eggleston*, p. 141. The full title is *Autobiography of a Pioneer: or, the Nativity, Experience, Travels, and
Ministerial Labors of Rev. Jacob Young* (Cincinnati, 1857).

at the outset of his notetaking for *The Circuit Rider* and
during the writing of early drafts, Eggleston leaned rather
heavily on Young; at one place in the notes he exclaimed,
"Young is full of suggestion—the best autobiographist of
all."[13] Some of the real-life personages in *The Circuit Rider*
—Bishop Asbury for instance—are featured in Young's
volume. Cap'n Lumsden's plight as a victim of "the jerks"
developed partly from Young's pages, and a Tennessee
evangelist "who wore himself out & died in five years"[14] may
have been a prototype of Preacher "Kike."

Without a doubt, Young's *Autobiography* at first was of
substantial aid to Eggleston. But, once under way, Eggleston developed and shaped the story as a creative enterprise
in accordance with his own techniques. To a degree, *The
Circuit Rider* benefited from Young's reminiscences in much
the same way as *The Hoosier School-Master* had benefited
from George Cary Eggleston's teaching experiences. Yet, as
the younger brother explained in 1886, Edward Eggleston
"was by nature too true an artist to adhere" rigidly to a
preconceived "photographic plan."[15] Long before he reached the halfway mark in his rough drafts, Eggleston's artistry
took over.

It was that artistry reinforced by hard work which led
Howells to assert in the *Atlantic* that *The Circuit Rider*
represented "a vast advance" upon Eggleston's earlier
stories.[16] *Scribner's*, edited by J. G. Holland, fully concurred
and had more to say than the *Atlantic* about the reasons for

13 Notes for *The Circuit Rider*, entry of 22 March 1873, Eggleston
Papers, Collection of Regional History and University Archives, Cor-
nell University, Ithaca, New York.

14 Ibid., entries of 20 and 22 March 1873.

15 James A. Rawley, "Some New Light on Edward Eggleston,"
American Literature 11 (January 1940): 457.

16 *Atlantic Monthly* 33 (June 1874): 745. While Howells in a
kindly manner criticized an authorial "blemish" or two, he praised
the book as a whole and quoted at some length from it.

improvement: *"The Circuit Rider* is in every way the best" of Eggleston's books. "As a study of backwoods life, it is more careful and real than *The Hoosier School-Master.* Its characters are drawn with a hand that has gained in firmness, and its action is more consistent and vigorous than . . . in any of his previous novels. . . . This is mainly due to the fact that the phase of frontier life with which it deals is the phase of which Mr. Eggleston knows most."[17]

The courage and indeed the heroism of itinerant preachers in a frontier environment inspired *The Circuit Rider.* It was no accident that Eggleston chose as his subtitle *A Tale of the Heroic Age.* Although George Rogers Clark's capture of Vincennes and William Henry Harrison's victory at Tippecanoe were woven into the fabric of early Indiana history, neither triumphant soldiers nor their Indian adversaries had for Eggleston anything like the appeal of Methodist evangelists. "More than any one else, the early circuit preachers brought order out of . . . chaos," he wrote. "In no other class was the real heroic element so finely displayed. . . . It is not possible to write of this heroic race of men without enthusiasm. But nothing has been further from my mind than the glorifying of a sect. . . . There are those, indeed, whose sectarian pride will be offended that I have frankly shown the rude as well as the heroic side of early Methodism. I beg they will remember the solemn obligation of a novelist to tell the truth. . . . No man is worthy to be called a novelist who does not endeavor with his whole soul to produce the higher form of history, by writing truly of men as they are, and dispassionately of those forms of life that come within his scope."[18]

Eggleston published later novels, including *Roxy* and *The Graysons,* which (especially *Roxy*) have long been considered superior in some ways to *The Circuit Rider.* More

[17] *Scribner's Monthly* 8 (July 1874): 375.
[18] Eggleston, *The Circuit Rider,* pp. vi-vii.

significant is the fact that, in the last twenty-two years of his life, Eggleston devoted most of his time and talent to the historical research and writing which resulted in *The Beginners of a Nation* (1896) and *The Transit of Civilization* (1901). *Beginners,* in particular, is an important book because of the social history it contains. Both have some serious limitations, as one would expect in the products of a man who was physically frail, frequently sick, and old before his time. Nevertheless, in 1941 one historian described Eggleston as "a pioneer in American historiography."[19] In 1960, another characterized the fragmentary *Transit* as "notable" and "a remarkably imaginative effort."[20] And in 1966 a third found both volumes significant as social history and their author a pioneer "in the writing of the history of ideas and intellectual life in America."[21]

Not long before his death in 1902, Eggleston became president of the American Historical Association. Advocating a "New History," he insisted that "never was a falser thing said than that history is dead politics and politics living history." When the American Historical Association "shall assemble . . . a hundred years hence," he predicted, "there will be, do not doubt it, gifted writers of the history of the people." Instead of old-fashioned political and military history, he foresaw a day when subsequent generations would present "the history of culture, the real history of men and women."[22]

This was exactly what Eggleston had sought to do—and,

[19] Charles Hirschfeld, "Edward Eggleston: Pioneer in Social History," in Eric F. Goldman, ed., *Historiography and Urbanization: Essays in American History in Honor of W. Stull Holt* (Baltimore, 1941), p. 193.

[20] Bernard Bailyn, *Education in the Forming of American Society* (Chapel Hill, 1960), p. 5.

[21] Robert A. Skotheim, *American Intellectual Histories and Historians* (Princeton, 1966), p. 64.

[22] Edward Eggleston, "The New History," *Annual Report of the American Historical Association,* 1900, 2 vols., 1: 39-40, 47.

to a great degree, did—in *Beginners* and *Transit* and in his novels of which *The Circuit Rider* is a prime example. Although in 1874 he termed his fourth novel a "love-story," he also asserted that "whatever is incredible in this story is true."[23] What made his fiction stand out, Eggleston told an interviewer five years before he died, was that his "characters were all treated in relation to social conditions —something of which I was quite unconscious at the time."[24] Actually, he had *not* been unconscious of it, as we have seen in the preface to *Metropolisville*.

More permanently satisfactory and more abidingly significant is Eggleston's 1890 statement: "What distinguishes . . . my own novels . . . from other works of fiction is the prominence . . . they give . . . social conditions." Thus he "treated . . . individual characters . . . as parts of a study of a society—as in some sense the logical results of the environment. Whatever may be the rank assigned to these stories as works of literary art, they will always have a certain value as materials for the student of social history."[25]

[23] Eggleston, *The Circuit Rider,* pp. v, vii.
[24] "Edward Eggleston: An Interview," *The Outlook* 55 (6 February 1897): 433.
[25] Eggleston, "Formative Influences," p. 286.

CONTENTS.

CONTENTS.

PREFACE.

———

WHATEVER is incredible in this story is true. The tale I have to tell will seem strange to those who know little of the social life of the West at the beginning of this century. These sharp contrasts of corn-shuckings and camp-meetings, of wild revels followed by wild revivals; these contacts of highwayman and preacher; this *mélange* of picturesque simplicity, grotesque humor and savage ferocity, of abandoned wickedness and austere piety, can hardly seem real to those who know the country now. But the books of biography and reminiscence which preserve the memory of that time more than justify what is marvelous in these pages.

Living, in early boyhood, on the very ground where my grandfather—brave old Indian-fighter!—had defended his family in a block-house built in a wilderness by his own hands, I grew up familiar with this strange wild life. At the age when other children hear fables and fairy stories, my childish fancy was filled with traditions of battles with Indians and highwaymen. Instead of imaginary giant-killers, children then heard of real Indian-slayers; instead of Blue-Beards, we had Murrell and his robbers; instead of Little Red Riding Hood's wolf, we were regaled with the daring adventures of the generation before us, in conflict with wild beasts on the very road we traveled to school. In many households the old customs still held sway; the wool was carded, spun, dyed, woven, cut and made up in the house: the corn-shucking, wood-chopping, quilting, apple-peeling and country "hoe-down" had not yet fallen into disuse.

In a true picture of this life neither the Indian nor the hunter is the center-piece, but the circuit-rider. More than any one else, the early circuit preachers brought order out of this chaos. In no other class was the real heroic element so finely displayed. How do I remember the forms and weather-beaten visages of the old preachers, whose constitutions had conquered starvation and exposure—who had survived swamps, alligators, Indians, highway robbers and bilious fevers! How was my boyish soul tickled with their anecdotes of rude experience—how was my imagination wrought upon by the recital of their hair-breadth escapes! How was my heart set afire by their contagious religious enthusiasm, so that at eighteen years of age I bestrode the saddle-bags myself and laid upon a feeble frame the heavy burden of emulating their toils! Surely I have a right to celebrate them, since they came so near being the death of me.

It is not possible to write of this heroic race of men without enthusiasm. But nothing has been further from my mind than the glorifying of a sect. If I were capable of sectarian pride, I should not come upon the platform of Christian union* to display it. There are those, indeed, whose sectarian pride will be offended that I have frankly shown the rude as well as the heroic side of early Methodism. I beg they will remember the solemn

* "The Circuit Rider" originally appeared as a serial in *The Christian Union.*

obligations of a novelist to tell the truth. Lawyers and even ministers are permitted to speak entirely on one side. But no man is worthy to be called a novelist who does not endeavor with his whole soul to produce the higher form of history, by writing truly of men as they are, and dispassionately of those forms of life that come within his scope.

Much as I have laughed at every sort of grotesquerie, I could not treat the early religious life of the West otherwise than with the most cordial sympathy and admiration. And yet this is not a "religious novel," one in which all the bad people are as bad as they can be, and all the good people a little better than they can be. I have not even asked myself what may be the "moral." The story of any true life is wholesome, if only the writer will tell it simply, keeping impertinent preachment of his own out of the way.

Doubtless I shall hopelessly damage myself with some good people by confessing in the start that, from the first chapter to the last, this is a love-story. But it is not my fault. It is God who made love so universal that no picture of human life can be complete where love is left out.

E. E.

Brooklyn, *March*, 1874.

THE CIRCUIT RIDER:

A TALE OF THE HEROIC AGE.

——o——

CHAPTER I.

THE CORN-SHUCKING.

SUBTRACTION is the hardest "ciphering" in the book. Fifty or sixty years off the date at the head of your letter is easy enough to the "organ of number," but a severe strain on the imagination. It is hard to go back to the good old days your grandmother talks about—that golden age when people were not roasted alive in a sleeping coach, but gently tipped over a toppling cliff by a drunken stage-driver.

Grand old times were those in which boys politely took off their hats to preacher or schoolmaster, solacing their fresh young hearts afterward by making mouths at the back of his great-coat. Blessed days! in which parsons wore stiff, white stocks, and walked with starched dignity, and yet were not too good to drink peach-brandy and cherry-bounce with folks; when Congressmen were so honorable that they scorned bribes, and were only kept from killing one another by the exertions of the sergeant-at-arms. It was in

those old times of the beginning of the reign of Mad-
ison, that the people of the Hissawachee settlement, in
Southern Ohio, prepared to attend "the corn-shuckin'
down at Cap'n Lumsden's."

There is a peculiar freshness about the entertainment that opens the gayeties of the season. The
shucking at Lumsden's had the advantage of being
set off by a dim back-ground of other shuckings, and
quiltings, and wood-choppings, and apple-peelings that
were to follow, to say nothing of the frolics pure and
simple—parties alloyed with no utilitarian purposes.

Lumsden's corn lay ready for husking, in a whitey-
brown ridge five or six feet high. The Captain was
not insensible to considerations of economy. He
knew quite well that it would be cheaper in the long
run to have it husked by his own farm hands; the
expense of an entertainment in whiskey and other
needful provisions, and the wasteful handling of the
corn, not to mention the obligation to send a hand
to other huskings, more than counter-balanced the
gratuitous labor. But who can resist the public sentiment that requires a man to be a gentleman according to the standard of his neighbors? Captain Lumsden had the reputation of doing many things which
were oppressive, and unjust, but to have "shucked" his
own corn would have been to forfeit his respectability
entirely. It would have placed him on the Pariah
level of the contemptible Connecticut Yankee who
had bought a place farther up the creek, and who
dared to husk his own corn, practise certain forbidden
economies, and even take pay for such trifles as but-

ter, and eggs, and the surplus veal of a calf which he
had killed. The propriety of "ducking" this Yankee
had been a matter of serious debate. A man "as
tight as the bark on a beech tree," and a Yankee besides, was next door to a horse-thief.

So there was a corn-shucking at Cap'n Lumsden's.
The "women-folks" turned the festive occasion into
farther use by stretching a quilt on the frames, and
having the ladies of the party spend the afternoon in
quilting and gossiping—the younger women blushing
inwardly, and sometimes outwardly, with hope and
fear, as the names of certain young men were mentioned. Who could tell what disclosures the evening frolic
might produce? For, though "circumstances alter
cases," they have no power to change human nature ;
and the natural history of the delightful creature
which we call a young woman, was essentially the same
in the Hissawachee Bottom, sixty odd years ago, that
it is on Murray or Beacon Street Hill in these mod-
ern times. Difference enough of manner and costume
—linsey-woolsey, with a rare calico now and then for
Sundays ; the dropping of "kercheys" by polite young
girls—but these things are only outward. The dainty
girl that turns away from my story with disgust, because
"the people are so rough," little suspects how entirely
of the cuticle is her refinement—how, after all, there
is a touch of nature that makes Polly Ann and Sary
Jane cousins-german to Jennie, and Hattie, and Blanche,
and Mabel.

It was just dark—the rising full moon was blazing
like a bonfire among the trees on Campbell's Hill,

across the creek—when the shucking party gathered
rapidly around the
Captain's ridge of
corn. The first com-
ers waited for the
others, and spent the
time looking at the
heap, and specula-
ting as to how many
bushels it would
"shuck out." Cap-
tain Lumsden, an
active, eager man,
under the medium
size, welcomed his
neighbors cordially,
but with certain re-

CAPTAIN LUMSDEN.

serves. That is to say, he spoke with hospitable warmth
to each new comer, but brought his voice up at the last
like a whip-cracker; there was a something in what
Dr. Rush would call the "vanish" of his enunciation,
which reminded the person addressed that Captain
Lumsden, though he knew how to treat a man with
politeness, as became an old Virginia gentleman, was
not a man whose supremacy was to be questioned for
a moment. He reached out his hand, with a "Howdy, Bill?" "Howdy, Jeems? how's your mother gittin',
eh?" and "Hello, Bob, I thought you had the shakes
—got out at last, did you?" Under this superficial familiarity a certain reserve of conscious superiority and
flinty self-will never failed to make itself appreciated.

Let us understand ourselves. When we speak of
Captain Lumsden as an old Virginia gentleman, we
speak from his own standpoint. In his native state
his hereditary rank was low—his father was an "up-
start," who, besides lacking any claims to "good
blood," had made money by doubtful means. But
such is the advantage of emigration that among outside barbarians the fact of having been born in " Ole
Virginny " was credential enough. Was not the Old
Dominion the mother of presidents, and of gentlemen? And so Captain Lumsden was accustomed to
tap his pantaloons with his raw-hide riding-whip,
while he alluded to his relationships to "the old
families," the Carys, the Archers, the Lees, the Peytons,
and the far-famed William and Evelyn Bird; and he
was especially fond of mentioning his relationship to
that family whose aristocratic surname is spelled
"Enroughty," while it is mysteriously and inexplicably
pronounced "Darby," and to the "Tolivars," whose
name is spelled "Taliaferro." Nothing smacks more
of hereditary nobility than a divorce betwixt spelling
and pronouncing. In 'all the Captain's strutting talk
there was this shade of truth, that he was related to
the old families through his wife. For Captain Lumsden would have scorned a *prima facie* lie. But, in his
fertile mind, the truth was ever germinal—little acorns
of fact grew to great oaks of fable.

How quickly a crowd gathers! While I have been
introducing you to Lumsden, the Captain has been
shaking hands in his way, giving a cordial grip, and
then suddenly relaxing, and withdrawing his hand as

if afraid of compromising dignity, and all the while
calling out, " Ho, Tom! Howdy, Stevens? Hello,
Johnson! is that you? Did come after all, eh?"

When once the company was about complete, the
next step was to divide the heap. To do this, judges
were selected, to wit: Mr. Butterfield, a slow-speaking
man, who was believed to know a great deal because
he said little, and looked at things carefully; and
Jake Sniger, who also had a reputation for knowing
a great deal, because he talked glibly, and was good
at off-hand guessing. Butterfield looked at the corn,
first on one side, and then on the end of the heap.
Then he shook his head in uncertainty, and walked
round to the other end of the pile, squinted one eye,
took sight along the top of the ridge, measured its
base, walked from one end to the other with long strides
as if pacing the distance, and again took bearings
with one eye shut, while the young lads stared at
him with awe. Jake Sniger strode away from the
corn and took a panoramic view of it, as one who
scorned to examine anything minutely. He pointed to
the left, and remarked to his admirers that he " 'low'd
they was a heap sight more corn in the left hand
eend of the pile, but it was the long, yaller gourd-seed,
and powerful easy to shuck, while t' other eend wuz
the leetle, flint, hominy corn, and had a right smart
sprinklin' of nubbins." He " 'low'd whoever got aholt
of them air nubbins would git sucked in. It was neck-
and-neck twixt this ere and that air, and fer his own
part, he thought the thing mout be nigh about even,
and had orter be divided in the middle of the pile.

Strange to say, Butterfield, after all his sighting, and pacing, and measuring, arrived at the same difficult and complex conclusion, which remarkable coincidence served to confirm the popular confidence in the infal- libility of the two judges.

So the ridge of corn was measured, and divided exactly in the middle. A fence rail, leaning against either side, marked the boundary between the territo- ries of the two parties. The next thing to be done was to select the captains. Lumsden, as a prudent man, desiring an election to the legislature, declined to appoint them, laughing his chuckling kind of laugh, and saying, "Choose for yourselves, boys, choose for yourselves."

Bill McConkey was on the ground, and there was no better husker. He wanted to be captain on one side, but somebody in the crowd objected that there was no one present who could "hold a taller dip to Bill's shuckin."

"Whar's Mort Goodwin?" demanded Bill; "he's the one they say kin lick me. I'd like to lay him out wunst."

"He ain't yer."

"That air's him a comin' through the cornstalks, I 'low," said Jake Sniger, as a tall, well-built young man came striding hurriedly through the stripped corn stalks, put two hands on the eight-rail fence, and cleared it at a bound.

"That's him! that's his jump," said "little Kike," a nephew of Captain Lumsden. "Could n't many fellers do that eight-rail fence so clean."

"Hello, Mort!" they all cried at once as he came

Mort Goodwin.

up taking off his wide-rimmed straw hat and wiping
his forehead. "We thought you wuzn't a comin',
Here, you and Conkey choose up."

"Let somebody else," said Morton, who was shy,
and ready to give up such a distinction to others.

"Backs out!" said Conkey, sneering.

"Not a bit of it," said Mort. "You don't appreciate kindness; where's your stick?"

By tossing a stick from one to the other, and then
passing the hand of one above that of the other, it
was soon decided that Bill McConkey should have the
first choice of men, and Morton Goodwin the first
choice of corn. The shuckers were thus all divided
into two parts. Captain Lumsden, as host, declining

to be upon either side. Goodwin chose the end of the corn which had, as the boys declared, "a desp'-rate sight of nubbins." Then, at a signal, all hands went to work.

The corn had to be husked and thrown into a crib, a mere pen of fence-rails.

"Now, boys, crib your corn," said Captain Lumsnen, as he started the whiskey bottle on its encouraging travels along the line of shuckers.

"Hurrah, boys!" shouted McConkey. "Pull away, my sweats! work like dogs in a meat-pot; beat 'em all to thunder, er bust a biler, by jimminy! Peel 'em off! Thunder and blazes! Hurrah!"

This loud hallooing may have cheered his own men, but it certainly stimulated those on the other side. Morton was more prudent; he husked with all his might, and called down the lines in an undertone, "Let them holler, boys, never mind Bill; all the breath he spends in noise we'll spend in gittin' the corn peeled. Here, you! don't you shove that corn back in the shucks! No cheats allowed on this side!"

Goodwin had taken his place in the middle of his own men, where he could overlook them and husk, without intermission, himself; knowing that his own dexterity was worth almost as much as the work of two men. When one or two boys on his side began to run over to see how the others were getting along, he ordered them back with great firmness. "Let them alone," he said, "you are only losing time; work hard at first, everybody will work hard at the last."

For nearly an hour the huskers had been stripping

husks with unremitting eagerness; the heap of un-
shucked corn had grown smaller, the crib was nearly
full of the white and yellow ears, and a great billow
of light husks had arisen behind the eager workers.

"Why don't you drink?" asked Jake Sniger, who
sat next to Morton.

"Want's to keep his breath sweet for Patty Lumsden," said Ben North, with a chuckle.

Morton did not knock Ben over, and Ben never
knew how near he came to getting a whipping.

It was now the last heavy pull of the shuckers.
McConkey had drunk rather freely, and his "Pull
away, sweats!" became louder than ever. Morton found
it necessary to run up and down his line once or
twice, and hearten his men by telling them that they
were "sure to beat if they only stuck to it well."

The two parties were pretty evenly matched; the
side led by Goodwin would have given it up once if
it had not been for his cheers; the others were so
near to victory that they began to shout in advance,
and that cheer, before they were through, lost them the
battle,—for Goodwin, calling to his men, fell to work
in a way that set them wild by contagion, and for
the last minute they made almost superhuman exertions, sending a perfect hail of white corn into the
crib, and licking up the last ear in time to rush with
a shout into the territory of the other party, and seize
on one or two dozen ears, all that were left, to show
that Morton had clearly gained the victory. Then
there was a general wiping of foreheads, and a general expression of good feeling. But Bill McConkey

vowed that he "knowed what the other side does with their corn," pointing to the husk pile.

"I'll bet you six bits," said Morton, "that I can find more corn in your shucks than you kin in mine." But Bill did not accept the wager.

After husking the corn that remained under the rails, the whole party adjourned to the house, washing their hands and faces in the woodshed as they passed into the old hybrid building, half log-cabin, the other half block-house fortification.

The quilting frames were gone; and a substantial supper was set in the apartment which was commonly used for parlor and sitting room, and which was now pressed into service for a dining room. The ladies stood around against the wall with a self-conscious air of modesty, debating, no doubt, the effect of their linsey-woolsey dresses. For what is the use of carding and spinning, winding and weaving cutting and sewing to get a new linsey dress, if you cannot have it admired?

B

CHAPTER II.

THE FROLIC.

THE supper was soon dispatched; the huskers eat-
ing with awkward embarrassment, as frontiermen
always do in company,—even in the company of each
other. To eat with decency and composure is the
final triumph of civilization, and the shuckers of Hissawachee Bottom got through with the disagreeable per-
formance as hurriedly as possible, the more so that
their exciting strife had given them vigorous relish for
Mrs. Lumsden's "chicken fixin's," and batter-cakes,
and "punkin-pies." The quilters had taken their
supper an hour before, the table not affording room
for both parties. When supper was over the "things"
were quickly put away, the table folded up and removed to the kitchen—and the company were then
ready to enjoy themselves. There was much gawky
timidity on the part of the young men, and not a little shy dropping of the eyes on the part of the young
women; but the most courageous presently got some of
the rude, country plays a-going. The pawns were sold
over the head of the blindfold Mort Goodwin, who, as
the wit of the company, devised all manner of penal-
ties for the owners. Susan Tomkins had to stand up
in the corner, and say,

"Here I stand all ragged and dirty,
Kiss me quick, or I 'll run like a turkey."

These lines were supposed to rhyme. When Aleck Tilley essayed to comply with her request, she tried to run like a turkey, but was stopped in time.

The good taste of people who enjoy society novels will decide at once that these boisterous, unrefined sports are not a promising beginning. It is easy enough to imagine heroism, generosity and courage in people who dance on velvet carpets; but the great heroes, the world's demigods, grew in just such rough social states as that of Ohio in the early part of this century. There is nothing more important for an over-refined generation than to understand that it has not a monopoly of the great qualities of humanity, and that it must not only tolerate rude folk, but sometimes admire in them traits that have grown scarce as refinement has increased. So that I may not shrink from telling that one kissing-play took the place of another until the excitement and merriment reached a pitch which would be thought not consonant with propriety by the society that loves round-dances with *roués,* and "the German" untranslated—though, for that matter, there are people old-fashioned enough to think that refined deviltry is not much better than rude freedom, after all.

Goodwin entered with the hearty animal spirits of his time of life into the boisterous sport; but there was one drawback to his pleasure — Patty Lumsden would not play. He was glad, indeed, that she did not; he could not bear to see her kissed by his companions. But, then, did Patty like the part he was taking in the rustic revel? He inly rejoiced that his

position as the blindfold Justice, meeting out punish-
ment to the owner of each forfeit, saved him, to some
extent, the necessity of going through the ordeal of
kissing. True, it was quite possible that the severest
prescription he should make might fall on his own
head, if the pawn happened to be his; but he was
saved by his good luck and the penetration which enabled him to guess, from the suppressed chuckle of the
seller, when the offered pawn was his own.

At last, "forfeits" in every shape became too dull
for the growing mirth of the company. They ranged
themselves round the room on benches and chairs,
and began to sing the old song:

> "Oats, peas, beans, and barley grow—
> Oats, peas, beans, and barley grow—
> You nor I, but the farmers, know
> Where oats, peas, beans, and barley grow.

> "Thus the farmer sows his seed,
> Thus he stands and takes his ease,
> Stamps his foot, and claps his hands,
> And whirls around and views his lands.

> "Sure as grass grows in the field,
> Down on this carpet you must knee
> Salute your true love, kiss her sweet,
> And rise again upon your feet."

It is not very different from the little children's
play—an old rustic sport, I doubt not, that has existed
in England from immemorial time. McConkey took
the handkerchief first, and, while the company were
singing, he pretended to be looking around and puz-
zling himself to decide whom he would favor with his

affection. But the girls nudged one another, and looked significantly at Jemima Huddlestone. Of course,
everybody knew that Bill would take Jemima. That
was fore-ordained. Everybody knew it except Bill and
Jemima! Bill fancied that he was standing in entire
indecision, and Jemima—radiant peony!—turned her
large, red-cheeked face away from Bill, and studied
meditatively a knot in a floor-board. But her averted
gaze only made her expectancy the more visible, and
the significant titter of the company deepened the hue
and widened the area of red in her cheeks. Attempts
to seem unconscious generally result disastrously. But
the tittering, and nudging, and looking toward Jemima,
did not prevent the singing from moving on; and now
the singers have reached the line which prescribes the
kneeling. Bill shakes off his feigned indecision, and
with a sudden effort recovers from his vacant and
wandering stare, wheels about, spreads the "handker-
cher" at the feet of the backwoods Hebe, and diffi-
dently kneels upon the outer edge, while she, in com-
pliance with the order of the play, and with reluctance
only apparent, also drops upon her knees on the handkerchief, and, with downcast eyes, receives upon her
red cheek· a kiss so hearty and unreserved that it
awakens laughter and applause. Bill now arises with
the air of a man who has done his whole duty under
difficult circumstances. Jemima lifts the handkerchief,
and, while the song repeats itself, selects some gentleman before whom she kneels, bestowing on him a kiss
in the same fashion, leaving him the handkerchief to
spread before some new divinity.

This alternation had gone on for some time.   Poor,
sanguine, homely
Samantha   Britton
had looked smiling-
ly and expectantly
at each successive
gentleman who bore
the   handkerchief ;
but in vain. "S'man-
thy " could never
understan why her
seductive   smiles
were so unavailing.
Presently, Betty
Harsha was chosen
by somebody—Bet-
ty had a pretty,

HOMELY S'MANTHY.

round face, and pink cheeks, and was sure to be
chosen, sooner or later.   Everybody knew whom she
would choose.   Morton Goodwin was the desire of
her heart.   She dressed to win him ; she fixed her
eyes on him in church ; she put herself adroitly in
his way ; she compelled him to escort her home
against his will ; and now that she held the handkerchief, everybody looked at Goodwin.   Morton, for
his part, was too young to be insensible to the
charms of the little round, impulsive face, the twinkling eyes, the red, pouting lips ; and he was not averse
to having the pretty girl, in her new, bright, linsey
frock, single him out for her admiration.   But just
at this moment he wished she might choose some

one else. For Patty Lumsden, now that all her guests were interested in the play, was relieved from her cares as hostess, and was watching the progress of the exciting amusement. She stood behind Jemima Huddleston, and never was there finer contrast than between the large, healthful, high-colored Jemima, a typical country belle, and the slight, intelligent, fair-skinned Patty, whose black hair and

{ PATTY AND JEMIMA. }

eyes made her complexion seem whiter, and whose resolute lips and proud carriage heightened the refinement of her face. Patty, as folks said, "favored" her mother, a woman of considerable pride and much refinement, who, by her unwillingness to accept the rude customs of the neighborhood, had about as bad a reputation as one can have in a frontier community. She was regarded as excessively "stuck up." This stigma of aristocracy was very pleasing to the Captain. His family was part of himself, and he liked to believe them better than anybody's else. But he heartily wished that Patty would sacrifice her dignity, at this juncture, to further his political aspirations.

Seeing the vision of Patty standing there in her bright new calico—an extraordinary bit of finery in those days—Goodwin wished that Betty would attack somebody else, for once. But Betty Harsha bore down on the perplexed Morton, and, in her eagerness, did not wait for the appropriate line to come—she did not give the farmer time to "stomp" his foot, and clap his hands, much less to whirl around and view his lands—but plumped down upon the handkerchief before Morton, who took his own time to kneel. But draw it out as he would, he presently found himself, after having been kissed by Betty, standing foolishly, handkerchief in hand, while the verses intended for Betty were not yet finished. Betty's precipitancy, and her inevitable gravitation toward Morton, had set all the players laughing, and the laugh seemed to Goodwin to be partly at himself. For, indeed, he was perplexed. To choose any other woman for his "true love" even in play, with Patty standing by, was more than he could do; to offer to kneel before *her* was more than he dared to do. He hesitated a moment; he feared to offend Patty; he must select some one. Just at the instant he caught sight of the eager face of S'manthy Britton stretched up to him, as it had been to the others, with an anxious smile. Morton saw a way out. Patty could not be jealous of S'manthy. He spread the handkerchief before the delighted girl, and a moment later she held in her hand the right to choose a partner.

The fop of the party was "Little Gabe," that is to say, Gabriel Powers, junior. His father was "Old

Gabe," the most miserly farmer of the neighborhood.
But Little Gabe had run away in boyhood, and had
been over the mountains, had made some money, nobody could tell how, and had invested his entire cap-
ital in "store clothes." He wore a mustache, too, which,
being an unheard-of innovation in those primitive times,
marked him as a man who had seen the world. Everybody laughed at him for a fop, and yet everybody admired him. None of the girls had yet dared to select
Little Gabe. To bring their linsey near to store-cloth
—to venture to salute his divine mustache—who could
be guilty of such profanity? But S'manthy was mor-
ally certain that she would not soon again have a
chance to select a "true love," and she determined to
strike high. The players did not laugh when she
spread her handkerchief at the feet of Little Gabe.
They were appalled. But Gabe dropped on one knee,
condescended to receive her salute, and lifted the
handkerchief with a delicate flourish of the hand
which wore a ring with a large jewel, avouched by
Little Gabe to be a diamond—a jewel that was at
least transparent.

Whom would Little Gabe choose? became at once
a question of solemn import to every young woman
of the company; for even girls in linsey are not free
from that liking for a fop, so often seen in ladies
better dressed. In her heart nearly every young woman
wished that Gabe would choose herself. But Gabe
was one of those men who, having done many things
by the magic of effrontery, imagine that any thing can
be obtained by impudence, if only the impudence be

sufficiently transcendent. He knew that Miss Lumsden held herself aloof from the kissing-plays, and he
knew equally that she looked favorably on Morton
Goodwin; he had divined Morton's struggle, and he
had already marked out his own line of action. He
stood in quiet repose while the first two stanzas were
sung. As the third began, he stepped quickly round
the chair on which Jemima Huddleston sat, and stood
before Patty Lumsden, while everybody held breath.
Patty's cheeks did not grow red, but pale, she turned
suddenly and called out toward the kitchen:

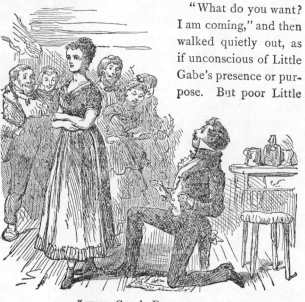

"What do you want?
I am coming," and then
walked quietly out, as
if unconscious of Little
Gabe's presence or pur-
pose. But poor Little

LITTLE GABE'S DISCOMFITURE.

Gabe had already begun to kneel; he had gone too far

to recover himself; he dropped upon one knee, and got up immediately, but not in time to escape the general chorus of laughter and jeers. He sneered at the departing figure of Patty, and said, "I knew I could make her run." But he could not conceal his discomfiture.

When, at last, the party broke up, Morton essayed to have a word with Patty. He found her standing in the deserted kitchen, and his heart beat quick with the thought that she might be waiting for him. The ruddy glow of the hickory coals in the wide fire-place made the logs of the kitchen walls bright, and gave a tint to Patty's white face. But just as Morton was about to speak, Captain Lumsden's quick, jerky tread sounded in the entry, and he came in, laughing his aggravating metallic little laugh, and saying, "Morton, where's your manners? There's nobody to go home with Betty Harsha."

"Dog on Betty Harsha!" muttered Morton, but not loud enough for the Captain to hear. And he escorted Betty home.

CHAPTER III.

EVERY history nas one quality in common with eternity. Begin where you will, there is always a beginning back of the beginning. And, for that matter, there is always a shadowy ending beyond the ending. Only because we may not always begin, like Knickerbocker, at the foundation of the world, is it that we get courage to break somewhere into the interlaced web of human histories—of loves and marriages, of births and deaths, of hopes and fears, of successes and disappointments, of gettings and havings, and spendings and losings. Yet, break in where we may, there is always just a little behind the beginning, something that needs to be told.

I find it necessary that the reader should understand how from childhood Morton had rather worship-ed than loved Patty Lumsden. When the long spelling-class, at the close of school, counted off its numbers, to enable each scholar to remember his relative standing, Patty was always "one," and Morton "two." On one memorable occasion, when the all but infallible Patty misspelled a word, the all but infallible Morton, disliking to "turn her down," missed also, and went down with her. When she afterward regained her place, he took pains to stand always "next to head." Bulwer calls first love a great "purifier of youth," and, despite his fondness for hunting, horse-racing, gaming, and the other wild excitements that were prevalent among the young men of that day, Morton was kept from worse vices by his devotion to Patty, and by a certain ingrained manliness.

Had he worshiped her less, he might long since have proposed to her, and thus have ended his suspense; but he had an awful sense of Patty's nobility, and of his own unworthiness. Moreover, there was a lion in the way. Morton trembled before the face of Captain Lumsden.

Lumsden was one of the earliest settlers, and was by far the largest land-owner in the settlement. In that day of long credit, he had managed to place himself in such a way that he could make his power felt, directly or indirectly, by nearly every man within twenty miles of him. The very judges on the bench were in debt to him. On those rare occasions when he had been opposed, Captain Lumsden had struck so ruthlessly, and with such regardlessness of means or consequences, that he had become a terror to everybody. Two or three families had been compelled to leave the settlement by his vindictive persecutions, so that his name had come to carry a sort of royal authority. Morton Goodwin's father was but a small farmer on the hill, a man naturally unthrifty, who had lost the greater part of a considerable patrimony How could Morton, therefore, make direct advances to so proud a girl as Patty, with the chances in favor of refusal by her, and the certainty of rejection by her father? Illusion is not the dreadfulest thing, but disillusion — Morton preferred to cherish his hopeless hope, living in vain expectation of some improbable change that should place him at better advantage in his addresses to Patty.

At first, Lumsden had left him in no uncertainty in regard to his own disposition in the matter. He had frowned upon Goodwin's advances by treating him with that sort of repellant patronage which is so aggravating, because it affords one no good excuse for knocking down the author of the insult. But of late, having observed the growing force and independence of Morton's character, and his ascendancy over the men of his own age, the Captain appreciated the necessity of attaching such a person to himself, particularly for the election which was to take place in the autumn. Not that he had any intention of suffering Patty to marry Morton. He only meant to play fast and loose a while. Had he even intended to give his approval to the marriage at last, he would have played fast and loose all the same, for the sake of making Patty and her lover feel his power as long as possible. At present, he meant to hold out just enough of hope to bind the ardent young man to his interest. Morton, on his part, reasoned that if Lumsden's kindness should continue to increase in the future as it had in the three weeks past, it would become even cordial, after a while. To young men in love, all good things are progressive.

On the Sunday morning following the shucking, Morton rose early, and went to the stable. Did you ever have the happiness to see a quiet autumn Sun-

day in the backwoods? Did you ever observe the
stillness, the solitude, the softness of sunshine, the gentleness of wind, the chip-chip-chlurr-r-r of great flocks
of blackbirds getting ready for migration, the lazy
cawing of crows, softened by distance, the half-laughing bark of cunning squirrel, nibbling his prism-shaped
beech-nut, and twinkling his jolly, child-like eye at
you the while, as if to say, "Don't you wish you
might guess?"

Not that Morton saw aught of these things. He
never heard voices, or saw sights, out of the common,
and that very October Sunday had been set apart for
a horse-race down at "The Forks." The one piece
of property which our young friend had acquired during his minority was a thorough-bred filley, and he
felt certain that she—being a horse of the first families—would be able to "lay out" anything that could
be brought against her. He was very anxious about
the race, and therefore rose early, and went out into
the morning light that he might look at his mare, and
feel of her perfect legs, to make sure that she was in
good condition.

"All right, Dolly?" he said—"all right this morning, old lady? eh? You'll beat all the scrubs; won't
you?"

In this exhilarating state of anxiety and expectation, Morton came to breakfast, only to have his
breath taken away. His mother asked him to ride to
meeting with her, and it was almost as hard to deny
her as it was to give up the race at "The Forks."

Rough associations had made young Goodwin a

rough man. His was a nature buoyant, generous, and complaisant, very likely to take the color of his surroundings. The catalogue of his bad habits is sufficiently shocking to us who live in this better day of Sunday - school morality. He often swore in a way that might have edified the army in Flanders. He spent his Sundays in hunting, fishing, and riding horse-races, except when he was needed to escort h:s mother to meeting. He bet on cards, and I am afraid he drank to intoxication sometimes. Though he was too proud and manly to lie, and too pure to be unchaste, he was not a promising young man. The chances that he would make a fairly successful trip through life did not preponderate over the chances that he would wreck himself by intemperance and gambling But his roughness was strangely veined by nobleness. This rude, rollicking, swearing young fellow had a chivalrous loyalty to his mother, which held him always ready to devote himself in any way to her service.

On her part, she was, indeed, a woman worthy of reverence. Her father had been one of those fine old Irish gentlemen, with grand manners, extravagant habits, generous impulses, brilliant wit, a ruddy nose, and final bankruptcy. His daughter, Jane Morton, had married Job Goodwin, a returned soldier of the Revolution—a man who was "a poor manager." He lost his patrimony, and, what is worse, lost heart. Upon his wife, therefore, had devolved heavy burdens. But her face was yet fresh, and her hair, even when anchored back to a great tuck-comb, showed an errant

Irish tendency to curl. Morton's hung in waves about
his neck, and he cherished his curls, proud of the resemblance to his mother, whom he considered a very
queen, to be served right royally.

But it was hard — when he had been training the
filley from a colt — when he had looked forward for
months to this race as a time of triumph—to have so
severe a strain put upon his devotion to his mother.
When she made the request, he did not reply. He
went to the barn and stroked the filley's legs — how
perfect they were! — and gave vent to some very old
and wicked oaths. He was just making up his mind
to throw the saddle on Dolly and be off to the Forks,
when his decision was curiously turned by a word from
his brother Henry, a lad of twelve, who had followed
Morton to the stable, and now stood in the door.

"Mort," said he, "I'd go anyhow, if I was you.
I wouldn't stand it. You go and run Doll, and lick
Bill Conkey's bay fer him. He'll think you're afeard,
ef you don't. The old lady hain't got no right to
make you set and listen to old Donaldson on sech a
purty day as this."

"Looky here, Hen!" broke out Morton, looking up
from the meditative scratching of Dolly's fetlocks,
"don't you talk that away about mother. She's every
inch a lady, and it's a blamed hard life she's had to
foller, between pappy's mopin' and the girls all a-dyin'
and Lew's bad end — and you and me not promisin'
much better. It's mighty little I kin do to make
things kind of easy for her, and I'll go to meetin' every day in the week, ef she says so."

IN THE STABLE.

"She'll make a Persbyterian outen you, Mort; see ef she don't."

"Nary Presbyterian. They's no Presbyterian in me. I'm a hard nut. I would like to be a elder, or a minister, if it was in me, though, just to see the smile spread all over her face whenever she'd think about it. Looky here, Hen! I'll tell you something. Mother's about forty times too good for us. When I had the scarlet fever, and was cross, she used to set on the side of the bed, and tell me stories, about knights and such like, that she'd read about in grandfather's books when she was a girl — jam up good stories, too, you better believe. I liked the knights, because they rode fine horses, and was always ready to fight anything that come along, but always fair and square, you know. And she told me how the knights fit fer their religion, and fer ladies, and fer everybody that had got tromped down by somebody else. I wished I'd been a knight myself. I 'lowed it would be *some* to fight for somebody in trouble, or somethin' good. But then it seemed as if I couldn't find nothin' worth the fightin' fer. One day I lay a-thinkin', and a-lookin' at mother's white lady hands, and face fit fer a queen's. And in them days she let her hair hang down in long curls, and her black eyes was bright like as if they had a light *inside* of 'em, you know. She *was* a queen, *I* tell you! And all at wunst it come right acrost me, like a flash, that I mout as well be mother's knight through thick and thin; and I've been at it ever since. I 'low I've give her a sight of trouble, with my plaguey wild ways, and I come mighty blamed nigh runnin' this mornin', dogged ef I didn't. But here goes."

And with that he proceeded to saddle the restless Dolly, while Henry put the side-saddle on old Blaze, saying, as he drew the surcingle tight, "For my part, I don't want to fight for nobody. I want to do as I dog-on please." He was meditating the fun he would have catching a certain ground-hog, when once his mother should be safely off to meeting.

Morton led old Blaze up to the stile and helped his mother to mount, gallantly put her foot in the stirrup, arranged her long riding-skirt, and then mounted his own mare. Dolly sprang forward prancing and

dashing, and chafing against the bit in a way highly
pleasing to Morton, who thought that going to meeting would be a dull affair, if it were not for the fun of
letting Dolly know who was her master.   The ride
to church was a long one, for there had never been
preaching nearer to the Hissawachee settlement than
ten miles away.   Morton found the sermon rather
more interesting than usual.   There still lingered in
the West at this time the remains of the controversy
between "Old-side" and "New-side" Presbyterians,
that dated its origin before the Revolution.   Parson
Donaldson belonged to the Old side.   With square,
combative face, and hard, combative voice, he made
war upon the laxity of New-side Presbyterians, and
the grievous heresies of the Arminians, and in particular upon the exciting meetings of the Methodists.
The great Cane Ridge Camp-meeting was yet fresh in
the memories of the people, and for the hundredth
time Mr. Donaldson inveighed against the Presbyterian ministers who had originated this first of camp-
meetings, and set agoing the wild excitements now
fostered by the Methodists.   He said that Presbyterians who had anything to do with this fanaticism
were led astray of the devil, and the Synod did right
in driving some of them out.   As for Methodists, they
denied "the Decrees."   What was that but a denial
of salvation by grace?   And this involved the over-
throw of the great Protestant doctrine of Justification
by Faith.   This is rather the mental process by which
the parson landed himself at his conclusions, than his
way of stating them to his hearers.   In preaching, he

did not find it necessary to say that a denial of the decrees logically involved the rest. He translated his conclusions into a statement of fact, and boldly asserted that these crazy, illiterate, noisy, vagabond circuit riders were traitors to Protestantism, denying the doctrine of Justification, and teaching salvation by the merit of works. There were many divines, on both sides, in that day who thought zeal for their creed justified any amount of unfairness. (But all that is past!)

Morton's combativeness was greatly tickled by this discourse, and when they were again in the saddle to ride the ten miles home, he assured his mother that he wouldn't mind coming to meeting often, rain or shine, if the preacher would only pitch into somebody every time. He thought it wouldn't be hard to be good, if a body could only have something bad to fight. "Don't you remember, mother, how you used to read to me out of that old " Pilgrim's Progress," and show me the picture of Christian thrashing Apollyon till his hide wouldn't hold shucks? If I could fight the devil that way, I wouldn't mind being a Christian."

Morton felt especially pleased with the minister to-day, for Mr. Donaldson delighted to have the young men come so far to meeting; and imagining that he might be in a "hopeful state of mind," had hospitably urged Morton and his mother to take some refreshment before starting on their homeward journey. It is barely possible that the stimulus of the good parson's cherry-bounce had quite as much to do with Morton's valiant impulses as the stirring effect of his discourse.

CHAPTER IV.

THE fight so much desired by Morton came soon enough.

As he and his mother rode home by a "near cut," little traveled, Morton found time to master Dolly's fiery spirit and yet to scan the woods with the habitual searching glance of a hunter. He observed on one of the trees a notice posted. A notice put up in this out-of-the-way place surprised him. He endeavored to make his restless steed approach the tree, that he might read, but her wild Arabian temper took fright at something—a blooded horse is apt to see visions— and she would not stand near the tree. Time after time Morton drove her forward, but she as often shied away. At last, Mrs. Goodwin begged him to give over the attempt and come on; but Morton's love of mastery was now excited, and he said,

"Ride on, mother, if you want to; this question between Dolly and me will have to be discussed and settled right here. Either she will stand still by this sugar-tree, or we will fight away till one or t'other lays down to rest."

The mother contented herself with letting old Blaze browse by the road-side, and with shaping her thoughts into a formal regret that Morton should spend the holy Sabbath in such fashion; but in her maternal heart she admired his will and courage. He was so like her own father, she thought—such a gentleman! And she could not but hope that he was one of God's elect. If so, what a fine Christian he would be when he should be converted! And, quiet as she was without, her heart was in a moment filled with agony and prayer and questionings. How could she live in heaven without Morton? Her eldest son had already died a violent death in prodigal wanderings from home. But Morton would surely be saved!

Morton, for his part, cared at the moment far less for anything in heaven than he did to master the rebellious Dolly. He rode her all round the tree; he circled that maple, first in one direction, then in another, until the mare was so dizzy she could hardly see. Then he held her while he read the notice, saying with exultation, "Now, my lady, do you think you can stand still?"

Beyond a momentary impulse of idle curiosity, Morton had not cared to know the contents of the paper. Even curiosity had been forgotten in his combat with Dolly. But as soon as he saw the signature, "Enoch Lumsden, administrator of the estate of Hezekiah Lumsden, deceased," he forgot his victory over his horse in his interest in the document itself. It was therein set forth that, by order of the probate court in and for the county aforesaid, the said Enoch Lumsden, administrator, would sell at public auction all that parcel of land belonging to the estate of the said Hezekiah Lumsden, deceased, known and described as follows, to wit, namely, etc., etc.

"By thunder!" broke out Morton, angrily, as he rode away (I am afraid he swore by thunder instead of by something else, out of a filial regard for his mother). "By thunder! if that ain't too devilish mean! I s'pose 'tain't enough for Captain Lumsden to mistreat little Kike—he has gone to robbing him. He means to buy that land himself; or, what's the same thing, git somebody to do it for him. That's what he put that notice in this holler fer. The judge is afraid of him; and so's everybody else. Poor Kike won't have a dollar when he's a man."

"Somebody ought to take Kike's part," said Mrs. Goodwin. "It's a shame for a whole settlement to be cowards, and to let one man rule them. It's worse than having a king."

Morton loved "Little Kike," and hated Captain Lumsden; and this appeal to the anti-monarchic feeling of the time moved him. He could not bear that his mother, of all, should think him cowardly. His pride was already chafed by Lumsden's condescension, and his provoking way of keeping Patty and himself apart. Why should he not break with him, and have done with it, rather than stand by and see Kike robbed? But to interfere in behalf of Kike was to put Patty Lumsden farther away from him. He was a knight who had suddenly come in sight of his long sought adversary while his own hands were tied. And so he fell into the brownest of studies, and scarcely spoke a word to his mother all the rest of his ride. For here were his friendship for little Kike, his innate antagonism to Captain Lumsden, and his strong sense of justice, on one side; his love for Patty—stronger than all the rest—on the other. In the stories of chivalry which his mother had told, the love of woman had always been a motive to valiant deeds for the right. And how often had he dreamed of doing some brave thing while Patty applauded! Now, when the brave thing offered, Patty was on the other side. This unexpected entanglement of motives irritated him, as such embarrassment always does a person disposed to act impulsively and in right lines. And so it happened that he rode on in moody silence, while the mother, always looking for signs of seriousness in the son, mentally reviewed the sermon of the day, in vain endeavor to recall some passages that might have "found a lodgment in his mind."

Had the issue been squarely presented to Morton, he might even then have chosen Patty, letting the interests of his friends take care of themselves. But he did not decide it squarely. He began by excusing himself to himself:—What could he do for Kike? He had no influence with the judge; he had no money to buy the land, and he had no influential friends. He might agitate the question and sacrifice his own hope, and, after all, accomplish nothing for Kike. No doubt all these considerations of futility had their weight with him; nevertheless he had an angry consciousness that he was not acting bravely in the matter. That he, Morton Goodwin, who had often vowed that he would not truckle to any man, was ready to shut his eyes to Captain Lumsden's rascality, in the hope of one day getting his consent to marry his daughter!

It was this anger with himself that made Morton rest-

MORT, DOLLY, AND KIKE.

less, and his restlessness took him down to the Forks that Sunday evening, and led him to drink two or three times, in spite of his good resolution not to drink more than once. It was this restlessness that carried him at last to the cabin of the widow Lumsden, that evening, to see her son Kike.

Kike was sixteen; one of those sallow-skinned boys with straight black hair that one sees so often in southern latitudes. He was called "Little Kike" only to

distinguish him from his father, who haa also borne
the name of Hezekiah. Delicate in health and quiet
in manner, he was a boy of profound feeling, and his
emotions were not only profound but persistent. Dressed in buck-skin breeches and homespun cotton over-
shirt, he was milking old Molly when Morton came
up. The fixed lines of his half-melancholy face relaxed a little, as with a smile deeper than it was broad,
he lifted himself up and said,

"Hello, Mort! come in, old feller!"

But Mort only sat still on Dolly, while Kike came
round and stroked her fine neck, and expressed his regret that she hadn't run at the Forks and beat Bill
McConkey's bay horse. He wished he owned such "a
beast."

"Never mind; one of these days, when I get a little stronger, I will open that crick bottom, and then I
shall make some money and be able to buy a blooded
horse like Dolly. Maybe it'll be a colt of Dolly's;
who knows?" And Kike smiled with a half-hopeful-
ness at the vision of his impending prosperity. But
Morton could not smile, nor could he bear to tell
Kike that his uncle had determined to seize upon that
very piece of land regardless of the air-castles Kike
had built upon it. Morton had made up his mind not
to tell Kike. Why should he? Kike would hear of
his uncle's fraud in time, and any mention on his part
would only destroy his own hopes without doing anything for Kike. But if Morton meant to be prudent
and keep silence, why had he not staid at home?
Why come here, where the sight of Kike's slender

frame was a constant provocation to speech? Was there a self contending against a self?

"Have you got over your chills yet?" asked Morton.

"No," said the black-haired boy, a little bitterly. "I was nearly well when I went down to Uncle Enoch's to work; and he made me work in the rain. 'Come, Kike,' he would say, jerking his words, and throwing them at me like gravel, 'get out in the rain. It'll do you good. Your mother has ruined you, keeping you over the fire. You want hardening. Rain is good for you, water makes you grow; you're a perfect baby.' I tell you, he come plaguey nigh puttin' a finishment to me, though."

Doubtless, what Morton had drunk at the Forks had not increased his prudence. As usual in such cases, the prudent Morton and the impulsive Morton stood the one over against the other; and, as always the imprudent self is prone to spring up without warning, and take the other by surprise, so now the young man suddenly threw prudence and Patty behind, and broke out with—

"Your uncle Enoch is a rascal!" adding some maledictions for emphasis.

That was not exactly telling what he had resolved not to tell, but it rendered it much more difficult to keep the secret; for Kike grew a little red in the face, and was silent a minute. He himself was fond of roundly denouncing his uncle. But abusing one's relations is a luxury which is labeled "strictly private," and this savage outburst from his friend touched Kike's family pride a little.

"I know that as well as you do," was all he said, however.

"He would swindle his own children," said Morton, spurred to greater vehemence by Kike's evident disrelish of his invective. "He will chisel you out of everything you've got before you're of age, and then make the settlement too hot to hold you if you shake your head." And Morton looked off down the road.

"What's the matter, Mort? What set you off on Uncle Nuck to-night? He's bad enough, Lord knows; but something must have gone wrong with you. Did he tell you that he did not want you to talk to Patty?"

"No, he didn't," said Morton. And now that Patty was recalled to his mind, he was vexed to think that he had gone so far in the matter. His tone provoked Kike in turn.

"Mort, you've been drinking! What brought you down here?"

Here the imprudent Morton got the upper hand again. Patty and prudence were out of sight at once, and the young man swore between his teeth.

"Come, old fellow; there's something wrong," said Kike, alarmed. "What's up?"

"Nothing; nothing," said Morton, bitterly. "Nothing, only your affectionate uncle has stuck a notice in Jackson's holler—on the side of the tree furthest from the road — advertising your crick bottom for sale. That's all. Old Virginia gentleman! Old Virginia *devil!* Call a horse-thief a parson, will you?" And then he added something about hell and damnation. These two last words had no grammatical relation

with the rest of his speech; but in the mind of Mor‹
ton Goodwin they had very logical relations with Cap‹
tain Lumsden and the subject under discussion. No‹
body is quite a Universalist in moments of indigna‹
tion. Every man keeps a private and select perdition
for the objects of his wrath.

When Morton had thus let out the secret he had
meant to retain, Kike trembled and grew white about
the lips. "I'll never forgive him," he said, huskily.
"I'll be even with him, and one to carry; see if I
ain't!" He spoke with that slow, revengeful, relentless
air that belongs to a black-haired, Southern race.

"Mort, loan me Doll to-morry?" he said, presently.

"Can you ride her? Where are you going?" Mor‹
ton was loth to commit himself by lending his horse.

"I am going to Jonesville, to see if I can stop that
sale; and I've got a right to choose a gardeen. I
mean to take one that will make Uncle Enoch open
his eyes. I'm goin' to take Colonel Wheeler; he hates
Uncle Enoch, and he'll see jestice done. As for ridin'
Dolly, you know I can back any critter with four legs."

"Well, I guess you can have Dolly," said Morton,
reluctantly. He knew that if Kike rode Dolly, the
Captain would hear of it; and then, farewell to Patty!
But looking at Kike's face, so full of pain and wrath,
he could not quite refuse. Dolly went home at a tre‹
mendous pace, and Morton, commonly full of good na‹
ture, was, for once, insufferably cross at supper-time.

"Mort, meetin' must 'a' soured on you," said Hen‹
ry, provokingly. "You're cross as a coon when its
cornered."

"Don't fret Morton; he's worried," said Mrs. Good-win. The fond mother still hoped that the struggle in his mind was the great battle of Armageddon that should be the beginning of a better life.

Morton went to his bed in the loft filled with a con-tempt for himself. He tried in vain to acquit himself of cowardice—the quality which a border man consid-ers the most criminal. Early in the morning he fed Dolly, and got her ready for Kike ; but no Kike came. After a while, he saw some one ascending the hill on the other side of the creek. Could it be Kike ? Was he going to walk to Jonesville, twenty miles away ? And with his ague-shaken body ? How roundly Mor-ton cursed himself for the fear that made him half re-fuse the horse! For, with one so sensitive as Kike, a half refusal was equivalent to the most positive denial. It was not too late. Morton threw the saddle and bridle on Dolly, and mounted. Dolly sprang forward, throwing her heels saucily in the air, and in fifteen minutes Morton rode up alongside Kike.

"Here, Kike, you don't escape that way! Take Dolly."

"No, I won't, Morton. I oughtn't to have axed you to let me have her. I know how you feel about Patty."

"Confound—no, I won't say confound Patty—but confound *me*, if I'm mean enough to let you walk to Jonesville. I was a devlish coward yesterday. Here, take the horse, dog on you, or I'll thrash you," and Morton laughed.

"I tell you, Mort, I won't do it," said Kike, "I'm goin' to walk."

D

"Yes, you look like it! You'll die before you git half-way, you blamed little fool you! If you won't take Dolly, then I'll go along to bury your bones. They's no danger of the buzzard's picking such bones, though."

Just then came by Jake Sniger, who was remarkable for his servility to Lumsden.

"Hello, boys, which ways?" he asked.

"No ways jest now," said Morton.

"Are you a travelin', or only a goin' some place?" asked Sniger, smiling.

"I 'low I'm travelin', and Kike's a goin' some place," said Morton.

When Sniger had gone on, Morton said, "Now Kike, the fat's all in the fire. When the Captain finds out what you've done, Sniger is sure to tell that he see us together. I've got to fight it out now anyhow, and you've got to take Dolly."

"No, Morton, I can't."

If Kike had been any less obstinate the weakness of his knees would have persuaded him to relent.

"Well, hold Dolly a minute for me, anyhow," said Morton, dismounting. As soon as Kike had obligingly taken hold of the bridle, Morton started toward home, singing Burns's "Highland Mary" at the top of his rich, melodious voice, never looking back at Kike till he had finished the song, and reached the summit of the hill. Then he had the satisfaction of seeing Kike in the saddle, laughing to think how his friend had outwitted him. Morton waved his hat heartily, and Kike, nodding his head, gave Dolly the rein, and she

plunged forward, carrying him out of sight in a few minutes.   Morton's mother was disappointed, when he came
in late to breakfast, to see that his brow was clear.   She
feared that the good impressions of the day before had
worn away.   How little does one know of the real na-

GOOD-BYE!

ture of the struggle between God and the devil, in the
heart of another! But long before Kike had brought
Dolly back to her stall, the exhilaration of self-sacrifice
in the mind of Morton had worn away, and the possible consequences of his action made him uncomfortable.

CHAPTER V.

WORK, Morton could not. After his noonday dinner he lifted his flint-lock gun from the forked
sticks upon the wall where it was laid, and set out to
seek for deer,—rather to seek forgetfulness of the anxiety that preyed upon him. Excitement was almost a
necessity with him, even at ordinary times; now, it
seemed the only remedy for his depression. But instead of forgetting Patty, he forgot everything but
Patty, and for the first time in his life he found it
impossible to absorb himself in hunting. For when a
frontierman loves, he loves with his whole nature.
The interests of his life are few, and love, having un-
disputed sway, becomes a consuming passion. After
two hours' walking through the unbroken forest he
started a deer, but did not see it in time to shoot.
He had tramped through the brush without caution or
vigilance. He now saw that it would be of no avail
to keep up this mockery of hunting. He was seized
with an eager desire to see Patty, and talk with her
once more before the door should be closed against
him. He might strike the trail, and reach the settlement in an hour, arriving at Lumsden's while yet the
Captain was away from the house. His only chance
was to see her in the absence of her father, who would
surely contrive some interruption if he were present.

So eagerly did Morton travel, that when his return was about half accomplished he ran headlong into the very midst of a flock of wild turkeys. They ran swiftly away in two or three directions, but not until the two barrels of Morton's gun had brought down two glossy young gobblers. Tying their legs together with a strip of paw-paw bark, he slung them across his gun, and laid his gun over his shoulder, pleased that he would not have to go home quite empty-handed.

As he steps into Captain Lumsden's yard that Autumn afternoon, he is such a man as one likes to see: quite six feet high, well made, broad, but not too broad, about the shoulders, with legs whose litheness indicate the reserve force of muscle and nerve coiled away somewhere for an emergency. His walk is direct, elastic, unflagging; he is like his horse, a clean stepper; there is neither slouchiness, timidity, nor craftiness in his gait. The legs are as much a test of character as the face, and in both one can read resolute eagerness. His forehead is high rather than broad, his blue eye and curly hair, and a certain sweetness and dignity in his smile, are from his Scotch-Irish mother. His picturesque coon-skin cap gives him the look of a hunter. The homespun "hunting shirt" hangs outside his buckskin breeches, and these terminate below inside his rawhide boots.

The great yellow dog, Watch, knows him well enough by this time, but, like a policeman on duty, Watch is quite unwilling to seem to neglect his function; and so he bristles up a little, meets Morton at

the gate, and snuffs at his cowhide boots with an air
of surly vigilance. The young man hails him with a
friendly "Hello, Watch!" and the old fellow smooths
his back hair a little, and gives his clumsy bobbed
til three solemn little wags of recognition, comical
nough if Goodwin were only in a mood to observe.

Morton hears the hum of the spinning-wheel in the
old cabin portion of the building, used for a kitchen
and loom-room. The monotonous rise and fall of the
wheel's tune, now buzzing gently, then louder and
louder till its whirr could be heard a furlong, then
slacking, then stopping abruptly, then rising to a new
climax — this cadenced hum, as he hears it, is made
rhythmical by the tread of feet that run back across
the room after each climax of sound. He knows the
quick, elastic step; he turns away from the straight-
ahead entrance to the house, and passes round to the
kitchen door. It is Patty, as he thought, and, as his
shadow falls in at the door, she is in the very act of
urging the wheel to it highest impetus; she whirls it
till it roars, and at the same time nods merrily at
Morton over the top of it; then she trips back across
the room, drawing the yarn with her left hand, which
she holds stretched out; when the impulse is somewhat spent, and the yarn sufficiently twisted, Patty
catches the wheel, winds the yarn upon the spindle,
and turns to the door. She changes her spinning stick
to the left hand, and extends her right with a genial
"Howdy, Morton? killed some turkeys, I see."

"Yes, one for you and one for mother."

"For me? much obliged! come in and take a chair."

"No, this'll do," and Morton sat upon the door-sill, doffing his coon-skin cap, and wiping his forehead with his red handkerchief. " Go on with your spinning, Patty, I like to see you spin."

"Well, I will. I mean to spin two dozen cuts to-day. I've been at it since five o'clock."

Morton was glad, indeed, to have her spin. He was, in his present perplexed state, willing to avoid all conversation except such broken talk as might be carried on while Patty wound the spun yarn upon the spindle, or adjusted a new roll of wool.

Nothing shows off the grace of the female figure as did the old spinning-wheel. Patty's perfect form was disfigured by no stays, or pads, or paniers—her swift tread backwards with her up-raised left hand, her movement of the wheel with the right, all kept her agile figure in lithe action. If plastic art were not an impossibility to us Americans, our stone-cutters might long since have ceased, like school-boys, to send us back from Rome imitation Venuses, and counterfeit Hebes, and lank Lincolns aping Roman senators, and stagey Washingtons on stage-horses;—they would by this time have found out that in our primitive life there are subjects enough, and that in mythology and heroics we must ever be dead copyists. But I do not believe Morton was thinking of art at all, as he sat there in the October evening sun and watched the little feet, yet full of unexhausted energy after traveling to and fro all day. He did not know, or care, that Patty, with her head thrown back and her left arm half out-stretched to guide her thread, was a glorious subject for a statue. He had never seen marble, and had never heard of statues except in the talk of the old schoolmaster. How should he think to call her statu-esque? Or how should he know that the wide old log-kitchen, with its loom in one corner, its vast fire-place, wherein sit the two huge, black andirons, and wherein swings an iron crane on which hang pot-hooks with iron pots depending—the old kitchen, with its bark - covered joists high overhead, from which are festooned strings of drying pumpkins—how should Morton Goodwin know that this wide old kitchen, with its rare centre-piece of a fine-featured, fresh-hearted young girl straining every nerve to spin two dozen cuts of yarn in a day, would make a *genre* piece, the subject of which would be good enough for one of the old Dutch masters? He could not know all this, but he did know, as he watched the feet treading swiftly and rhythmically back and forth, and as he saw the fine face, ruddy with the vigorous exer-cise, looking at him over the top of a whirling wheel whose spokes were invisible—he did know that Patty Lumsden was a little higher than angels, and he shud-dered when he remembered that to-morrow, and indefi-nitely afterward, he might be shut out from her fa-ther's house.

It was while he sat thus and listened to Patty's broken patches of sprightly talk and the monotonous symphony of her wheel, that Captain Lumsden came into the yard, snapping his rawhide whip against his boots, and walking, in his eager, jerky fashion, around to the kitchen door.

"Hello, Morton! here, eh? Been hunting? This don't pay. A young man that is going to get on in the world oughtn't to set here in the sunshine talking to the girls. Leave that for nights and Sundays. I'm afeard you won't get on if you don't work early and late. Eh?" And the captain chuckled his hard little laugh.

Morton felt all the pleasure of the glorious afternoon vanish, as he rose to go. He laid the turkey destined for Patty inside the door, took up the other, and was about to leave. Meantime the captain had lifted the white gourd at the well-curb, to satisfy his thirst.

"I saw Kike just now," he said, in a fragmentary way, between his sips of water—and Morton felt his face color at the first mention of Kike. "I saw Kike crossing the creek on your mare. You oughtn't to let him ride her; she'll break his fool neck yet. Here comes Kike himself. I wonder where he's been to?"

Morton saw, in the fixed look of Kike's eyes, as he opened the gate, evidence of deep passion; but Captain Enoch Lumsden was not looking for anything remarkable about Kike, and he was accustomed to treat him with peculiar indignity because he was a relative.

"Hello, Kike!" he said, as his nephew approached, while Watch faithfully sniffed at his heels, "where've you been cavorting on that filley to-day? I told Mort he was a fool to let a snipe like you ride that she-devil. She'll break your blamed neck some day, and then there'll be one fool less." And the captain chuckled triumphantly at the wit in his way of putting the thing. "Don't kick the dog! What an ill-natured ground-hog you air! If I had the training of you, I'd take some of that out."

"You haven't got the training of me, and you never will have."

Kike's face was livid, and his voice almost inaudible.

"Come, come, don't be impudent, young man," chuckled Captain Lumsden.

"I don't know what you call impudence," said Kike, stretching his slender frame up to its full height, and shaking as if he had an ague-chill; "but you are a tyrant and a scoundrel!"

"Tut! tut! Kike, you're crazy, you little brute. What's up?"

"You know what's up. You want to cheat me out of that bottom land; you have got it advertised on the back side of a tree in North's holler, without consulting mother or me. I have been over to Jonesville to-day, and picked out Colonel Wheeler to act as my gardeen."

"Colonel Wheeler? Why, that's an insult to me!" And the captain ceased to laugh, and grew red.

"I hope it is. I couldn't get the judge to take back the order for the sale of the land; he's afeard of you. But now let me tell you something, Enoch Lumsden! If you sell my land by that order of the court, you'll lose more'n you'll make. I ain't afeard of the devil nor none of his angels; and I recken you're one of the blackest. It'll cost you more burnt barns and dead hosses and cows and hogs and sheep than what you make will pay for. You cheated pappy, but you shan't make nothin' out of Little Kike. I'll turn Ingin, and take Ingin law onto you, you old thief and—"

Here Captain Lumsden stepped forward and raised

THE ALTERCATION.

his cowhide. "I'll teach you some manners, you impudent little brat!"

Kike quivered all over, but did not move hand or foot. "Hit me if you dare, Enoch Lumsden, and they'll be blood betwixt us then. You hit me wunst, and they'll be one less Lumsden alive in a year. You or me'll have to go to the bone-yard."

Patty had stopped her wheel, had forgotten all about her two dozen a day, and stood frightened in the door, near Morton. Morton advanced and took hold of Kike.

"Come, Kike! Kike! don't be so wrothy," said he.

"Keep hands offen me, Mort Goodwin," said Kike, shaking loose. "I've got an account to settle, and ef he tetches a thread of my coat with a cowhide, it'll be a bad day fer both on us. We'll settle with blood then."

"It's no use for you to interfere, Mort," snarled the captain. "I know well enough who put Kike up to this. I'll settle with both of you, some day." Then, with an oath, the captain went into the house, while the two young men moved away down the road, Morton not daring to look at Patty.

What Morton dreaded most had come upon him. As for Kike, when once they were out of sight of Lumsden's, the reaction on his feeble frame was terrible. He sat down on a log and cried with grief and anger.

"The worst of it is, I've ruined your chances, Mort," said he.

And Morton did not reply.

CHAPTER VI

MORTON led Kike home in silence, and then returned to his father's house, deposited his turkey
outside the door, and sat down on a broken chair by
the fire-place. His father, a hypochondriac, hard of
hearing, and slow of thought and motion, looked at
him steadily a moment, and then said:

"Sick, Mort? Goin' to have a chill?"

"No, sir."

"You look powerful dauncy," said the old man, as
he stuffed his pipe full of leaf tobacco which he had
chafed in his hand, and sat down on the other side of
the fire-place. "I feel a kind of all-overishness myself. I 'low we'll have the fever in the bottoms this
year. Hey?"

"I don't know, sir."

"What?"

"I said I didn't know." Morton found it hard to
answer his father with decency. The old man said
"Oh," when he understood Morton's last reply; and
perceiving that his son was averse to talking, he devoted himself to his pipe, and to a cheerful revery on
the awful consequences that might result if "the fever,"
which was rumored to have broken out at Chilicothe,
should spread to the Hissawachee bottom. Mrs. Goodwin took Morton's moodiness to be a fresh evidence

of the working of the Divine Spirit in his heart, and
she began to hope more than ever that he might
prove to be one of the elect. Indeed, she thought it
quite probable that a boy so good to his mother would
be one of the precious few; for though she knew that
the election was unconditional, and of grace, she could
not help feeling that there was an antecedent proba-
bility of Morton's being chosen. She went quietly and
cheerfully to her work, spreading the thin corn-meal
dough on the clean hoe used in that day instead of a
griddle, for baking the "hoe-cake," and putting the
hoe in its place before the fire, setting the sassafras
tea to draw, skimming the milk, and arranging the
plates—white, with blue edges—and the yellow cups
and saucers on the table, and all the while praying
that Morton might be found one of those chosen before the foundation of the world to be sanctified and
saved to the glory of God.

The revery of Mr. Goodwin about the possible
breaking out of the fever, and the meditation of his
wife about the hopeful state of her son, and the painful reflections of Morton about the disastrous break
with Captain Lumsden—all three set agoing primarily
by one cause—were all three simultaneously interrupted by the appearance of the younger son, Henry, at
the door, with a turkey.

"Where did you get that?" asked his mother.

"Captain Lumsden, or Patty, sent it."

"Captain Lumsden, eh?" said the father. "Well,
the captain's feeling clever, I 'low."

"He sent it to Mort by little black Bob, and said

it was with Miss Patty's somethin' or other — *couple-ments*, Bob called 'em."

"Compliments, eh?" and the father looked at Morton, smiling. "Well, you're gettin' on there mighty fast, Mort; but how did Patty come to send a turkey?" The mother looked anxiously at her son, seeing he did not evince any pleasure at so singular a present from Patty. Morton was obliged to explain the state of affairs between himself and the captain, which he did in as few words as possible. Of course, he knew that the use of Patty's name in returning the turkey was a ruse of Lumsden's, to give him additional pain.

"It's bad," said the father, as he filled his pipe again, after supper. "Quarreled with Lumsden! He'll drive us off. We'll all take the fever "—for every evil that Job Goodwin thought of immediately became inevitable, in his imagination—"we'll all take the fever, and have to make a new settlement in winter time." Saying this, Goodwin took his pipe out of his mouth, rested his elbow on his knee, and his head on his hand, diligently exerting his imagination to make real and vivid the worst possible events conceivable from this new and improved stand-point of despair.

But the wise mother set herself to planning; and when eight o'clock had come, and Job Goodwin had forgotten the fever, having fallen into a doze in his shuck-bottom chair, Mrs. Goodwin told Morton that the best thing for him and Kike would be to get out of the settlement until the captain should have time to cool off.

"Kike ought to be got away before he does any.
thing desperate. We want some meat for winter; and
though it's a little early yet, you'd better start off with
Kike in the morning," she said.

Always fond of hunting, anxious now to drown
pain and forebodings in some excitement, Morton did
not need a second suggestion from his mother. He
feared bad results from Kike's temper; and though he
had little hope of any relenting on Lumsden's part, he
had an eager desire to forget his trouble in a chase
after bears and deer. He seized his cap, saddled and
mounted Dolly, and started at once to the house of
Kike's mother. Soon after Morton went, his father
woke up, and, finding his son gone out, complained,
as he got ready for bed, that the boy would "ketch the
fever, certain, runnin' 'round that away at night."

THE IRISH SCHOOL-MASTER.

Morton found Kike
in a state of exhaus-
tion—pale, angry, and
sick. Mr. Brady, the
Irish school-master,
from whom the boys
had received most of
their education and
many a sound whip-
ping, was doing his
best to divert Kike
from his revengeful
mood. It is a singu-
lar fact in the history
of the West, that so

large a proportion of the first school-masters were Irish-men of uncertain history.

"Ha! Moirton, is it you?" said Brady. "I'm roight glad to see ye. Here's this b'y says hay'd a shot his own uncle as shore as hay'd a toiched him with his roidin'-fwhip. An' I've been a-axin ov him fwoi hay hain't blowed out me brains a dozen times, sayin' oive lathered him with baich switches. I didn't guiss fwat a saltpayter kag hay wuz, sure. Else I'd a had him sarched for foire-arms before iver I'd a ven-ter'd to inform him which end of the alphabet was the bayginnin'. Hay moight a busted me impty pate for tellin' him that A wusn't B."

It was impossible for Morton to keep from smiling at the good old fellow's banter. Brady was bent on mollifying Kike, who was one of his brightest and most troublesome pupils, standing next to Patty and Morton in scholarship though much younger.

Kike's mother, a shrewd but illiterate woman, was much troubled to see him in so dangerous a passion. "I wish he was leetle-er, ur bigger," she said.

"An' fwoi air ye afther wishing that same, me dair madam?" asked the Irishman.

"Bekase," said the widow, "ef he was leetle-er, I could whip it outen him; ef he was bigger, he wouldn't be sich a fool. Boys is allers powerful troublesome when they're kinder 'twixt and 'tween—nary man nor boy. They air boys, but they feel so much bigger'n they used to be, that they think theirselves men, and talk about shootin', and all sich like. Deliver me from a boy jest a leetle too big to be laid acrost your lap, and larnt what's what. Tho', ef I do say it, Kike's been a oncommon good sort of boy to me mostly, on'y he's got a oncommon lot of red pepper into him, like his pappy afore him, and he's one of them you can't turn. An', as for Enoch Lumsden, I *would* be glad ef he wuz shot, on'y I don't want no little fool like Kike to go to fightin' a man like Nuck Lumsden. Nobody but God A'mighty kin ever do jestice to his case; an' it's a blessed comfort to me that I'll meet him at the Jedgment-day. Nothin' does my heart so much good, like, as to think what a bill Nuck 'll have to settle *then*, and how he can't browbeat the Jedge, nor shake a mortgage in *his* face. It's the on'y rale nice thing about the Day of Jedgment, akordin' to my thinkin'. I mean to call his attention to some things then. He won't say much about his wife's belongin' to fust families thar, I 'low."

Brady laughed long and loud at this sally of Mrs. Hezekiah Lumsden's; and even Kike smiled a little, partly at his mother's way of putting things, and partly from the contagion of Brady's merry disposition.

Morton now proposed Mrs. Goodwin's plan, that he and Kike should leave early in the morning, on the fall hunt. Kike felt the first dignity of manhood on him; he knew that, after his high tragic stand with his uncle, he ought to stay, and fight it out; but then the opportunity to go on a long hunt with Morton was a rare one, and killing a bear would be almost as pleasant to his boyish ambition as shooting his uncle.

"I don't want to run away from him. He'll think I've backed out," he said, hesitatingly.

"Now, I'll tell ye fwat," said Brady, winking; "you put out and git some bear's ile for your noice black hair. If the cap'n makes so bowld as to sell ye out of house and home, and crick bottom, fwoile ye're gone, it's yerself as can do the burnin' afther ye git back. The barn's noo, and 'tain't quoit saysoned yit. It'll burn a dale better fwen ye're ray-turned, me lad. An', as for the shootin' part, practice on the bears fust! 'Twould be a pity to miss foire on the captain, and him ye're own dair uncle, ye know. He'll keep till ye come back. If I say anybody a goin' to crack him owver, I'll jist spake a good word for ye, an' till him as the captin's own affictionate niphew has got the fust pop at him, by roight of bayin' blood kin, sure."

Kike could not help smiling grimly at this presentation of the matter; and while he hesitated, his mother said he should go. She'd bundle him off in the early morning. And long before daylight, the two boys, neither of whom had slept during the night, started, with guns on their shoulders, and with the venererable Blaze for a pack-horse. Dolly was a giddy young thing, that could not be trusted in business so grave.

D

CHAPTER VII.

HAD I but bethought myself in time to call this history by one of those gentle titles now in vogue, as " The Wild Hunters of the Far West," or even by one of the labels with which juvenile and Sunday-school literature—milk for babes—is now made attractive, as, for instance, " Kike, the Young Bear Hunter." I might here have entertained the reader with a vigorous description of the death of Bruin, fierce and fat, at the hands of the triumphant Kike, and of the exciting chase after deer under the direction of Morton.

After two weeks of such varying success as hunters have, they found that it would be necessary to forego the discomforts of camp-life for a day, and visit the nearest settlement in order to replenish their stock of ammunition. Wilkins' store, which was the center of a settlement, was a double log-building. In one end the proprietor kept for sale powder and lead, a few bonnets, cheap ribbons, and artificial flowers, a small stock of earthenware, and cheap crockery, a little homespun cotton cloth, some bolts of jeans and linsey, hanks of yarn and skeins of thread, tobacco for smoking and tobacco for " chawing," a little " store-tea "—so called in contradistinction to the sage, sassafras and crop-vine teas in general use—with a plentiful stock of whisky, and some apple-brandy. The other end of this building was a large room, festooned with strings of drying pumpkin, cheered by an enormous fireplace, and lighted by one small window with four lights of glass. In this room, which contained three beds, and in the loft above, Wilkins and his family lived and kept a first-class hotel.

In the early West, Sunday was a day sacred to Diana and Bacchus. Our young friends visited the settlement at Wilkins' on that day, not because they wished to rest, but because they had begun to get lonely, and they knew that Sunday would not fail to find some frolic in progress, and in making new acquaintances, fifty miles from home, they would be able to relieve the tedium of the wilderness with games at cards, and other social enjoyments.

Morton and Kike arrived at Wilkins' combined store and tavern at ten o'clock in the morning, and found the expected crowd of loafers. The new-comers "took a hand" in all the sports, the jumping, the foot-racing, the quoit-pitching, the "wras'lin'," the target-shooting, the poker-playing, and the rest, and were soon accepted as clever fellows. A frontierman could bestow no higher praise—to be a clever fellow in his sense was to know how to lose at cards, without grumbling, the peltries hard-earned in hunting, to be always ready to change your coon-skins into "drinks for the crowd," and to be able to hit a three-inch "mark" at two hundred paces without bragging.

Just as the sports had begun to lose their zest a littr'e, there walked up to the tavern door a man in homespun dress, carrying one of his shoes in his hand,

and yet not seeming to be a plain backwoodsman.

ELECTIONEERING.

He looked a trifle over thirty years of age, and an acute observer might have guessed from his face that his life had been one of daring adventure, and many vicissitudes. There were traces also of conflicting purposes, of a certain strength, and a certain weakness of character; the melancholy history of good intentions overslaughed by bad passions and evil associations was written in his countenance.

"Some feller 'lectioneerin', I'll bet," said one of Morton's companions.

The crowd gathered about the stranger, who spoke

to each one as though he had known him always. He proposed " the drinks " as the surest road to an acquaintance, and when all had drunk, the stranger paid the score, not in skins but in silver coin.

"See here, stranger," said Morton, mischievously, "you're mighty clever, by hokey. What are you running fer?"

Well, gentlemen, you guessed me out that time. I 'low to run for sheriff next heat," said the stranger, who affected dialect for the sake of popularity.

"What mout your name be?" asked one of the company.

"Marcus Burchard's my name when I'm at home. I live at Jenkinsville. I sot out in life a poor boy. I'm so used to bein' bar'footed that my shoes hurts my feet an' I have to pack one of 'em in my hand most of the time."

Morton here set down his glass, and looking at the stranger with perfect seriousness said, dryly : "Well, Mr. Burchard, I never heard that speech so well done before. We're all goin' to vote for you, without t'other man happens to do it up slicker'n you do. I don't believe he can, though. That was got off very nice."

Burchard was acute enough to join in the laugh which this sally produced, and to make friends with Morton, who was clearly the leader of the party and whose influence was worth securing.

Nothing grows wearisome so soon as idleness and play, and as evening drew on, the crowd tired even of Mr. Burchard's choice collection of funny anecdotes—little stories that had been aired in the same order at every other tavern and store in the county. From sheer *ennui* it was proposed that they should attend Methodist preaching at a house two miles away. They could at least get some fun out of it. Burchard, foreseeing a disturbance, excused himself. He wished he might enjoy the sport, but he must push on. And "push on" he did. In a closely contested election even Methodist votes were not to be thrown away.

Morton and Kike relished the expedition. They had heard that the Methodists were a rude, canting, illiterate race, cloaking the worst practices under an appearance of piety. Mr. Donaldson had often fulminated against them from the pulpit, and they felt almost sure that they could count on his apostolic approval in their laudable enterprise of disturbing a Methodist meeting.

The preacher whom they heard was of the roughest type. His speech was full of dialectic forms and ungrammatical phrases. His illustrations were exceedingly uncouth. It by no means followed that he was not an effective preacher. All these defects were rather to his advantage,—the backwoods rhetoric was suited to move the backwoods audience. But the party from the tavern were in no mood to be moved by anything. They came for amusement, and set themselves diligently to seek it. Morton was ambitious to lead among his new friends, as he did at home, and on this occasion he made use of his rarest gift. The preacher, Mr. Mellen, was just getting "warmed up" with his theme; he was beginning to sling his rude metaphors to the right and left, and the audience was

fast coming under his influence, when Morton Goodwin, who had cultivated a ventriloquial gift for the
diversion of country parties, and the disturbance of
Mr. Brady's school, now began to squeak like a rat
in a trap, looking all the while straight at the preacher,
as if profoundly interested in the discourse. The
women were startled and the grave brethren turned
their austere faces round to look stern reproofs at the
young men. In a moment the squeaking ceased, and
there began the shrill yelping of a little dog, which
seemed to be on the women's side of the room. Brother
Mellen, the preacher, paused, and was about to request
that the dog should be removed, when he began to
suspect from the sensation among the young men that
the disturbance was from them.

"You needn't be afeard, sisters," he said, "puppies
will bark, even when they walk on two legs instid of
four."

This rude joke produced a laugh, but gained no
permanent advantage to the preacher, for Morton, being
a stranger, did not care for the good opinion of the
audience, but for the applause of the young revelers
with whom he had come. He kept silence now, until
the preacher again approached a climax, swinging his
stalwart arms and raising his voice to a tremendous
pitch in the endeavor to make the day of doom seem
sufficiently terrible to his hearers. At last, when he
got to the terror of the wicked, he cried out dra-
matically, "What are these awful sounds I hear?" At
this point he made a pause, which would have been
very effective, had it not been for young Goodwin.

"Caw! caw! caw-aw! cah!" he said, mimicking a crow.

"Young man," roared the preacher, "you are hair-hung and breeze-shaken over that pit that has no bottom."

"Oh, golly!" piped the voice of Morton, seeming to come from nowhere in particular. Mr. Mellen now ceased preaching, and started toward the part of the room in which the young men sat, evidently intending to deal out summary justice to some one. He was a man of immense strength, and his face indicated that he meant to eject the whole party. But they all left in haste except Morton, who staid and met the preacher's gaze with a look of offended innocence. Mr. Mellen was perplexed. A disembodied voice wandering about the room would have been too much for Hercules himself. When the baffled orator turned back to begin to preach again, Morton squeaked in an aggravating falsetto, but with a good imitation of Mr. Mellen's inflections, "Hair-hung and breeze-shaken!"

And when the angry preacher turned fiercely upon him, the scoffer was already fleeing through the door.

CHAPTER VIII.

THE young men were gone until the latter part of November. Several persons longed for their return. Mr. Job Goodwin, for one, began to feel a strong conviction that Mort had taken the fever and died in the woods. He was also very sure that each succeeding day would witness some act of hostility toward himself on the part of Captain Lumsden; and as each day failed to see any evil result from the anger of his powerful neighbor, or to bring any tidings of disaster to Morton, Job Goodwin faithfully carried forward the dark foreboding with compound interest to the next day. He abounded in quotations of such Scripture texts as set forth the fact that man's days were few and full of trouble. The book of Ecclesiastes was to him a perennial fountain of misery —he delighted to found his despairing auguries upon the superior wisdom of Solomon. He looked for Morton's return with great anxiety, hoping to find that nothing worse had happened to him than the shooting away of an arm. Mrs. Goodwin, for her part, dreaded the evil influences of the excitements of hunting. She feared lest Morton should fall into the bad habits that had carried away from home an older brother, for whose untimely death in an affray she had never ceased to mourn.

And Patty! When her father had on that angry afternoon discovered the turkey that Morton had given her, and had sent it home with a message in her name, Patty had borne herself like the proud girl that she was. She held her head aloft; she neither indicated pleasure nor displeasure at her father's course, she would not disclose any liking for Morton, nor any complaisance toward her father. This air of defiance about her Captain Lumsden admired. It showed her mettle, he said to himself. Patty would almost have finished that two dozen cuts of yarn if it had cost her life. She even managed to sing, toward the last of her weary day of work; and when, at nine o'clock, she reeled off her twenty-fourth cut,—drawing a sigh of relief when the reel snapped,—and hung her twelve hanks up together, she seemed as blithe as ever. Her sickly mother sitting, knitting in hand, with wan face bordered by white cap-frill, looked approvingly on Patty's achievement. Patty showed her good blood, was the mother's reflection.

But Patty? She did not hurry. She put everything away carefully. She was rather slow about retiring. But when at last she went aloft into her room in the old block-house part of the building, and shut and latched her door, and set her candle-stick on the high, old-fashioned, home-made dressing-stand, she looked at herself in the little looking-glass and did not see there the face she had been able to keep while the eyes of others were upon her. She saw weariness, disappointment, and dejection. Her strong will held her up. She undressed herself with habitual quietness. She even stopped to look again in self-pity at her face as she stood by the glass to tie on her

night-cap. But when at last she had blown out the candle, and carefully extinguished the wick, and had climbed into the great, high, billowy feather-bed under the rafters, she buried her tired head in

PATTY IN HER CHAMBER.

the pillow and cried a long time, hardly once admitting to herself what she was crying about.

And as the days wore on, and her father ceased to speak of Kike or Morton, and she heard that they were out of the settlement, she found in herself an ever-increasing desire to see Morton. The more she tried to smother her feeling, and the more she denied to herself the existence of the feeling, the more intense did it become. Whenever hunters passed the gate, going after or returning laden with game, she stopped involuntarily to gaze at them. But she never failed, a moment later, to affect an indifferent expression of countenance and to rebuke herself for curiosity so idle. What were hunters to her?

But one evening the travelers whom she looked for went by. They were worse for wear; their buckskin pantaloons were torn by briers; their tread was heavy, for they had traveled since daylight; but Patty, peering through one of the port-holes of the blockhouse, did not fail to recognize old Blaze, burdened as he was with venison, bear-meat and skins, nor to note how Morton looked long and steadfastly at Captain Lumsden's house as if hoping to catch a glimpse of herself. That look of Morton's sent a blush of pleasure over her face, which she could not quite conceal when she met the inquiring eyes of a younger brother a minute later. But when she saw her father gallop rapidly down the road as if in pursuit of the young men, her sense of pleasure changed quickly to foreboding.

Morton and Kike had managed, for the most part, to throw off their troubles in the excitement of hunting. But when at last they had accumulated all the meat old Blaze could carry and all the furs they could " pack," they had turned their steps toward home. And with the turning of their steps toward home had come the inevitable turning of their thoughts toward old perplexities. Morton then confided to Kike his intention of leaving the settlement and leading the life of a hermit in the wilderness in case it should prove to be "all off" between him and Patty. And Kike said that his mind was made up. If he found that his uncle Enoch had sold the land, he would be revenged in some way and then run off and live with the Indians. It is not uncommon for boys now-a-days to make stern resolutions in moments of wretchedness which they never attempt to carry out. But the rude life of the West developed deep feeling and a hardy persistence in a purpose once formed. Many a young man crossed in love or incited to revenge had already taken to the wilderness, becoming either a morose hermit or a desperado among the savages. At the period of life when the animal fights hard for supremacy in the soul of man, destiny often hangs very perilously balanced. It was at that day a question in many cases whether a young man of force would become a rowdy or a class-leader.

When once our hunters had entered the settlement they became more depressed than ever. Morton's eyes searched Captain Lumsden's house and yard in vain for a sight of Patty. Kike looked sternly ahead of him, full of rage that he should have to be reminded of his uncle's existence. And when, five minutes later, they heard horse-hoofs behind them, and, looking back, saw Captain Lumsden himself galloping after them on his sleek, "clay-bank" saddle-horse, their hearts beat fast with excitement. Morton wondered what the Captain could want with them, seeing it was not his way to carry on his conflicts by direct attack; and Kike contented himself with looking carefully to the prim ing of his flintlock, compressing his lips and walking straight forward.

"Hello, boys! Howdy? Got a nice passel of furs, eh? Had a good time?"

"Pretty good, thank you, sir!" said Morton, astonished at the greeting, but eager enough to be on good terms again with Patty's father. Kike said not a word, but grew white with speechless anger.

"Nice saddle of ven'son that!" and the Captain tapped it with his cow-hide whip. "Killed a bar, too; who killed it?"

"Kike," said Morton.

"Purty good fer you, Kike! Got over your pout about that land yet?"

Kike did not speak, for the reason that he could not.

"What a little fool you was to make sich a fuss about nothing! I didn't sell it, of course, when you didn't want me to, but you ought to have a little manners in your way of speaking. Come to me next time, and don't go running to the judge and old Wheeler. If you won't be a fool, you'll find your own kin your best friends. Come over and see me to-morry, Mort. I've got some business with you. Good-by!" and the Captain galloped home.

Nor did he fail to observe how inquiringly Patty looked at his face to see what had been the nature of his interview with the boys. With a characteristic love of exerting power over the moods of another, he said, in Patty's hearing: "That Kike is the sulkiest little brute I ever did see."

And Patty spent most of her time during the night in trying to guess what this saying indicated. It was what Captain Lumsden had wished.

Neither Morton nor Kike could guess what the Captain's cordiality might signify. Kike was pleased that his land had not been sold, but he was not in the least mollified by that fact. He was glad of his victory and hated his uncle all the more.

After the weary weeks of camping, Morton greatly enjoyed the warm hoe-cakes, the sassafras tea, the milk and butter, that he got at his mother's table. His father was pleased to have his boy back safe and sound, but reckoned the fever was *shore* to ketch them all before Christmas or Noo Years. Morton told of his meeting with the Captain in some elation, but Job Goodwin shook his head. He "knowed what that meant," he said. " The Cap'n always wuz sorter deep. He'd hit sometime when you didn't know whar the lick come from. And he'd hit powerful hard when he *did* hit, you be shore."

Before the supper was over, who should come in but Brady. He had heard, he said, that Morton had come home, and he was dayloighted to say him agin. Full of quaint fun and queer anecdotes, knowing all the gossip of the settlement, and having a most miscellaneous and disordered lot of information besides, Brady was always welcome; he filled the place of a local newspaper. He was a man of much reading, but with no mental discipline. He had treasured all the strange and delightful things he had ever heard or read—the bloody murders, the sudden deaths, the wonderful accidents and incidents of life, the ups and downs of noted people, and especially a rare fund or humorous stories. He had so many of these at command that it was often surmised that he manufactured them. He "boarded 'round" during school-time, and sponged 'round the rest of the year, if, indeed, a man can be said to sponge who paid for his board so amply in amusement, information, flattery, and a thousand other good offices. Good company is scarcer and higher in price in the back settlements than in civilization; and many a backwoods housewife, perishing of *ennui*, has declared that the genial Brady's " company wuz worth his keep,"—an opinion in which husbands and children always coincided. For welcome belongs primarily to woman; no man makes another's reception sure until he is pretty certain of his wife's disposition toward the guest.

Mrs. Goodwin set a place for the "master" with right good will, and Brady catechised "Moirton" about his adventures. The story of Kike's first bear roused the good Irishman's enthusiasm, and when Morton told of his encounter with the circuit-rider, Brady laughed merrily. Nothing was too bad in his eyes for " a man that undertook to prache afore hay could parse." Brady's own grammatical knowledge, indeed, had more influence on his parsing than on his speech.

At last, when supper was ended, Morton came to the strangest of all his adventures—the meeting with Captain Lumsden; and while he told it, the school-master's eyes were brimming full of fun. By the time he story was finished, Morton began to suspect that Brady knew more about it than he affected to.

"Looky here, Mr. Brady," he said, "I believe you could tell something about this thing. What made the coon come down so easy?"

"Tut! tut! and ye shouldn't call yer own dair father-in-law (that is to bay) a coun. Ye ought to have larn't some manners agin this toime, with all the batins I've gin ye for disrespect to yer supayriors. An' ispicially to thim as is closte akin to ye."

Little Henry, who sat squat upon the hearth, tickling the ears of a sleepy dog with a straw, saw an infinite deal of fun in this rig on Morton.

"Well, but you didn't answer my question, Mr. Brady. How did you fetch the Captain round? For I think you did it."

"Be gorra I did!" and Brady looked up from under his eyebrows with his face all a-twinkle with fun. "I jist parsed the sintince in sich a way as to put the Captin in the nominative case. He loikes to be put in the nominative case, does the Captin. If iver yer goin' to win the devoine craycher that calls him father ye'll hev to larn to parse with Captin Lumsden for the nominative." Here Brady gave the whole party a look of triumphant mystery, and dropped his head reflectively upon his bosom.

"Well, but you'll have to teach me that way of parsing. You left that rule of syntax out last winter." said Morton, seeking to draw out the master by humoring his fancy. "How did you parse the sentence with him, while Kike and I were gone?"

"Aisy enough! don't you say? the nominative gov‑ arns the varb, and thin the varb governs 'most all the rist of the sintince."

"Give an instance," said Morton, mimicking at the same time the pompous air and authoritative voice with which Brady was accustomed to make such a demand of a pupil.

"Will, thin, I'll till ye, Moirton. But ye must all be quiet about it. I wint to say the Captin soon af‑ ther yerself and Koike carried yer two impty skulls into the woods. An' I looked koind of confidintial‑ loike at the Captin, an' I siz, 'Captin, ye ought to riprisint this county in the ligislater,' siz I."

"'Do you think so, Brady?' siz he.

"'It's fwat I've been a-sayin' down at the Forks,' siz I, 'till the folks is all a-gittin' of me opinion,' siz I; 'ye've got more interest in the county,' siz I, 'than the rist,' siz I, 'an' ye've got the brains to exart an anfluence whin ye git thar,' siz I. Will, ye see, Moir‑ ton, the Captin loiked that, and he siz, 'Will, Brady,' siz he, 'I'm obleeged fer yer anfluence,' siz he. An' I saw I had 'im. I'd jist put 'im in the nominative case governin' the varb. And I was the varb. An' I mint to govern the rist." Here Brady stopped to smile complacently and enjoy the mystification of the rest.

"Will, I said to 'im afther that: 'Captain' siz I, 'ye must be moighty keerful not to give the inimy any handle onto ye,' siz I. An' he siz 'Will, Brady, I'll be keerful,' siz he. An' I siz, 'Captin, be pertik'ler keerful about that matter of Koike, if I may make so bowld,' siz I. 'Fer they'll use that ivery fwere,

They're a-talkin' about it now.' An' the Captin siz,
'Will, Brady, I say I kin thrust ye,' siz he. An' I
siz, 'That ye kin, Captain Lumsden : ye kin thrust
the honor of an Oirish gintleman,' siz I. 'Brady,'
siz he, 'this mess of Koike's is a bad one fer me,
since the little brat's gone and brought ole Whayler
into it,' siz he. 'Ye bitter belave it is, Captin, siz I.
'Fwat shill I do, Brady?' siz he. 'Spoike the guns,
Captin,' siz I. 'How?' siz he. 'Make it all roight
with Koike and Moirton,' siz I. 'As fer Moirton,' siz
I, 'he's the smartest *young* man,' siz I (puttin' im-
phasis on '*young*,' you say), he's the smartest *young*
man,' siz I, 'in the bottoms; and if ye kin make an
alloiance with him,' siz I, 'ye've got the smartest old
man managin' the smartest young man. An' if ye kin
make a matrimonial alloiance,' siz I, a-winkin' me oi
at 'im, 'atwixt that devoine young craycher, yer charm-
in' dauther Patty,' siz I, 'and Moirton, ye've got him
tethered for loife, and the guns is spoiked,' siz I. An'
he siz, 'Brady, yer Oirish head is good, afther all.
I'll think about it,' siz he. An' that's how I made
Captin Lumsden the nominative case governin' the
varb—that's myself—and thin the varb rigilates the
rist. "But I must go and say Koike, or the little black-
hidded fool 'll spoil all me conthrivin' and parsin' wid
the captin. Betwixt Moirton and Koike and the captin, it's meself as has got a hard sum in the rule of
thray. This toime I hope the answer 'll come out all
roight, Moirton, me b'y !" and Brady slapped him on
the shoulder and went out. Then he put his head
into the door again to say that the answer set down
in the book was: "Misthress Patty Goodwin."

CHAPTER IX.

THE COMING OF THE CIRCUIT RIDER.

COLONEL Wheeler was the standard-bearer of the flag of independence in the Hissawachee bottom. He had been a Captain in the Revolution; but Revolutionary titles showed a marked tendency to grow during the quarter of a century that followed the close of the war. An ex-officer's neighbors carried him forward with his advancing age; a sort of ideal promotion by brevet gauged the appreciation of military titles as the Revolution passed into history and heroes became scarcer. And emigration always advanced a man several degrees—new neighbors, in their uncertainty about his rank, being prone to give him the benefit of all doubts, and exalt as far as possible the lustre which the new-comer conferred upon the settlement. Thus Captain Wheeler in Maryland was Major Wheeler in Western Pennsylvania, and a full-blown Colonel by the time he had made his second move, into the settlement on Hissawachee Creek. And yet I may be wrong. Perhaps it was not the transplanting that did it. Even had he remained on the "Eastern Shore," he might have passed through a process of canonization as he advanced in life that would have brought him to a colonelcy: other men did. For what is a Colonel but a Captain gone to seed?

"Gone to seed" may be considered a slang expression; and, as a conscientious writer, far be it from me to use slang. And I take great credit to myself for avoiding it just now, since nothing could more perfectly describe Wheeler. His hair was grizzling, his shoulders had a chronic shrug, his under lip protruded in an expression of perpetual resistance, and his prominent chin and brow seemed to have been jammed together; the space between was too small. He had an air of defense; his nature was always in a "guard-against-cavalry" attitude. He had entered into the spirit of colonial resistance from childhood; he was born in antagonism to kings and all that are in authority; it was a family tradition that he had been flogged in boyhood for shooting pop-gun wads into the face of a portrait of the reigning monarch.

When he settled in the Hissawachee bottom, he of course looked about for the power that was to be resisted, and was not long in finding it in his neighbor, Captain Lumsden. He was the one opponent whom Lumsden could not annoy into submission or departure. To Wheeler this fight against Lumsden was the one delightful element of life in the Bottoms. He had now the comfortable prospect of spending his declining years in a fertile valley where there was a powerful foe, whose encroachments on the rights and privileges of his neighbors would afford him an inexhaustible theme for denunciation, and a delightful incitement to the exercise of his powers of resistance. And thus for years he had eaten his dinners with better relish because of his contest with Lumsden. Mordecai could not have had half so much pleasure in staring stiffly at the wicked Haman as Isaiah Wheeler found in meeting Captain Lumsden on the road without so much as a nod of recognition. And Haman's feelings were not more deeply wounded than Lumsden's.

Colonel Wheeler was not very happily married; for at home he could find no encroachments to resist. The perfect temper of his wife disarmed even his opposition. He had begun his married life by fighting his wife's Methodism; but when he came to the Hissawachee and found Methodism unpopular, he took up arms in its defense.

Such was the man whom Kike had selected as guardian—a man who, with all his disagreeableness, was possessed of honesty, a virtue not inconsistent with oppugnancy. But Kike's chief motive in choosing him was that he knew that the choice would be a stab to his uncle's pride. Moreover, Wheeler was the only man who would care to brave Lumsden's anger by taking the trust.

Wheeler lived in a log house on the hillside, and to this house, on the day after the return of Morton and Kike, there rode a stranger. He was a broad-shouldered, stalwart, swarthy man, of thirty-five, with a serious but aggressive countenance, a broad-brim white hat, a coat made of country jeans, cut straight-breasted and buttoned to the chin, rawhide boots, and "linsey" leggings tied about his legs below the knees. He rode a stout horse, and carried an ample pair of saddle-bags.

Reining his horse in front of the colonel's double

cabin, he shouted, after the Western fashion, "Hello!
Hello the house!"

At this a quartette of dogs set up a vociferous
barking, ranging in key all the way from the contemptible treble of an ill-natured "fice" to the deep
baying of a huge bull-dog.

"Hello the house!" cried the stranger.

COLONEL WHEELER'S DOORYARD.

"Hello! hello!" answered back Isaiah Wheeler,
opening the door, and shouting to the dogs, "You,
Bull, come here! Git out, pup! Clear out, all of
you!" And he accompanied this command by threat-
eningly lifting a stick, at which two of the dogs scam-

pered away, and a third sneakingly retreated; but the bull-dog turned with reluctance, and, without smoothing his bristles at all, slowly marched back toward the house, protesting with surly growls against this authoritative interruption.

"Hello, stranger, howdy?" said Colonel Wheeler, advancing with caution, but without much cordiality. He would not commit himself to a welcome too rashly; strangers needed inspection. "'Light, won't you?" he said, presently; and the stranger proceeded to dismount, while the Colonel ordered one of his sons who came out at that moment to "put up the stranger's horse, and give him some fodder and corn." Then turning to the new-comer, he scanned him a moment, and said: "A preacher, I reckon, sir?"

"Yes, sir, I'm a Methodist preacher, and I heard that your wife was a member of the Methodist Church, and that you were very friendly; so I came round this way to see if you wouldn't open your doors for preaching. I have one or two vacant days on my round, and thought maybe I might as well take Hissawachee Bottom into the circuit, if I didn't find anything to prevent."

By this time the colonel and his guest had reached the door, and the former only said, "Well, sir, let's go in, and see what the old woman says. I don't agree with you Methodists about everything, but I do think that you are doing good, and so I don't allow anybody to say anything against circuit riders without taking it up."

Mrs. Wheeler, a dignified woman, with a placidly

religious face—a countenance in which scruples are balanced by evenness of temperament—was at the moment engaged in dipping yarn into a blue dye that stood in a great iron kettle by the fire. She made haste to wash and dry her hands, that she might have a "good, old-fashioned Methodist shake-hands" with Brother Magruder, "the first Methodist preacher she had seen since she left Pittsburg."

Colonel Wheeler readily assented that Mr. Magruder should preach in his house. Methodists had just the same rights in a free country that other people had. He "reckoned the Hissawachee settlement didn't belong to one man, and he had fit aginst the King of England in his time, and was jist as ready to fight aginst the King of Hissawachee Bottom." The Colonel almost relaxed his stubborn lips into a smile when he said this. Besides, he proceeded, his wife was a Methodist; and she had a right to be, if she chose. He was friendly to religion himself, though he wasn't a professor. If his wife didn't want to wear rings or artificials, it was money in his pocket, and nobody had a right to object. Colonel Wheeler plumed himself before the new preacher upon his general friendliness toward religion, and really thought it might be set down on the credit side of that account in which he imagined some angelic book-keeper entered all his transactions. He felt in his own mind "middlin' certain," as he would have told you, that "betwixt the prayin' for he got from *such* a wife as his, and his own gineral friendliness to the preachers and the Methodis' meetings, he would be saved at the last, *somehow or*

E

nother." It was not in the man to reflect that his
"gineral friendliness" for the preacher had its origin
in a gineral spitefulness toward Captain Lumsden.

Colonel Wheeler's son was dispatched through the
settlement to inform everybody that there would be
preaching in his house that evening. The news was
told at the Forks, where there was always a crowd of
loafers; and each individual loafer, in riding home
that afternoon, called a "Hello!" at every house he
passed; and when the salutation from within was answered, remarked that he "thought liker'n not they
had'n heern tell of the preacher's comin' to Colonel
Wheeler's." And then the eager listener, generally the
woman of the house, would cry out, "Laws-a-massy!
You don't say! A Methodis'? One of the shoutin'
kind, that knocks folks down when he preaches!
What will the Captin' do? They do say he *does* hate
the Methodis' worse nor copperhead snakes, now.
Some old quarrel, liker'n not. Well, I'm agoin', jist to
see how *red*ikl'us them Methodis' *does* do!"

The news was sent to Brady's school, which had
"tuck up" for the winter, and from this centre also it
soon spread throughout the neighborhood. It reached
Lumsden's very early in the forenoon.

"Well!" said Lumsden, excitedly, but still with his
little crowing chuckle; "so Wheeler's took the Methodists in! We'll have to see about that. A man that
brings such people to the settlement ought to be
lynched. But I'll match the Methodists. Where's
Patty? Patty! O, Patty! Bob, run and find Miss
Patty."

And the little negro ran out, calling, "Miss Patty! O! Miss Patty! Whah is ye?"

He looked into the smoke-house, and then ran down toward the barn, shouting, "Miss Patty! O! Miss Patty!"

Where was Patty?

CHAPTER X.

PATTY had that morning gone to the spring-house, as usual, to strain the milk.

Can it be possible that any benighted reader does not know what a spring-house is? A little log cabin six feet long by five feet wide, without floor, built where the great stream of water issues clear and icy cold from beneath the hill. The little cabin-like spring-house sits always in the hollow; as you approach it you look down upon the roof of rough shingles which Western people call "clapboards," you see the green moss that overgrows them and the logs, you see the new-born brook rush out from beneath the logs that hide its cradle, you lift the home-made latch and open the low door which creaks on its wooden hinges, you see the great perennial spring rushing up eagerly from its subterranean prison, you note how its clear cold waters lave the sides of the earthen crocks, and in the dim light and the fresh coolness, in the presence of the rich creaminess, you feel whole eclogues of poetry which you can never turn into words.

It was in just such a spring-house that Patty Lumsden had hidden herself.

She brought clean crocks—earthenware milk pans —from the shelf outside, where they had been airing to keep them sweet; she held the strainer in her left hand and poured the milk through it until each crock was nearly full; she adjusted them in their places among the stones, so that they stood half immersed in the cold current of spring water; she laid the smooth pine cover on each crock, and put a clean stone atop that to secure it.

While she was thus putting away the milk her mind was on Morton. She wondered what her father had said to him yesterday. In the heart of her heart she resolved that if Morton loved her she would marry him in the face of her father's displeasure. She had never rebelled against the iron rule, but she felt herself full of power and full of endurance. She could go off into the wilderness with Morton; they would build them a cabin, with chinking and daubing, with puncheon floor and stick chimney; they would sleep, like other poor settlers, on beds of dry leaves, and they would subsist upon the food which Morton's unerring rifle would bring them from the forest. These were the humble cabin castles she was building. All girls weave a tapestry of the future; on Patty's the knight wore buck-skin clothes and a wolf-skin cap, and brought home, not the shields or spoils of the enemy, but saddles of venison and luscious bits of bear-meat to a lady in linsey or cheap cotton who looked out of no balcony but a cabin window, and who smoked her eyes with hanging pots upon a crane in a great fire-place. I know it sounds old-fashioned and sentimental in me to say so, and yet how can it matter to a heart like Patty's what may be the scenery on the tapestry, if love be the warp and faith the woof?

Morton on his part was at the same time endeavoring to plan his own and Patty's partnership future, but he drew a more cheerful picture than she did, for he had no longer any reason to fear Captain Lumsden's displeasure. He was at the moment going to meet the Captain, walking down the foot-path through the woods, kicking the dry beech leaves into billows before him

PATTY IN THE SPRING-HOUSE.

and singing a Scotch love-song of Burns's which he had learned from his mother.

He planned one future, she another; and in after
years they might have laughed to think how far wrong
were both guesses. The path which Morton followed
led by the spring-house, and Patty, standing on the
stones inside, caught the sound of his fine baritone
voice as he approached, singing tender words that
made her heart stand still:

> " Ghaist nor bogle shalt thou fear;
> Thou'rt to love and heaven sae dear
> Nocht of ill shall come thee near,
> My bonnie dearie."

And as he came right by the spring-house, he
sang, now in a lower tone lest he should be heard at
the house, but still more earnestly, and so audibly
that the listening Patty could hear every word, the
last stanza :

> " Fair and lovely as thou art,
> Thou hast stown my very heart;
> I can die—but cannot part,
> My bonnie dearie."

And even as she listened to the last line, Morton
had discovered that the spring-house door was ajar,
and turned, shading his eyes, to see if perchance Patty
might not be within. He saw her and reached out
his hand, greeting her warmly ; but his eyes yet unaccustomed to the imperfect light did not see how
full of blushes was her face—for she feared that he
might guess all that she had just been dreaming. But
she was resolved at any rate to show him more kindness than she would have shown had it not been for
the displeasure which she supposed her father had

manifested And so she covered the last crock and came and stood by him at the door of the spring-house, and he talked right on in the tender strain of his song. And she did not protest, but answered back timidly and almost as warmly.

And that is how little negro Bob at last found Patty at the spring-house and found Morton with her. "Law's sake! Miss Patty, done look for ye mos' ev-erywhah. Yer paw wants ye." And with that Bob rolled the whites of his eyes up, parted his black lips into a broad white grin, and looked at Morton know-ingly.

CHAPTER XI

THE VOICE IN THE WILDERNESS.

"HA! ha! good morning, Morton!" said the Captain. "You've been keeping Patty down at the spring-house when she should have been at the loom by this time. In my time young men and women didn't waste their mornings. Nights and Sundays are good enough for visiting. Now, see here, Patty, there's one of them plagued Methodist preachers brought into the settlement by Wheeler. These circuit riders are worse than third day fever 'n' ager. They go against dancing and artificials and singing songs and reading novels and all other amusements. They give people the jerks wherever they go. The devil's in 'em. Now I want you to go to work and get up a dance to-night, and ask all you can get along with. Nothing 'll make the preacher so mad as to dance right under his nose; and we'll keep a good many people away who might get the jerks, or fall down with the power and break their necks, maybe."

Patty was always ready to dance, and she only said: "If Morton will help me send the invitations."

"I'll do that," said Morton, and then he told of the discomfiture he had wrought in a Methodist meeting while he was gone. And he had the satis-faction of seeing that the narrative greatly pleased Captain Lumsden.

"We'll have to send Wheeler afloat sometime, eh, Mort?" said the Captain, chuckling interrogatively. Morton did not like this proposition, for, notwithstanding theological differences about election, Mrs. Wheeler was a fast friend of his mother. He evaded an answer by hastening to consult with Patty and her mother concerning the guests.

Those who got "invites" danced cotillions and reels nearly all night. Morton danced with Patty to his heart's content, and in the happiness of Morton's assured love and of a truce in her father's interruptions she was a queen indeed. She wore the antique earrings that were an heir-loom in her mother's family, and a showy breast-pin which her father had bought her. These and her new dress of English calico made her the envy of all the others. Pretty Betty Harsha was led out by some one at almost every dance, but she would have given all of these for one dance with Morton Goodwin.

Meantime Mr. Magruder was preaching. Behold in Hissawachee Bottom the world's evils in miniature! Here are religion and amusement divorced—set over the one against the other as hostile camps.

Brady, who was boarding for a few days with the widow Lumsden, went to the meeting with Kike and his mother, explaining his views as he went along.

"I'm no Mithodist, Mrs. Lumsden. Me father was a Catholic and me mother a Prisbytarian, and they compromised on me by making me a mimber of the Episcopalian Church and throyin' to edicate me for orders, and intoirely spoilĭng me for iverything

else but a school taycher in these haythen backwoods.
But it does same to me that the Mithodists air the
only payple that can do any good among sich pagans
as we air. What would a parson from the ould coun-
thry do here? He moight spake as grammathical as
Lindley Murray himsilf, and nobody would be the
better of it. What good does me own grammathical
acquoirements do towards reforming the sittlement?
With all me grammar I can't kape me boys from
makin' God's name the nominative case before very bad
words. Hey, Koike? Now, the Mithodists air a narry sort of a payple. But if you want to make a strame
strong you hev to make it narry. I've read a good
dale of history, and in me own estimation the ould
Anglish Puritans and the Mithodists air both torrents,
because they're both shet up by narry banks. The
Mithodists is ferninst the wearin' of jewelry and danc-
in' and singin' songs, which is all vairy foolish in me
own estimation. But it's kind o' nat'ral for the mill-
race that turns the whale that fades the worruld to
git mad at the babblin', oidle brook that wastes its
toime among the mossy shtones and grinds nobody's
grist. But the brook ain't so bad afther all. Hey,
Mrs. Lumsden?"

Mrs. Lumsden answered that she didn't think it
was. It was very good for watering stock.

"Thrue as praychin', Mrs. Lumsden," said the
schoolmaster, with a laugh. "And to me own oi the
wanderin' brook, a-goin' where it chooses and doin'
what it plazes, is a dale plizenter to look at than the
sthraight-travelin' mill-race. But I wish these Mithod-

ists would convart the souls of some of these young·
sters, and make 'em quit their gamblin' and swearin
and bettin' on horses and gettin' dthrunk. And may·
be if some of 'em would git convarted, they wouldn'
be quoite so anxious to skelp their own uncles. Hey
Koike?"

Kike had no time to reply if he had cared to, for
by this time they were at the door of Colonel Wheeler's house. Despite the dance there were present,
from near and far, all the house would hold. For
those who got no "invite" to Lumsden's had a double
motive for going to meeting; a disposition to resent
the slight was added to their curiosity to hear the
Methodist preacher. The dance had taken away those
who were most likely to disturb the meeting; people
left out did not feel under any obligation to gratify
Captain Lumsden by raising a row. Kike had been
invited, but had disdained to dance in his uncle's
house.

Both lower rooms of Wheeler's log house were
crowded with people. A little open space was left at
the door between the rooms for the preacher, who
presently came edging his way in through the crowd.
He had been at prayer in that favorite oratory of the
early Methodist preacher, the forest.

Magruder was a short, stout man, with wide shoulders, powerful arms, shaggy brows, and bristling black
hair. He read the hymn, two lines at a time, and led
the singing himself. He prayed with the utmost sincerity, but in a voice that shook the cabin windows
and gave the simple people a deeper reverence for the

dreadfulness of the preacher's message. He prayed as
a man talking face to face with the Almighty Judge of
the generations of men; he prayed with an undoubt-
ing assurance of his own acceptance with God, and
with the sincerest conviction of the infinite peril of
his unforgiven hearers. It is not argument that reaches men, but conviction; and for immediate, practical
purposes, one Tishbite Elijah, that can thunder out of
a heart that never doubts, is worth a thousand acute
writers of ingenious apologies.

When Magruder read his text, which was, "Grieve
not the Holy Spirit of God," he seemed to his hearers a prophet come to lay bare their hearts. Magruder had not been educated for his ministry by years
of study of Hebrew and Greek, of Exegesis and Sys-
tematics; but he knew what was of vastly more consequence to him—how to read and expound the hearts
and lives of the impulsive, simple, reckless race among
whom he labored. He was of their very fibre.

He commenced with a fierce attack on Captain
Lumsden's dance, which was prompted, he said, by the
devil, to keep men out of heaven. With half a dozen
quick, bold strokes, he depicted Lumsden's selfish ar-
rogance and proud meanness so exactly that the audience fluttered with sensation. Magruder had a vicarious conscience; but a vicarious conscience is good
for nothing unless it first cuts close at home. Whitefield said that he never preached a sermon to others till
he had first preached it to George Whitefield; and Magruder's severities had all the more effect that his audience could see that they had full force upon himself.

It is hard for us to understand the elements that produced such incredible excitements as resulted from the early Methodist preaching. How at a camp-meeting, for instance, five hundred people, indifferent enough to everything of the sort one hour before, should be seized during a sermon with terror—should cry aloud to God for mercy, some of them falling in trances and cataleptic unconsciousness; and how, out of all this excitement, there should come forth, in very many cases, the fruit of transformed lives seems to us a puzzle beyond solution. But the early Westerners were as inflammable as tow; they did not deliberate, they were swept into most of their decisions by contagious excitements. And never did any class of men understand the art of exciting by oratory more perfectly than the old Western preachers. The simple hunters to whom they preached had the most absolute faith in the invisible. The Day of Judgment, the doom of the wicked, and the blessedness of the righteous were as real and substantial in their conception as any facts in life. They could abide no refinements. The terribleness of Indian warfare, the relentlessness of their own revengefulness, the sudden lynchings, the abandoned wickedness of the lawless, and the ruthlessness of mobs of "regulators" were a background upon which they founded the most materialistic conception of hell and the most literal understanding of the Day of Judgment. Men like Magruder knew how to handle these few positive ideas of a future life so that they were indeed terrible weapons.

On this evening he seized upon the particular sins

of the people as things by which they drove away the Spirit of God. The audience trembled as he moved on in his rude speech and solemn indignation. Every man found himself in turn called to the bar of his own conscience. There was excitement throughout the house. Some were angry, some sobbed aloud, as he alluded to "promises made to dying friends," "vows offered to God by the new-made graves of their children,"—for pioneer people are very susceptible to all such appeals to sensibility.

When at last he came to speak of revenge, Kike, who had listened intently from the first, found himself breathing hard. The preacher showed how the re vengeful man was "as much a murderer as if he had already killed his enemy and hid his mangled body in the leaves of the woods where none but the wolf could ever find him !"

At these words he turned to the part of the room where Kike sat, white with feeling. Magruder, looking always for the effect of his arrows, noted Kike's emotion and paused. The house was utterly still, save now and then a sob from some anguish-smitten soul. The people were sitting as if waiting their doom. Kike already saw in his imagination the mutilated form of his uncle Enoch hidden in the leaves and scented by hungry wolves. He waited to hear his own sentence. Hitherto the preacher had spoken with vehemence. Now, he stopped and began again with tears, and in a tone broken with emotion, looking in a general way toward where Kike sat : " O, young man, there are stains of blood on your hands!

How dare you hold them up before the Judge of all? You are another Cain, and God sends his messenger to you to-day to inquire after him whom you have already killed in your heart. *You are a murderer!* Nothing but God's mercy can snatch you from hell!"

No doubt all this is rude in refined ears. But is it nothing that by these rude words he laid bare Kike's sins to Kike's conscience? That in this moment Kike heard the voice of God denouncing his sins, and trembled? Can you do a man any higher service than to make him know himself, in the light of the highest sense of right that he capable of? Kike, for his part, bowed to the rebuke of the preacher as to the rebuke of God. His frail frame shook with fear and penitence, as it had before shaken with wrath. "O, God! what a wretch I am!" cried he, hiding his face in his hands.

"Thank God for showing it to you, my young friend," responded the preacher. "What a wonder that your sins did not drive away the Holy Ghost, leaving you with your day of grace sinned away, as good as damned already!" And with this he turned and appealed yet more powerfully to the rest, already excited by the fresh contagion of Kike's penitence, until there were cries and sobs in all parts of the house. Some left in haste to avoid yielding to their feeling, while many fell upon their knees and prayed.

The preacher now thought it time to change, and offer some consolation. You would say that his view of the atonement was crude, conventional and commercial; that he mistook figures of speech in Scripture for general and formulated postulates. But however imperfect his symbols, he succeeded in making known to his hearers the mercy of God. And surely that is the main thing. The figure of speech is but the vessel; the great truth that God is merciful to the guilty, what is this but the water of life?—not less refreshing because the jar in which it is brought is rude! The preacher's whole manner changed. Many weeping and sobbing people were swept now to the other extreme, and cried aloud with joy. Perhaps Magruder exaggerated the change that had taken place in them. But is it nothing that a man has bowed his soul in penitence before God's justice, and then lifted his face in childlike trust to God's mercy? It is hard for one who has once passed through this experience not to date from it a revolution. There were many who had not much root in themselves, doubtless, but among Magruder's hearers this day were those who, living half a century afterward, counted their better living from the hour of his forceful presentation of God's antagonism to sin, and God's tender mercy for the sinner.

It was not in Kike to change quickly. Smitten with a sense of his guilt, he rose from his seat and slowly knelt, quivering with feeling. When the preacher had finished preaching, amid cries of sorrow and joy, he began to sing, to an exquisitely pathetic tune, Watts' hymn:

> " Show pity, Lord, O ! Lord, forgive,
> Let a repenting rebel live.
> Are not thy mercies large and free?
> May not a sinner trust in thee?"

The meeting was held until late. Kike remained quietly kneeling, the tears trickling through his fingers. He did not utter a word or cry. In all the confusion he was still. What deliberate recounting of his own misdoings took place then, no one can know. Thoughtless readers may scoff at the poor backwoods boy in his trouble. But who of us would not be better if we could be brought thus face to face with our own souls? His simple penitent faith did more for him than all our philosophy has done for us, maybe.

At last the meeting was dismissed. Brady, who had been awe-stricken at sight of Kike's agony of contrition, now thought it best that he and Kike's mother should go home, leaving the young man to follow when he chose. But Kike staid immovable upon his knees. His sense of guilt had become an agony. All those allowances which we in a more intelligent age make for inherited peculiarities and the defects of education, Kike knew nothing about. He believed all his revengefulness to be voluntary; he had a feeling that unless he found some assurance of God's mercy then he could not live till morning. So the minister and Mrs. Wheeler and two or three brethren that had come from adjoining settlements staid and prayed and talked with the distressed youth until after midnight. The early Methodists regarded this persistence as a sure sign of a "sound" awakening.

At last the preacher knelt again by Kike, and asked "Sister Wheeler" to pray. There was nothing in the old Methodist meetings so excellent as the audible prayers of women. Women oftener than men have a genius for prayer. Mrs. Wheeler began tenderly, penitently to confess, not Kike's sins, but the sins of all of them; her penitence fell in with Kike's; she confessed the very sins that he was grieving over. Then slowly—slowly, as one who waits for another to follow—she began to turn toward trustfulness. Like a little child she spoke to God; under the influence of her praying Kike sobbed audibly. Then he seemed to feel the contagion of her faith; he, too, looked to God as a father; he, too, felt the peace of a trustful child.

The great struggle was over. Kike was revengeful no longer. He was distrustful and terrified no longer. He had "crept into the heart of God" and found rest. Call it what you like, when a man passes through such an experience, however induced, it separates the life that is passed from the life that follows by a great gulf.

Kike, the new Kike, forgiving and forgiven, rose up at the close of the prayer, and with a peaceful face shook hands with the preacher and the brethren, rejoicing in this new fellowship. He said nothing, but when Magruder sang

> "Oh! how happy are they
> Who their Saviour obey,
>   And have laid up their treasure above!
> Tongue can never express
> The sweet comfort and peace
>   Of a soul in its earliest love,"

Kike shook hands with them all again, bade them good-night, and went home about the time that his friend Morton, flushed and weary with dancing and pleasure, laid himself down to rest.

CHAPTER XII.

MR. BRADY PROPHESIES.

THE Methodists had actually made a break in the settlement. Dancing had not availed to keep them out. It was no longer a question of getting "shet" of Wheeler and his Methodist wife, thus extirpating the contagion. There would now be a "class" formed, a leader appointed, a regular preaching place established; Hissawachee would become part of that great wheel called a circuit; there would be revivals and conversions; the peace of the settlement would be destroyed. For now one might never again dance at a "hoe-down," drink whiskey at a shuckin', or race "hosses" on Sunday, without a lecture from somebody. It might be your own wife, too. Once let the Methodists in, and there was no knowin'.

Lumsden, for his part, saw more serious consequences. By his opposition, he had unfortunately spoken for the enmity of the Methodists in advance. The preacher had openly defied him. Kike would join the class, and the Methodists would naturally resist his ascendancy. No concession on his part short of absolute surrender would avail. He resolved therefore that the Methodists should find out "who they were fighting."

Brady was pleased. Gossips are always delighted to have something happen out of the usual course. It gives them a theme, something to exercise their wits upon. Let us not be too hard upon gossip. It is one form of communicative intellectual activity. Brady, under different conditions, might have been a journalist, writing relishful leaders on "topics of the time." For what is journalism but elevated and organized gossip? The greatest benefactor of an out-of-the-way neighborhood is the man or woman with a talent for good-natured gossip. Such an one averts absolute mental stagnation, diffuses intelligence, and keeps alive a healthful public opinion on local questions.

Brady wanted to taste some of Mrs. Goodwin's "ry-al hoe-cake." That was the reason he assigned for his visit on the evening after the meeting. He was always hungry for hoe-cake when anything had happened about which he wanted to talk. But on this evening Job Goodwin got the lead in conversation at first.

"Mr. Brady," said he, "what's going to happen to us all? These Methodis' sets people crazy with the jerks, I've hearn tell. Hey? I hear dreadful things about 'em. Oh dear, it seems like as if everything come upon folks at once. Hey? The fever's spreadin' at Chilicothe, they tell me. And then, if we should git into a war with England, you know, and the Indians should come and skelp us, they'd be precious few left, betwixt them that went crazy and them that got skelped. Precious few, *I* tell you. Hey?"

Here Mr. Goodwin knocked the ashes out of his pipe and laid it away, and punched the fire meditatively, endeavoring to discover in his imagination some

new and darker pigment for his picture of the future.
But failing to think of anything more lugubrious than
Methodists, Indi-
ans, and fever, he
set the tongs in the
corner, heaved a
sigh of discourage-
ment, and looked at
Brady inquiringly.

" Ye're loike the
hootin' owl, Mis-
ther Goodwin; it's
the black side ye're
afther lookin' at all
the toime. Where's
Moirton? He aint
been to school yet
since this quarter
took up."

" Morton? He's
got to stay out, I

Job Goodwin.

expect. My rheumatiz is mighty bad, and I'm powerful
weak. I don't think craps 'll be good next year, and
I expect we'll have a hard row to hoe, partic'lar if we
all have the fever, and the Methodis' keep up their
excitement and driving people crazy with jerks, and
war breaks out with England, and the Indians come on
us. But here's Mort now."

" Ha! Moirton, and ye wasn't at matin' last noight?
Ye heerd fwat a toime we had. Most iverybody got
struck harmless, excipt mesilf and a few other hard.

ened sinners. Ye heerd about Koike? I reckon the
Captain's good and glad he's got the blissin'; it's a
warrantee on the Captain's skull, maybe. Fwat would
ye do for a crony now, Moirton, if Koike come to be
a praycher?"

"He aint such a fool, I guess," said Morton, with
whom Kike's "getting religion" was an unpleasant
topic. "It'll all wear off with Kike soon enough."

"Don't be too shore, Moirton. Things wear off
with you, sometoimes. Ye swear ye'll niver swear no
more, and ye're willin' to bet that ye'll niver bet agin,
and ye're always a-talkin' about a brave loife; but the
flesh is ferninst ye. When Koike's bad, he's bad all
over; lickin' won't take it out of him; I've throid it
mesilf. Now he's got good, the divil 'll have as hard
a toime makin' him bad as I had makin' him good.
I'm roight glad it's the divil now, and not his schoolmasther, as has got to throy to handle the lad. Got
ivery lisson to-day, and didn't break a single rule of
the school! What do you say to that, Moirton? The
divil's got his hands full thair. Hey, Moirton?"

"Yes, but he'll never be a preacher. He wants to
get rich just to spite the Captain."

"But the spoite's clean gone with the rist, Moirton.
And he'll be a praycher yit. Didn't he give me a
talkin' to this mornin', at breakfast? Think of the impudent little scoundrel a-venturin' to tell his ould masther that he ought to repint of his sins! He talked
to his mother, too, till she croid. He'll make her belave she is a great sinner whin she aint wicked a bit,
excipt in her grammar, which couldn't be worse. I've

talked to her about that mesilf. Now, Moirton, I'll tell ye the symptoms of a praycher among the Mith. odists. Those that take it aisy, and don't bother a body, you needn't be afeard of. But those that git it bad, and are throublesome, and middlesome, and ag- gravatin', ten to one 'll turn out praychers. The lad that'll tackle his masther and his mother at breakfast the very mornin' afther he's got the blissin, while he's yit a babe, so to spake, and pray he to 'em single- handed, two to one, is a-takin' the short cut acrost the faild to be a praycher of the worst sort ; one of the kind that's as thorny as a honey-locust."

"Well, why can't they be peaceable, and let other people alone ? That meddling is just what I don't like," growled Morton.

"Bedad, Moirton, that's jist fwat Ahab and Jizebel thought about ould Elijy ! We don't any of us loike to have our wickedness or laziness middled with. 'Twas middlin', sure, that the Pharisays objicted to ; and if the blissed Jaysus hadn't been so throublesome, he wouldn't niver a been crucified."

"Why, Brady, you'll be a Methodist yourself," said Mr. Job Goodwin.

"Niver a bit of it, Mr. Goodwin. I'm rale lazy. This lookin' at the state of me moind's insoides, and this chasin' afther me sins up hill and down dale all the toime, would niver agray with me frail constitoo- tion. This havin' me spiritooal pulse examined ivery wake in class-matin', and this watchin' and prayin', aren't for sich oidlers as me. I'm too good-natered to trate mesilf that wav. sure. Didn't you iver notice that the highest vartoos ain't possible to a rale good-nater'd man?"

Here Mrs. Goodwin looked at the cake on the hoe in front of the fire, and found it well browned. Supper was ready, and the conversation drifted to Morton's prospective arrangement with Captain Lumsden to cultivate his hill farm on the "sheers." Morton's father shook his head ominously. Didn't believe the Captain was in 'arnest. Ef he was, Mort mout git the fever in the winter, or die, or be laid up. 'Twouldn't do to depend on no sech promises, no way.

But, notwithstanding his father's croaking, Morton did hold to the Captain's promise, and to the hope of Patty. To the Captain's plans for mobbing Wheeler he offered a strong resistance. But he was ready enough to engage in making sport of the despised religionists, and even organized a party to interrupt Magruder with tin horns when he should preach again. But all this time Morton was uneasy in himself. What had become of his dreams of being a hero? Here was Kike bearing all manner of persecution with patience, devoting himself to the welfare of others, while all his own purposes of noble and knightly living were hopelessly sunk in a morass of adverse circumstances. One of Morton's temperament must either grow better or worse, and, chafing under these embarassments, he played and drank more freely than ever.

F

CHAPTER XIII.

TWO TO ONE.

MAGRUDER had been so pleased with his success in organizing a class in the Hissawachee settlement that he resolved to favor them with a Sunday sermon on his next round. He was accustomed to preach twice every week-day and three times on every Sunday, after the laborious manner of the circuit-rider of his time. And since he expected to leave Hissawachee as soon as meeting should be over, for his next appointment, he determined to reach the settlement before breakfast that he might have time to confirm the brethren and set things in order.

When the Sunday set apart for the second sermon drew near, Morton, with the enthusiastic approval of Captain Lumsden, made ready his tin horns to interrupt the preacher with a serenade. But Lumsden had other plans of which Morton had no knowledge.

John Wesley's rule was, that a preacher should rise at four o'clock and spend the hour until five in reading, meditation and prayer. Five o'clock found Magruder in the saddle on his way to Hissawachee, reflecting upon the sermon he intended to preach. When he had ridden more than an hour, keeping himself company by a lusty singing of hymns, he came suddenly out upon the brow of a hill overlooking the Hissawachee valley. The gray dawn was streaking the clouds, the preacher checked his horse and looked forth on the valley just disclosing its salient features in the twilight, as a General looks over a battle-field before the engagement begins. Then he dismounted, and, kneeling upon the leaves, prayed with apostolic fervor for victory over "the hosts of sin and the devil." When at last he got into the saddle again the winter sun was sending its first horizontal beams into his eyes, and all the eastern sky was ablaze. Magruder had the habit of turning the whole universe to spiritual account, and now, as he descended the hill, he made the woods ring with John Wesley's hymn, which might have been composed in the presence of such a scene :

> "O sun of righteousness, arise
> With healing in thy wing ;
> To my diseased, my fainting soul,
> Life and salvation bring.

> " These clouds of pride and sin dispel,
> By thy all-piercing beam ;
> Lighten my eyes with faith ; my heart
> With holy hopes inflame."

By the time he had finished the second stanza, the bridle-path that he was following brought him into a dense forest of beech and maple, and he saw walking toward him two stout men, none other than our old acquaintances, Bill McConkey and Jake Sniger.

"Looky yer," said Bill, catching the preacher's horse by the bridle : "you git down !"

"What for ?" said Magruder.

"We're goin' to lick you tell you promise to go

back and never stick your head into the Hissawachee
Bottom agin."

"But I won't promise."

"Then we'll put a finishment to ye."

Two to One.

"You are two to one. Will you give me time to
draw my coat?"

"Wal, yes, I 'low we will."

The preacher dismounted with quiet deliberation,

tied his bridle to a beech limb, offering a mental
prayer to the God of Samson, and then laid his coat
across the saddle.

"My friends," he said, "I don't want to whip you.
I advise you now to let me alone. As an American
citizen, I have a right to go where I please. My
father was a revolutionary soldier, and I mean to
fight for my rights."

"Shet up your jaw!" said Jake, swearing, and approaching the preacher from one side, while Bill came
up on the other. Magruder was one of those short,
stocky men who have no end of muscular force and
endurance. In his unregenerate days he had been
celebrated for his victories in several rude encounters.
Never seeking a fight even then, he had, nevertheless,
when any ambitious champion came from afar for the
purpose of testing his strength, felt himself bound to
"give him what he came after." He had now greatly
the advantage of the two bullies in his knowledge of
the art of boxing.

Before Jake had fairly finished his preliminary
swearing the preacher had surprised him by delivering
a blow that knocked him down. But Bill had taken
advantage of this to strike Magruder heavily on the
cheek. Jake, having felt the awful weight of Magruder's fist, was a little slow in coming to time, and the
preacher had a chance to give Bill a most polemical
blow on his nose; then turning suddenly, he rushed
like a mad bull upon Sniger, and dealt him one tremendous blow that fractured two of his ribs and felled
him to the earth. But Bill struck Magruder behind,

knocked him over, and threw himself upon him after the fashion of the Western free fight. Nothing saved Magruder but his immense strength. He rose right up with Bill upon him, and then, by a deft use of his legs, tripped his antagonist and hurled him to the ground. He did not dare take advantage of his fall, however, for Jake had regained his feet and was coming up on him cautiously. But when Sniger saw Magruder rushing at him again, he made a speedy retreat into the bushes, leaving Magruder to fight it out with Bill, who, despite his sorry-looking nose, was again ready. But he now "fought shy," and kept retreating slowly backward and calling out, "Come up on him behind, Jake! Come up behind!" But the demoralized Jake had somehow got a superstitious notion that the preacher bristled with fists before and behind, having as many arms as a Hindoo deity. Bill kept backing until he tripped and fell over a bit of brush, and then picked himself up and made off, muttering:

"I aint a-goin' to try to handle him alone! He must have the very devil into him!"

About nine o'clock on that same Sunday morning, the Irish school-master, who was now boarding at Goodwin's, and who had just made an early visit to the Forks for news, accosted Morton with: "An' did ye hear the nooze, Moirton? Bill Conkey and Jake Sniger hev had a bit of Sunday morning ricreation. They throid to thrash the praycher as he was a-comin' through North's Holler, this mornin'; but they didn't make no allowance for the Oirish blood Magruder's got in him. He larruped 'em both single-handed, and Jake's ribs are cracked, and ye'd lawf to see Bill's nose! Captain must 'a' had some proivate intherest in that muss; hey, Moirton?"

"It's thunderin' mean!' said Morton; "two men on one, and him a preacher; and all I've got to say is, I wish he'd killed 'em both."

"And yer futer father-in-law into the bargain? Hey, Moirton? But fwat did I tell ye about Koike? The praycher's jaw is lamed by a lick Bill gave him, and Koike's to exhort in his place. I tould ye he had the botherin' sperit of prophecy in him."

The manliness in a character like Morton's must react, if depressed too far; and he now notified those who were to help him interrupt the meeting that if any disturbance were made, he should take it on himself to punish the offender. He would not fight alongside Bill McConkey and Jake Sniger, and he felt like seeking a quarrel with Lumsden, for the sake of justitifying himself to himself.

CHAPTER XIV.

DURING the time that had intervened between
Kike's conversion and Magruder's second visit
to the settlement, Kike had developed a very considerable gift for earnest speech in the class meetings.
In that day every influence in Methodist association
contributed to make a preacher of a man of force.
The reverence with which a self-denying preacher was
regarded by the people was a great compensation for
the poverty and toil that pertained to the office. To
be a preacher was to be canonized during one's life-
time. The moment a young man showed zeal and
fluency he was pitched on by all the brethren and
sisters as one whose duty it was to preach the Gospel; he was asked whether he did not feel that he
had a divine call; he was set upon watching the
movements within him to see whether or not he
ought to be among the sons of the prophets. Often-
times a man was made to feel, in spite of his own
better judgment, that he was a veritable Jonah, slink-
ing from duty, and in imminent peril of a whale in
the shape of some providential disaster. Kike, indeed,
needed none of these urgings to impel him toward
the ministry. He was a man of the prophetic temperament—one of those men whose beliefs take hold
of them more strongly than the objects of sense. The

future life, as preached by the early Methodists, with all its joys and all its awful torments, became the most substantial of realities to him. He was in constant astonishment that people could believe these things theoretically and ignore them in practice. If men were going headlong to perdition, and could be saved and brought into a paradise of eternal bliss by preaching, then what nobler work could there be than that of saving them? And, let a man take what view he may of a future life, Kike's opinion was the right one—no work can be so excellent as that of helping men to better living.

Kike had been poring over some works of Methodist biography which he had borrowed, and the sublimated life of Fletcher was the only one that fulfilled his ideal. Methodism preached consecration to its disciples. Kike had already learned from Mrs. Wheeler, who was the class-leader at Hissawachee settlement, and from Methodist literature, that he must "keep all on the altar." He must be ready to do, to suffer, or to perish, for the Master. The sternest sayings of Christ about forsaking father and mother, and hating one's own life and kindred, he heard often repeated in exhortations. Most people are not harmed by a literal understanding of hyperbolical expressions. Laziness and selfishness are great antidotes to fanaticism, and often pass current for common sense. Kike had no such buffers; taught to accept the words of the Gospel with the dry literalness of statutory enactments, he was too honest to evade their force, too earnest to slacken his obedience. He was already prepared to accept any burden and endure any trial that might be given as a test of discipleship. All his natural ambition, vehemence, and persistence, found exercise in his religious life; and the simple-hearted brethren, not knowing that the one sort of intensity was but the counterpart of the other, pointed to the transformation as a "beautiful conversion," a standing miracle. So it was, indeed, and, like all moral miracles, it was worked in the direction of individuality, not in opposition to it.

It was a grievous disappointment to the little band of Methodists that Brother Magruder's face was so swollen, after his encounter, as to prevent his preaching. They had counted much upon the success of this day's work, and now the devil seemed about to snatch the victory. Mrs. Wheeler enthusiastically recommended Kike as a substitute, and Magruder sent for him in haste. Kike was gratified to hear that the preacher wanted to see him personally. His sallow face flushed with pleasure as he stood, a slender stripling, before the messenger of God.

"Brother Lumsden," said Mr. Magruder, "are you ready to do and to suffer for Christ?"

"I trust I am," said Kike, wondering what the preacher could mean.

"You see how the devil has planned to defeat the Lord's work to-day. My lip is swelled, and my jaw so stiff that I can hardly speak. Are you ready to do the duty the Lord shall put upon you?"

Kike trembled from head to foot. He had often fancied himself preaching his first sermon in a strange neighborhood, and he had even picked out his text;

but to stand up suddenly before his school-mates, before his mother, before Brady, and, worse than all, before Morton, was terrible. And yet, had he not that very morning made a solemn vow that he would not shrink from death itself!

"Do you think I am fit to preach?" he asked, evasively.

"None of us are fit; but here will be two or three hundred people hungry for the bread of life. The Master has fed you; he offers you the bread to distribute among your friends and neighbors. Now, will you let the fear of man make you deny the blessed Lord who has taken you out of a horrible pit and set your feet upon the Rock of Ages?"

Kike trembled a moment, and then said: "I will do whatever you say, if you will pray for me."

"I'll do that, my brother. And now take your Bible, and go into the woods and pray. The Lord will show you the way, if you put your whole trust in him."

The preacher's allusion to the bread of life gave Kike his subject, and he soon gathered a few thoughts which he wrote down on a fly-leaf of the Bible, in the shape of a skeleton. But it occurred to him that he had not one word to say on the subject of the bread of life beyond the sentences of his skeleton. The more this became evident to him, the greater was his agony of fear. He knelt on the brown leaves by a prostrate log; he made a "new consecration" of himself; he tried to feel willing to fail, so far as his own feelings were involved; he reminded the Lord of his promises to be with them he had sent; and then there came into his memory a text of Scripture: "For it shall be given you in that same hour what ye shall speak." Taking it, after the manner of the early Methodist mysticism, that the text had been supernaturally "suggested" to him, he became calm; and finding, from the height of the sun, that it was about the hour for meeting, he returned to the house of Colonel Wheeler, and was appalled at the sight that met his eyes. All the settlement, and many from other settlements, had come. The house, the yard, the fences, were full of people. Kike was seized with a tremor. He did not feel able to run the gauntlet of such a throng. He made a detour, and crept in at the back door like a criminal. For stage-fright—this fear of human presence—is not a thing to be overcome by the will. Susceptible natures are always liable to it, and neither moral nor physical courage can avert it.

A chair had been placed in the front door of the log house, for Kike, that he might preach to the congregation indoors and the much larger one outdoors. Mr. Magruder, much battered up, sat on a wooden bench just outside. Kike crept into the empty chair in the doorway with the feeling of one who intrudes where he does not belong. The brethren were singing, as a congregational voluntary, to the solemn tune of "Kentucky," the hymn which begins:

> "A charge to keep I have,
> A God to glorify;
> A never-dying soul to save
> And fit it for the sky."

Magruder saw Kike's fright, and, leaning over to
aim, said: "If you get confused, tell your own expe‹
rience." The early preacher's universal refuge was his
own experience. It was a sure key to the sympathies
of the audience.

Kike got through the opening exercises very well.
He could pray, for in praying he shut his eyes and
uttered the cry of his trembling soul for help. He
had been beating about among two or three texts,
either of which would do for a head-piece to the re-
marks he intended to make; but now one fixed itself
in his mind as he stood appalled by his situation in
the presence of such a throng. He rose and read,
with a tremulous voice:

> "There is a lad here which hath five barley loaves and two
> small fishes; but what are they among so many?"

The text arrested the attention of all. Magruder,
though unable to speak without pain, could not refrain
from saying aloud, after the free old Methodist fashion: "The Lord multiply the loaves! Bless and break
to the multitude!" "Amen!" responded an old brother from another settlement, "and the Lord help the
lad!" But Kike felt that the advantage which the text
had given him would be of short duration. The nov-
elty of his position bewildered him. His face flushed;
his thoughts became confused; he turned his back on
the audience out of doors, and talked rapidly to the
few friends in the house: the old brethren leaned their
heads upon their hands and began to pray. Whatever
spiritual help their prayers may have brought him,

their lugubrious groaning, and their doleful, audible prayers of " Lord, help !" depressed Kike immeasurably, and kept the precipice on which he stood constantly present to him. He tried in succession each division that he had sketched on the fly-leaf of the Bible, and found little to say on any of them. At last, he could not see the audience distinctly for confusion —there was a dim vision of heads swimming before him. He stopped still, and Magruder, expecting him to sit down, resolved to " exhort " if the pain should kill him. The Philistines meanwhile were laughing at Kike's evident discomfiture.

But Kike had no notion of sitting down. The laughter awakened his combativeness, and his combativeness restored his self-control. Persistent people begin their success where others end in failure. He was through with the sermon, and it had occupied just six minutes. The lad's scanty provisions had not been multiplied. But he felt relieved. The sermon over, there was no longer necessity for trying to speak against time, nor for observing the outward manner of a preacher.

" Now," he said, doggedly, " you have all seen that I cannot preach worth a cent. When David went out to fight, he had the good sense not to put on Saul's armor. I was fool enough to try to wear Brother Magruder's. Now, I'm done with that. The text and sermon are gone. But I'm not ashamed of Jesus Christ. And before I sit down, I am going to tell you all what he has done for a poor lost sinner like me."

Kike told the story with sincere directness. His recital of his own sins was a rebuke to others; with a trembling voice and a simple earnestness absolutely electrical, he told of his revengefulness, and of the effect of Magruder's preaching on him. And now that the flood-gates of emotion were opened, all trepidation departed, and there came instead the fine glow of martial courage. He could have faced the universe. From his own life the transition to the lives of those around him was easy. He hit right and left. The excitable crowd swayed with consternation as, in a rapid and vehement utterance, he denounced their sins with the particularity of one who had been familiar with them all his life. Magruder forgot to respond; he only leaned back and looked in bewilderment, with open eyes and mouth, at the fiery boy whose contagious excitement was fast setting the whole audience ablaze. Slowly the people pressed forward off the fences. All at once there was a loud bellowing cry from some one who had fallen prostrate outside the fence, and who began to cry aloud as if the portals of an endless perdition were yawning in his face. Magruder pressed through the crowd to find that the fallen man was his antagonist of the morning — Bill McConkey! Bill had concealed his bruised nose behind a tree, but had been drawn forth by the fascination of Kike's earnestness, and had finally fallen under the effect of his own terror. This outburst of agony from McConkey was fuel to the flames, and the excitement now spread to all parts of the audience. Kike went from man to man, and exhorted and rebuked each one in

particular. Brady, not wishing to hear a public com-
mentary on his own life, waddled away when he saw
Kike coming; his mother wept bitterly under his exhortation; and Morton sat stock still on the fence listening, half in anguish and half in anger, to Kike's
public recital of his sins.

At last Kike approached his uncle; for Captain
Lumsden had come on purpose to enjoy Morton's
proposed interruption. He listened a minute to Kike's
exhortation, and the contrary emotions of alarm at
the thought of God's judgment and anger at Kike's
impudence contended within him until he started for
his horse and was seized with that curious nervous
affection which originated in these religious excitements and disappeared with them.* He jerked violently—his jerking only adding to his excitement, which
in turn increased the severity of his contortions. This
nervous affection was doubtless a natural physical result of violent excitement; but the people of that day
imagined that it was produced by some supernatural
agency, some attributing it to God, others to the devil,
and yet others to some subtle charm voluntarily exer-
cised by the preachers. Lumsden went home jerking
all the way, and cursing the Methodists more bitterly
than ever.

---

* It bore, however, a curious resemblance to the "dancing disease" which prevailed in Italy in the Middle Ages.

CHAPTER XV.

MORTON'S RETREAT.

IT would be hard to analyze the emotions with which Morton had listened to Kike's hot exhortation. In vain he argued with himself that a man need not be a Methodist and "go shouting and crying all over the country," in order to be good. He knew that Kike's life was better than his own, and that he had not force enough to break his habits and associations unless he did so by putting himself into direct antagonism with them. He inwardly condemned himself for his fear of Lumsden, and he inly cursed Kike for telling him the blunt truth about himself. But ever as there came the impulse to close the conflict and be at peace with himself by "putting himself boldly on the Lord's side," as Kike phrased it, he thought of Patty, whose aristocratic Virginia pride would regard marriage with a Methodist as worse than death.

And so, in mortal terror, lest he should yield to his emotions so far as to compromise himself, he rushed out of the crowd, hurried home, took down his rifle, and rode away, intent only on getting out of the excitement.

As he rode away from home he met Captain Lumsden hurrying from the meeting with the jerks, and leading his horse—the contortions of his body not allowing him to ride. With every step he took he grew more and more furious. Seeing Morton, he endeavored to vent his passion upon him.

"Why didn't—you—blow—why didn't—why didn't you blow your tin horns, this——" but at this point the jerks became so violent as to throw off his hat and shut off all utterance, and he only gnashed his teeth and hurried on with irregular steps toward home, leaving Morton to gauge the degree of the Captain's wrath by the involuntary distortion of his visage.

Goodwin rode listlessly forward, caring little whither he went; endeavoring only to allay the excitement of his conscience, and to imagine some sort of future in which he might hope to return and win Patty in spite of Lumsden's opposition. Night found him in front of the "City Hotel," in the county-seat village of Jonesville; and he was rejoiced to find there, on some political errand, Mr. Burchard, whom he had met awhile before at Wilkins', in the character of a candidate for sheriff.

"How do you do, Mr. Morton? Howdy do?" said Burchard, cordially, having only heard Morton's first name and mistaking it for his last. "I'm lucky to meet you in this town. Do you live over this way? I thought you lived in our county and 'lectioneered you—expecting to get your vote."

The conjunction of Morton and Burchard on a Sunday evening (or any other) meant a game at cards, and as Burchard was the more skillful and just now in great need of funds, it meant that all the contents of Morton's pockets should soon transfer themselves *to* Burchard's, the more that Morton in his contending with the religious excitement of the morning rushed easily into the opposite excitement of gambling. The violent awakening of a religious revival has a sharp polarity—it has sent many a man headlong to the devil. When Morton had frantically bet and lost all

GAMBLING.

his money, he proceeded to bet his rifle, then his grandfather's watch—an ancient time-piece, that Burchard examined with much curiosity. Having lost this, he staked his pocket-knife, his hat, his coat, and offered to put up his boots, but Burchard refused them. The madness of gambling was on the young man, however. He had no difficulty in persuading Burchard to take his mare as security for a hundred dollars, which he proceeded to gamble away by the easy process of winning once and losing twice.

When the last dollar was gone, his face was very white and calm. He leaned back in the chair and looked at Burchard a moment or two in silence.

" Burchard," said he, at last, " I'm a picked goose. I don't know whether I've got any brains or not. But if you'll lend me the rifle you won long enough for me to have a farewell shot, I'll find out what's inside this good-for-nothing cocoa-nut of mine."

Burchard was not without generous traits, and he was alarmed. " Come, Mr. Morton, don't be desperate. The luck's against you, but you'll have better another time. Here's your hat and coat, and you're welcome. I've been flat of my back many a time, but I've always found a way out. I'll pay your bill here to-morrow morning. Don't think of doing anything desperate. There's plenty to live for yet. You'll break some girl's heart if you kill yourself, maybe."

This thrust hurt Morton keenly. But Burchard was determined to divert him from his suicidal impulse.

"Come, old fellow, you're excited. Come out into the air. Now, don't kill yourself. You looked troubled when you got here. I take it, there's some trouble at home. Now, if there is "—here Burchard hesitated—" if there is trouble at home, I can put you on the track of a band of fellows that have been in trouble themselves. They help one another. Of course, I haven't anything to do with them; but they'll be mighty glad to get a hold of a fellow like you, that's a good shot and not afraid."

For a moment even outlawry seemed attractive to Morton, so utterly had hope died out of his heart. But only for a moment; then his moral sense recoiled.

"No; I'd rather shoot myself than kill somebody else. I can't take that road, Mr. Burchard."

"Of course you can't," said Burchard, affecting to laugh. "I knew you wouldn't. But I wanted to turn your thoughts away from bullets and all that. Now, Mr. Morton——"

"My name's not Morton. My last name is Goodwin—Morton Goodwin." This correction was made as a man always attends to trifles when he is trying to decide a momentous question.

"Morton Goodwin?" said Burchard, looking at him keenly, as the two stood together in the moonlight. Then, after pausing a moment, he added: "I had a crony by the name of Lew Goodwin, once. Devilish hard case he was, but good-hearted. Got killed in a fight in Pittsburg."

"He was my brother," said Morton.

"Your brother? thunder! You don't mean it. Let's see; he told me once his father's name was Moses—no; Job. Yes, that's it—Job. Is that your father's name?"

"Yes."

"I reckon the old folks must a took Lew's devil-try hard. Didn't kill 'em, did it?"

" No. "

" Both alive yet?"

" Yes."

"And now you want to kill both of 'em by committing suicide. You ought to think a little of your mother——"

"Shut your mouth," said Morton, turning fiercely on Burchard; for he suddenly saw a vision of the agony his mother must suffer.

"Oh! don't get mad. I'm going to let you have back your horse and gun, only you must give me a bill of sale so that I may be sure you won't gamble them away to somebody else. You must redeem them on your honor in six months, with a hundred and twenty-five dollars. I'll do that much for the sake of my old friend, Lew Goodwin, who stood by me in many a tight place, and was a good-hearted fellow after all."

Morton accepted this little respite, and Burchard left the tavern. As it was now past midnight, Goodwin did not go to bed. At two o'clock he gave Dolly corn, and before daylight he rode out of the village. But not toward home. His gambling and losses would be speedily reported at home and to Captain Lumsden. And moreover, Kike would persecute him worse than ever. He rode out of town in the direction opposite to that he would have taken in returning to Hissawachee, and he only knew that it was opposite. He was trying what so many other men have tried in vain to do—to run away from himself.

But not the fleetest Arabian charger, nor the swiftest lightning express, ever yet enabled a man to leave a disagreeable self behind. The wise man knows better, and turns round and faces it.

About noon Morton, who had followed an obscure and circuitous trail of which he knew nothing, drew near to a low log-house with deer's horns over the door, a sign that the cabin was devoted to hotel purposes—a place where a stranger might get a little food, a place to rest on the floor, and plenty of whiskey. There were a dozen horses hitched to trees about it, and Goodwin got down and went in from a spirit of idle curiosity. Certainly the place was not attractive. The landlord had a cut-throat way of looking closely at a guest from under his eye-brows; the guests all wore black beards, and Morton soon found reason to suspect that these beards were not indigenous. He was himself the object of much disagreeable scrutiny, but he could hardly restrain a mischievous smile at thought of the disappointment to which any highwayman was doomed who should attempt to rob him in his present penniless condition. The very worst that could happen would be the loss of Dolly and his rifle. It soon occurred to him that this lonely place was none other than " Brewer's Hole," one of the favorite resorts of Micajah Harp's noted band of desperadoes, a place into which few honest men ever ventured.

One of the men presently stepped to the window, rested his foot upon the low sill, and taking up a piece of chalk, drew a line from the toe to the top

of his boot.* Several others imitated him; and Morton, in a spirit of reckless mischief and adventure,
took the chalk and marked his right boot in the same
way.

"Will you drink?" said the man who had first
chalked his boot.

Goodwin accepted the invitation, and as they stood
near together, Morton could plainly discover the false-
ness of his companion's beard. Presently the man
fixed his eyes on Goodwin and asked, in an indifferent tone: "Cut or carry?"

"Carry," answered Morton, not knowing the meaning of the lingo, but finding himself in a predicament
from which there was no escape but by drifting with
the current. A few minutes later a bag, which seemed
to contain some hundreds of dollars, was thrust into
his hand, and Morton, not knowing what to do with
it thought best to "carry" it off. He mounted his
mare and rode away in a direction opposite to that in
which he had come. He had not gone more than
three miles when he met Burchard.

"Why, Burchard, how did you come here?"

"Oh, I came by a short cut."

But Burchard did not say that he had traveled in
the night, to avoid observation.

"Hello! Goodwin," cried Burchard, "you've got

---

* In relating this incident, I give the local tradition as it is
yet told in the neighborhood. It does not seem that chalking
one's boot is a very prudent mode of recognizing the members of
a secret band, but I do not suppose that men who follow a high
wayman's life are very wise people.

chalk on your boot! I hope you haven't joined
the—"

"Well, I'll tell you, Burchard, how that come. I
found the greatest set of disguised cut-throats you ever
saw, at this little hole back here. You hadn't better
go there, if you don't want to be relieved of all the
money you got last night. I saw them chalking their
boots, and I chalked mine, just to see what would
come of it. And here's what come of it;" and with
that, Morton showed his bag of money. "Now," he
said, "if I could find the right owner of this money,
I'd give it to him; but I take it he's buried in some
holler, without nary coffin or grave-stone. I 'low to
pay you what I owe you, and take the rest out to Vincennes, or somewheres else, and use it for a nest-egg.
'Finders, keepers,' you know."

Burchard looked at him darkly a moment. "Look
here, Morton—Goodwin, I mean. You'll lose your
head, if you fool with chalk that way. If you don't
give that money up to the first man that asks for it,
you are a dead man. They can't be fooled for long.
They'll be after you. There's no way now but to
hold on to it and give it up to the first man that
asks; and if he don't shoot first, you'll be lucky. I'm
going down this trail a way. I want to see old
Brewer. He's got a good deal of political influence.
Good-bye!"

Morton rode forward uneasily until he came to a
place two miles farther on, where another trail joined
the one he was traveling. Here there stood a man
with a huge beard, a blanket over his shoulders, holes

cut through for arms, after the frontier fashion, a belt
with pistols and knives, and a bearskin cap. The
stranger stepped up to him, reaching out his hand and
saying nothing. Morton was only too glad to give up
the money. And he set Dolly off at her best pace,
seeking to get as far as possible from the head-quarters
of the cut-or-carry gang. He could not but wonder
how Burchard should seem to know them so well. He
did not much like the thought that Burchard's forbearance had bound him to support that gentleman's political aspirations when he had opportunity. This
friendly relation with thieves was not what he would
have liked to see in a favorite candidate, but a cursed
fatality seemed to be dragging down all his high aspirations. It was like one of those old legends he had
heard his mother recite, of men who had begun by
little bargains with the devil, and had presently found
themselves involved in evil entanglements on every
hand.

CHAPTER XVI.

SHORT SHRIFT.

BUT Morton had no time to busy himself now with nice scruples. Bread and meat are considerations more imperative to a healthy man than conscience. He had no money. He might turn aside from the trail to hunt; indeed this was what he had meant to do when he started. But ever, as he traveled, he had become more and more desirous of getting away from himself. He was now full sixty or seventy miles from home, but he could not make up his mind to stop and devote himself to hunting. At four o'clock the valley of the Mustoga lay before him, and Morton, still purposeless, rode on. And now at last the habitual thought of his duty to his mother was returning upon him, and he began to he hesitant about going on. After all, his flight seemed foolish. Patty might not yet be lost; and as for Kike's revival, why should he yield to it, unless he chose?

In this painful indecision he resolved to stop and crave a night's lodging at the crossing of the river. He was the more disposed to this that Dolly, having been ridden hard all day without food, showed unmistakable signs of exhaustion, and it was now snowing. He would give her a night's rest, and then perhaps take the road back to the Hissawachee, or go into the wilderness and hunt

"Hello the house!" he called. "Hello!"

A long, lank man, in butternut jeans, opened the door, and responded with a "Hello!"

"Can I get to stay here all night?"

"Wal, no, I 'low not, stranger. Kinder full tonight. You mout git a place about a mile furder on whar you could hang up for the night, mos' likely; but I can't keep you, no ways."

"My mare's dreadful tired, and I can sleep anywhere," plead Morton.

"She does look sorter tuckered out, sartain; blamed if she don't! Whar did you git her?"

"Raised her," said Morton.

"Whar abouts?"

"Hissawachee."

"You don't say! How far you rid her to-day?"

"From Jonesville."

"Jam up fifty miles, and over tough roads! Mighty purty critter, that air. Powerful clean legs. She's number one. Is she your'n, did you say?"

"Well, not exactly mine. That is—". Here Morton hesitated.

"Stranger," said the settler, "you can't put up here, no ways. I tuck in one of your sort a month ago, and he rid my sorrel mare off in the middle of the night. I'll bore a hole through him, ef I ever set eyes on him." And the man had disappeared in the house before Morton could reply.

To be in a snow-storm without shelter was unpleasant; to be refused a lodging and to be mistaken for a horse-thief filled the cup of Morton's bitterness. He reluctantly turned his horse's head toward the river. There was no ferry, and the stream was so swollen that he must needs swim Dolly across.

He tightened his girth and stroked Dolly affectionately, with a feeling that she was the only friend he had left. "Well, Dolly," he said, "it's too bad to make you swim, after such a day; but you must. If we drown, we'll drown together."

The weary Dolly put her head against his cheek in a dumb trustfulness.

There was a road cut through the steep bank on the other side, so that travelers might ride down to the water's edge. Knowing that he would have to come out at that place, young Goodwin rode into the water as far up the stream as he could find a suitable place. Then, turning the mare's head upward, he started across. Dolly swam bravely enough until she reached the middle of the stream; then, finding her strength well nigh exhausted after her travel, and under the burden of her master, she refused his guidance, and turned her head directly toward the road, which offered the only place of exit. The rapid current swept horse and rider down the stream; but still Dolly fought bravely, and at last struck land just below the road. Morton grasped the bushes over his head, urged Dolly to greater exertions, and the well-bred creature, rousing all the remains of her magnificent force, succeeded in reaching the road. Then the young man got down and caressed her, and, looking back at the water, wondered why he should have struggled to preserve a life that he was not able to regulate, and

that promised him nothing but misery and embarrassment.

The snow was now falling rapidly, and Morton
pushed his tired filley on another mile. Again he hal-
looed. This time he was welcomed by an old woman,
who, in answer to his inquiry, said he might put the
mare in the stable. She didn't ginerally keep no travelers, but it was too orful a night fer a livin' human
bein' to be out in. Her son Jake would be in thireckly, and she 'lowed he wouldn't turn nobody out
in sech a night. 'Twuz good ten miles to the next
house.

Morton hastened to stable Dolly, and to feed her,
and to take his place by the fire.

Presently the son came in.

"Howdy, stranger?" said the youth, eyeing Morton
suspiciously. "Is that air your mar in the stable?"

"Ye-es," said Morton, hesitatingly, uncertain whether he could call Dolly his or not, seeing she had been
transferred to Burchard.

"Whar did you come from?"

"From Hissawachee."

"Whar you makin' fer?"

"I don't exactly know."

"See here, mister! Akordin' to my tell, that air's
a mighty peart sort of a hoss fer a feller to ride what
don' know, to save his gizzard, whar he mout be a
travelin'. We don't keep no sich people as them what
rides purty hosses and can't giv no straight account of
theirselves. Akordin' to my tell, you'll hev to hitch up
yer mar and putt. It mout gin us trouble to keep you."

"You ain't going to send me out such a night as this, when I've rode fifty mile a'ready?" said Morton.

"What in thunder'd you ride fifty mile to-day fer? Yer health, I reckon. Now, stranger, I've jist got one word to say to you, and that is this ere: *Putt!* PUTT THIRECKLY! Clar out of these 'ere diggin's! That's all. Jist putt!"

The young man pronounced the vowel in "put" very flat, as it is sounded in the first syllable of "putty," and seemed disposed to add a great many words to this emphatic imperative when he saw how much Morton was disinclined to leave the warm hearth. "Putt out, I say! I ain't afeard of none of yer gang. I hain't got nary 'nother word."

"Well," said Morton, "I have only got one word— I *won't!* You haven't got any right to turn a stranger out on such a night."

"Well, then, I'l let the reggilators know abouten you."

"Let them know, then," said Morton; and he drew nearer the fire.

The strapping young fellow straitened himself up and looked at Morton in wonder, more and more convinced that nobody but an outlaw would venture on a move so bold, and less and less inclined to attempt to use force as his conviction of Morton's desperate character increased. Goodwin, for his part, was not a little amused; the old mischievous love of fun reasserted itself in him as he saw the decline of the young man's courage.

"If you think I am one of Micajah Harp's band,

why don't you be careful how you treat me? The band might give you trouble. Let's have something to eat. I haven't had anything since last night; I am starving."

"Marm," said the young man, "git him sompin'. He's tuck the house and we can't help ourselves."

Morton had eaten nothing for twenty-four hours, and in his amusement at the success of his ruse and in the comfortable enjoyment of food after his long fast his good spirits returned.

When he awoke the next morning in his rude bed in the loft, he became aware that there were a number of men in the room below, and he could gather that they were talking about him. He dressed quickly and came down-stairs. The first thing he noticed was that the settler who had refused him lodging the night before was the centre of the group, the next that they had taken possession of his rifle. This settler had roused the "reggilators," and they had crossed the creek in a flat-boat some miles below and come up the stream determined to capture this young horse-thief. It is a singular tribute to the value of the horse that among barbarous or half-civilized peoples horse-stealing is accounted an offense more atrocious than homicide. In such a community to steal a man's horse is the grandest of larcenies—it is to rob him of the stepping-stone to civilization.

For such philosophical reflections as this last, however, Morton had no time. He was in the hands of an indignant crowd, some of whom had lost horses and other property from the depredations of the famous band of Micajah Harp, and all of whom were bent on exacting the forfeit from this indifferently dressed young man who rode a horse altogether too good for him.

Morton was conducted three miles down the river 'to a log tavern, that being a public and appropriate place for the rendering of the decisions of Judge Lynch, and affording, moreover, the convenient refreshments of whiskey and tobacco to those who might become exhausted in their arduous labors on behalf of public justice. There was no formal trial. The evidence was given in in a disjointed and spontaneous fashion; the jury was composed of the whole crowd, and what the Quakers call the "sense of the meeting" was gathered from the general outcry. Educated in Indian wars and having been left at first without any courts or forms of justice, the settlers had come to believe their own expeditious modes of dealing with the enemies of peace and order much superior to the prolix method of the lawyers and judges.

And as for Morton, nothing could be much clearer than that he was one of the gang. The settler who had refused him a lodging first spoke:

"You see, I seed in three winks," he began, "that that feller didn't own the hoss. He looked kinder sheepish. Well, I poked a few questions at him and I reckon I am the beatin'est man to ax questions in this neck of timber. I axed him whar he come from, and he let it out that he'd rid more'n fifty miles. And I kinder blazed away at praisin' his hoss tell I got him off his guard, and then, unbeknownst to him,

I treed him suddenly. I jest axed him ef the hoss was his'n and he hemmed and hawed and says, says he: 'Well, not exactly mine.' Then I tole him to putt out."

" Did he tell you the mar wuzn't adzackly his'n? put in the youth whose unwilling hospitality Morton had enjoyed.

"Yes."

" Well, then, he lied one time or nuther, that's sartain shore. He tole me she wuz. And when I axed him whar he was agoin', he tole me he didn' know. I suspicioned him then, and I tole him to clar out; and he wouldn'. Well, I wuz agoin' to git down my gun and blow his brains out; but marm got skeered and didn' want me to, and I 'lowed it was better to let him stay, and I 'low'd you fellers mout maybe come over and cotch him, or liker'n not some feller'd come along and *in*quire arter that air mar. Then he ups and says ef the ole woman don' give him sompin' to eat she'd ketch it from Micajah Harp's band. He said as how he was a member of that gang. An' he said he hadn't had nothin' to eat sence the night before, havin' rid fer twenty-four hours."

" I didn't say —" began Morton.

"Shet up your mouth tell I'm done. Haint you got no manners? I tole him as how I didn't keer three continental derns* fer his whole band weth Micajah Harp throw'd onto the top, but the ole wom-

---

* A saying having its origin, no doubt, in the worthlessness of the paper money issued by the Continental Congress.

an wuz kinder sorter afeared to find she'd cotch a
rale hoss-thief and she gin him a little sompin' to eat.
And he did gobble it, I tell *you* !"

Young rawbones had repeated this statement a
dozen times already since leaving home with the
prisoner. But he liked to tell it. Morton made the
best defense he could, and asked them to send to
Hissawachee and inquire, but the crowd thought that
this was only a ruse to gain time, and that if they
delayed his execution long, Micajah Harp and his
whole band would be upon them.

The mob-court was unanimously in favor of hanging. The cry of " Come on, boys, let's string him
up," was raised several times, and " rushes " at him
were attempted, but these rushes never went further
than the incipient stage, for the very good reason
that while many were anxious to have him hung,
none were quite ready to adjust the rope. The law
threatened them on one side, and a dread of the
vengeance of Micajah Harp's cut-throats appalled them
on the other. The predicament in which the crowd
found themselves was a very embarrassing one, but
these administrators of impromptu justice consoled
themselves by whispering that it was best to wait till
night.

And the rawboned young man, who had given
such eager testimony that he " warn't afeard of the
whole gang with ole Micajah throw'd onto the top,"
concluded about noon that he had better go home—the
ole woman mout git skeered, you know. She wuz powerful skeery and mout git fits liker'n not, you know.

The weary hours of suspense drew on. However ready Morton may have been to commit suicide in a moment of rash despair, life looked very attractive to him now that its duration was measured by the descending sun. And what a quickener of conscience is the prospect of immediate death! In these hours the voice of Kike, reproving him for his reckless living, rang in his memory ceaselessly. He saw what a distorted failure he had made of life; he longed for a chance to try it over again. But unless help should come from some unexpected quarter, he saw that his probation was ended.

It is barely possible that the crowd might have become so demoralized by waiting as to have let Morton go, or at least to have handed him over to the authorities, had there not come along at that moment Mr. Mellen, the stern and ungrammatical Methodist preacher of whom Morton had made so much sport in Wilkins's Settlement. Having to preach at fifty-eight appointments in four weeks, he was somewhat itinerant, and was now hastening to a preaching place near by. One of the crowd, seeing Mr. Mellen, suggested that Morton had orter be allowed to see a preacher, and git "fixed up," afore he died. Some of the others disagreed. They warn't nothin' in the nex' world too bad fer a hoss-thief, by jeeminy hoe-cakes. They warn't a stringin' men up to send 'em to heaven, but to t' other place.

Mellen was called in, however, and at once recognized Morton as the ungodly young man who had insulted him and disturbed the worship of God. He

exhorted him to repent, and to tell who was the owner of the horse, and to seek a Saviour who was ready
to forgive even the dying thief upon the cross. In
vain Morton protested his innocence. Mellen told him
that he could not escape, though he advised the crowd
to hand him over to the sheriff. But Mellen's additional testimony to Morton's bad character had destroyed his last chance of being given up to the
courts. As soon as Mr. Mellen went away, the arrangements for hanging him at nightfall began to take
definite shape, and a rope was hung over a limb, in
full sight of the condemned man. Mr. Mellen used
with telling effect, at every one of the fifty-eight places
upon his next round, the story of the sad end of this
hardened young man, who had begun as a scoffer and
ended as an impenitent thief.

Morton sat in a sort of stupor, watching the sun
descending toward the horizon. He heard the rude
voices of the mob about him. But he thought of Patty
and his mother.

While the mob was thus waiting for night, and
Morton waiting for death, there passed upon the road
an elderly man. He was just going out of sight, when
Morton roused himself enough to observe him. When
he had disappeared, Goodwin was haunted with the
notion that it must be Mr. Donaldson, the old Presbyterian preacher, whose sermons he had so often heard
at the Scotch Settlement. Could it be that thoughts
of home and mother had suggested Donaldson? At
least, the faintest hope was worth clutching at in a
time of despair.

"Call him back!" cried Morton. "Won't somebody call that old man back? He knows me."

Nobody was disposed to serve the culprit. The

A LAST HOPE.

leaders looked knowingly the one at the other, and
shrugged their shoulders.

"If you don't call him back you will be a set of
murderers!" cried the despairing Goodwin

PARSON DONALDSON was journeying down to Cincinnati—at that time a thriving village of about two thousand people — to attend Presbytery and to contend manfully against the sinful laxity of some of his brethren in the matters of doctrine and revivals. In previous years Mr. Donaldson had been beaten a little in his endeavors to have carried through the extremest measures against his more progressive "new-side" brethren. He considered the doctrines of these zealous Presbyterians as very little better than the crazy ranting of the ungrammatical circuit riders. At the moment of passing the tavern where Morton sat, condemned to death, he was eagerly engaged in "laying out" a speech with which he intended to rout false doctrines and annihilate forever incipient fanaticism. His square head had fallen forward, and he only observed that there was a crowd of godless and noisy men about the tavern. He could not spare time to note anything farther, for the fate of Zion seemed to hang upon the weight and cogency of the speech which he meant to deliver at Cincinnati. He had almost passed out of sight when Morton first caught sight of him; and when the young man, finding that no one would go after him, set up a vigorous calling of his name, Mr. Donaldson did not hear it.

or at least did not think for an instant that anybody in that crowd could be calling his own name. How should he hear Morton's cry? For just at that moment he had reached the portion of his argument in which he triumphantly proved that his new-side friends, however unconscious they might be of the fact, were of necessity Pelagians, and, hence, guilty of fatal error.

Morton's earnest entreaties at last moved one of the crowd.

"Well, I don't mind," he said; "I'll call him. 'Pears like as ef he's a-lyin' any how. I don't 'low as he knows the ole coon, or the ole coon knows him —liker'n not he's a-foolin' by lettin' on; but 't wont do no harm to call him back." Saying which, he mounted his gaunt horse and rode away after Mr. Donaldson.

"Hello, stranger! I say, there! Mister! O, mister! Hello, you ole man on horseback!"

This was the polite manner of address with which the messenger interrupted the theological meditations of the worthy Mr. Donaldson at the moment of his most triumphant anticipations of victory over his opponents.

"Well, what is it?" asked the minister, turning round on the messenger a little tartly; much as one would who is suddenly awakened and not at all pleased to be awakened.

"They's a feller back here as we tuck up fer a hoss-thief, and we had three-quarters of a notion of stringin' on him up; but he says as how as he knows you, and ef you kin do him any good, I hope you'll do it, for I *do* hate to see a feller being hung, that's sartain shore."

"A horse-thief says that he knows me?" said the parson, not yet fairly awake to the situation. "Indeed? I'm in a great hurry. What does he want? Wants me to pray with him, I suppose. Well, it is never too late. God's election is of grace, and often he seems to select the greatest sinners that he may thereby magnify his grace and get to himself a great name. I'll go and see him."

And with that, Donaldson rode back to the tavern, endeavoring to turn his thoughts out of the polemical groove in which they had been running all day, that he might think of some fitting words to say to a malefactor. But when he stood before the young man he started with surprise.

"What! Morton Goodwin! Have you taken to stealing horses? I should have thought that the unhappy career of your brother, so soon cut short in God's righteousness, would have been a warning to you. My dear young man, how could you bring such disgrace and shame on the gray hairs —— "

Before Mr. Donaldson had gotten to this point, a murmur of excitement went through the crowd. They believed that the prisoner's own witness had turned against him and that they had a second *quasi* sanction from the clergy for the deed of violence they were meditating. Perceiving this, Morton interrupted the minister with some impatience, crying out:

"But, Mr. Donaldson, hold on; you have judged

me too quick. These folks are going to hang me
without any evidence at all, except that I was riding
a good horse. Now, I want you to tell them whose
filley yon is."

Mr Donaldson looked at the mare and declared
to the crowd that he had seen this young man riding
that colt for more than a year past, and that if they
were proceeding against him on a charge of stealing
that mare, they were acting most unwarrantably.

"Why couldn't he tell a feller whose mar he had,
and whar he was a-goin'?" said the man from the
other side of the river."

"I don't know. How did you come here, Morton?"

"Well, I'll tell you a straight story. I was gambling on Sunday night —— "

"Breaking two Commandments at once," broke in
the minister.

"Yes, sir, I know it; and I lost everything I had
—horse and gun and all—I seemed clean crazy. I
lost a hundred dollars more'n I had, and I give the
man I was playing with a bill of sale for my horse and
gun. Then he agreed to let me go where I pleased
and keep 'em for six months and I was ashamed
to go home; so I rode off, like a fool, hoping to find
some place where I could make the money to redeem
my colt with. That's how I didn't give straight
answers about whose horse it was, and where I was
going."

"Well, neighbors, it seems clear to me that you'll
have to let the young man go. You ought to be
thankful that God in his good providence has saved

you from the guilt of those who shed innocent blood. He is a very respectable young man, indeed, and often attends church with his mother. I am sorry he has got into bad habits."

"I'm right glad to git shed of a ugly job," said one of the party; and as the rest offered no objection, he cut the cords that bound Morton's arms and let him go. The landlord had stabled Dolly and fed her, hoping that some accident would leave her in his hands; the man from the other side of the creek had taken possession of the rifle as "his sheer, considerin' the trouble he'd tuck." The horse and gun were now reluctantly given up, and the party made haste to disperse, each one having suddenly remembered some duty that demanded immediate attention. In a little while Morton sat on his horse listening to some very earnest words from the minister on the sinfulness of gambling and Sabbath-breaking. But Mr. Donaldson, having heard of the Methodistic excitement in the Hissawachee settlement, slipped easily to that, and urged Morton not to have anything whatever to do with this mushroom religion, that grew up in a night and withered in a day. In fact the old man delivered to Morton most of the speech he had prepared for the Presbytery on the evil of religious excitements. Then he shook hands with him, exacted a promise that he would go directly home, and, with a few seasonable words on God's mercy in rescuing him from a miserable death, he parted from the young man. Somehow, after that he did not get on quite so well with his speech. After all, was it not better, perhaps, that this young man should be drawn into the whirl-pool of a Methodist excitement than that he should become a gambler? After thinking over it a while, however, the logical intellect of the preacher luckily enabled him to escape this dangerous quicksand, in reaching the sound conclusion that a religious excitement could only result in spiritual pride and Pelagian doctrine, and that the man involved in these would be lost as certainly as a gambler or a thief.

Now, lest some refined Methodist of the present day should be a little too severe on our good friend Mr. Donaldson, I must express my sympathy for the worthy old gentleman as he goes riding along toward the scene of conflict. Dear, genteel, and cultivated Methodist reader, you who rejoice in the patristic glory of Methodism, though you have so far departed from the standard of the fathers as to wear gold and costly apparel and sing songs and read some novels, be not too hard upon our good friend Donaldson. Had you, fastidious Methodist friend, who listen to organs and choirs and refined preachers, as you sit in your cushioned pew —had you lived in Ohio sixty years ago, would you have belonged to the Methodists, think you? Not at all! your nerves would have been racked by their shouting, your musical and poetical taste outraged by their ditties, your grammatical knowledge shocked beyond recovery by their English; you could never have worshiped in an excitement that prostrated people in religious catalepsy, and threw weak saints and obstinate sinners alike into the contortions of the jerks. It is easy to build the tombs of the prophets while you reap the harvest they sowed, and after they have been already canonized. It is easy to build the tombs of the early prophets now while we stone the prophets of our own time, maybe. Permit me, Methodist brother, to believe that had you lived in the days of Parson Donaldson, you would have condemned these rude Tishbites as sharply as he did. But you would have been wrong, as he was. For without them there must have been barbarism, worse than that of Arkansas and Texas. Methodism was to the West all that Puritanism was to New England. Both of them are sublime when considered historically; neither of them were very agreeable to live with, maybe.

But, alas! I am growing as theological as Mr. Donaldson himself. Meantime Morton has forded the creek at a point more favorable than his crossing of the night before, and is riding rapidly homeward; and ever, as he recedes from the scene of his peril and approaches his home, do the embarrassments of his situation become more appalling. If he could only be sure of himself in the future, there would be hope. But to a nature so energetic as his, there is no action possible but in a right line and with the whole heart.

In returning, Morton had been directed to follow a "trace" that led him toward home by a much nearer way than he had come. After riding twenty miles, he emerged from the wilderness into a settlement just as the sun was sitting. It happened that the house where he found a hospitable supper and lodging was already set apart for Methodist preaching that evening. After supper the shuck-bottom chairs and rude benches were arranged about the walls, and the intermediate space was left to be filled by seats which should be brought in by friendly neighbors. Morton gathered from the conversation that the preacher was none other than the celebrated Valentine Cook, who was held in such esteem that it was even believed that he had a prophetic inspiration and a miraculous gift of healing. This "class" had been founded by his preaching, in the days of his vigor. He had long since given up "traveling," on account of his health. He was now a teacher in Kentucky, being, by all odds, the most scholarly of the Western itinerants. He had set out on a journey among the churches with whom he had labored, seeking to strengthen the hands of the brethren, who were like a few sheep in the wilderness. The old Levantine churches did not more heartily welcome the final visit of Paul the Aged than did the backwoods churches this farewell tour of Valentine Cook.

Finding himself thus fairly entrapped again by a Methodist meeting, Morton felt no little agitation. His mother had heard Cook in his younger days, in Pennsylvania, and he was thus familiar with his fame as a man and as a preacher. Morton was not only curious to hear him; he entertained a faint hope that the great preacher might lead him out of his embarrassment.

After supper Goodwin strolled out through the trees trying to collect his thoughts; determined at one moment to become a Methodist and end his struggles, seeking, the next, to build a breastwork of resistance against the sermon that he must hear. Having walked some distance from the house into the bushes, he came suddenly upon the preacher himself, kneeling in earnest audible prayer. So rapt was the old man in his devotion that he did not note the approach of Goodwin, until the latter, awed at sight of a man talking face to face with God, stopped, trembling, where he stood. Cook then saw him, and, arising, reached out his hand to the young man, saying in a voice tremulous with emotion : " Be thou faithful unto death, and I will give thee a crown of life." Morton endeavored, in a few stammering words, to explain his accidental intrusion, but the venerable man seemed almost at once to have forgotten his presence, for he had taken his seat upon a log and appeared absorbed in thought. Morton retreated just in time to secure a place in the cabin, now almost full. The members of the church, men and women, as they entered, knelt in silent prayer before taking their seats. Hardly silent either, for the old Methodist could do nothing without noise, and even while he knelt in what he considered silent prayer, he burst forth continually in audible ejaculations of "Ah—ah!" " O my Lord, help!" "Hah!" and other groaning expressions of his inward wrestling—groanings easily uttered, but entirely without a possible orthography. With most, this was the simple habit of an uncultivated and unreserved nature ; in later times the ostentatious and hypocritical did not fail to cultivate it as an evidence of superior piety.

But now the room is full. People are crowding the doorways. The good old-class leader has shut his eyes and turned his face heavenward. Presently he strikes up lustily, leading the congregation in singing:

> " How tedious and tasteless the hours
>   When Jesus no longer I see !"

When he reached the stanza that declares :

> "While blest with a sense of his love
>   A palace a toy would appear;
> And prisons would palaces prove,
>   If Jesus would dwell with me there,"

there were shouts of " Halleluiah !" " Praise the Lord ! " and so forth. At the last quatrain, which runs,

> " O ! drive these dark clouds from my sky !
>   Thy soul-cheering presence restore ;
> Or take me to thee up on high,
>   Where winter and clouds are no more !"

there were the heartiest " Amens," though they must have been spoken in a poetic sense. I cannot believe that any of the excellent brethren, even in that moment of exaltation, would really have desired translation to the world beyond the clouds.

The preacher, in his meditations, had forgotten his congregation—a very common bit of absent-minded-ness with Valentine Cook; and so, when this hymn was finished, a sister, with a rich but uncultivated soprano, started, to the tune called " Indian Philos-opher," that inspiring song which begins:

> " Come on, my partners in distress,
>   My comrades in this wilderness,
>   Who still your bodies feel ;
>   Awhile forget your griefs and tears,
>   Look forward through this vale of tears
>   To that celestial hill."

The hymn was long, and by the time it was com-
pleted the preacher, having suddenly come to himself,
entered hurriedly, and pushed forward to the place
arranged for him. The festoons of dried pumpkin
hanging from the joists reached nearly to his head;
a tallow dip, sitting in the window, shed a feeble
light upon his face. as he stood there, tall, gaunt,
awkward, weather-beaten, with deep-sunken, weird,
hazel eyes, a low forehead, a prominent nose, coarse
black hair resisting yet the approach of age, and a
tout ensemble unpromising, but peculiar. He began
immediately to repeat his hymn :

> "I saw one hanging on a tree
> In agony and blood ;
> He fixed his languid eye on me,
> As near the cross I stood."

His tone was monotonous, his eyes seemed to have
a fascination, and the pathos of his voice, quivering
with suppressed emotion, was indescribable. Before
his prayer was concluded the enthusiastic Morton felt
that he could follow such a leader to the world's end.

He repeated his text : "*Behold, the day cometh,*" and
launched at once into a strongly impressive introduction about the all-pervading presence of God, until the
whole house seemed full of God, and Morton found
himself breathing fearfully, with a sense of God's presence and ineffable holiness. Then he took up that
never-failing theme of the pioneer preacher—the sinfulness of sin — and there were suppressed cries of
anguish over the whole house. Morton could hardly
feel more contempt for himself than he had felt for

two days past; but when the preacher advanced to
his climax of the Atonement and the Forgiveness of
Sins, Goodwin felt himself carried away as with a flood.
In that hour, with God around, above, beneath, without
and within—with a feeling that since his escape he
held his life by a sort of reprieve—with the inspiring
and persuasive accents of this weird prophet ringing
in his ears, he cast behind him all human loves, all
ambitious purposes, all recollections of theological puz-
zles, and set himself to a self-denying life. With one
final battle he closed his conflict about Patty. He
would do right at all hazards.

Morton never had other conversion than this. He
could not tell of such a struggle as Kike's. All he
knew was that there had been conflict. When once
he decided, there was harmony and peace. When Valentine Cook had concluded his rapt peroration, setting
the whole house ablaze with feeling, and then proceeded to "open the doors of the church" by singing,

> "Am I a soldier of the Cross,
>   A follower of the Lamb,
> And shall I fear to own his cause,
>   Or blush to speak his name?"

it was with a sort of military exaltation—a defiance
of the world, the flesh, and the devil—that Morton
went forward and took the hand of the preacher, as
a sign that he solemnly enrolled himself among those
who meant to

> " —— conquer though they die."

He was accustomed to say in after years, using

the Methodist phraseology, that " God spoke peace to his soul the moment he made up his mind to give up all." That God does speak to the heart of man in its great crises I cannot doubt; but God works with, and not against, the laws of mind. When Morton ceased to contend with his highest impulses there was no more discord, and he was of too healthful and objective a temperament to have subjective fights with fanciful Apollyons. When peace came he accepted it. One of the old brethren who crowded round him that night and questioned him about his experience was " afeard it warn't a rale deep conversion. They wuzn't wras'lin' and strugglin' enough." But the wise Valentine Cook said, when he took Morton's hand to say good-bye, and looked into his clear blue eye, " Hold fast the beginning of thy confidence, brother."

CHAPTER XVIII.

THE PRODIGAL RETURNS.

AT last the knight was in the saddle. Much as Morton grieved when he thought of Patty, he rejoiced now in the wholeness of his moral purpose. Vacillation was over. He was ready to fight, to sacrifice, to die, for a good cause. It had been the dream of his boyhood; it had been the longing of his youth, marred and disfigured by irregularities as his youth had been. In the early twilight of the winter morning he rode bravely toward his first battle field, and, as was his wont in moments of cheerfulness, he sang. But not now the "Highland Mary," or "Ca' the yowe's to the knowes," but a hymn of Charles Wesley's he had heard Cook sing the night before, some stanzas of which had strongly impressed him and accorded exactly with his new mood, and his anticipation of trouble and the loss of Patty, perhaps, from his religious life:

> "In hope of that immortal crown
> I now the Cross sustain,
> And gladly wander up and down,
> And smile at toil and pain;
> I suffer on my threescore years,
> Till my Deliv'rer come

And wipe away his servant's tears,
And take his exile home.

•   •   •   •   •   •   •   •

"O, what are all my sufferings here
    If, Lord, thou count me meet
With that enraptured host to appear
    And worship at thy feet !
Give joy or grief, give ease or pain,
    Take life or friends away,
But let me find them all again
    In that eternal day."

Long before he had reached Hissawachee he had ceased to sing. He was painfully endeavoring to imagine how he would be received at home and at Captain Lumsden's.

At home, the wan mother sat in the dull winter twilight, trying to keep her heart from fainting entirely. The story of Morton's losses at cards had quickly reached the settlement—with the easy addition that he had fled to escape paying his debt of dishonor, and had carried off the horse and gun which another had won from him in gambling. This last, the mother steadily refused to believe. It could not be that Morton would quench all the manly impulses of his youth and follow in the steps of his prodigal brother, Lewis. For Morton was such a boy as Lewis had never been, and the thought of his deserting his home and falling finally into bad practices, had brought to Mrs. Goodwin an agony that was next door to heart-break. Job Goodwin had abandoned all work and taken to his congenial employment of sighing and croaking in the chimney-corner, building innumer-able Castles of Doubt for the Giant Despair.

Mrs. Wheeler came in to comfort her friend. "I am sure, Mrs. Goodwin," she said, "Morton will yet be saved; I have been enabled to pray for him with faith."

In spite of her sorrow, Mrs. Goodwin could not help thinking that it was very inconsistent for an Arminian to believe that God would convert a man in answer to prayer, when Arminians professed to believe that a man could be a Christian or not as he pleased. Willing, however, to lay the blame of her misfortune on anybody but Morton, she said, half peevishly, that she wished the Methodists had never come to the settlement. Morton had been in a hope-ful state of mind, and they had driven him to wicked-ness. Otherwise he would doubtless have been a Christian by this time.

And now Mrs. Wheeler, on her part, thought — but did not say — that it was most absurd for Mrs. Goodwin to complain of anything having driven Morton away from salvation, since, according to her Calvinistic doctrine, he must be saved anyhow if he were elected. It is so easy to be inconsistent when we try to reason about God's relation to his creatures; and so easy to see absurdity in any creed but our own!

The twilight deepened, and Mrs. Goodwin, unable now to endure the darkness, lit her candle. Then there was a knock at the door. Ever since Sunday the mother, waiting between hope and despair, had turned pale at every sound of footsteps without. Now she called out, "Come in!" in a broken voice, and Mr. Brady entered, having just dismissed his school.

"Troth, me dair madam, it's not meself that can give comfort. I'm sure to say something not intoirely proper to the occasion, whiniver I talk to anybody in throuble—something that jars loike a varb that disagrees with its nominative in number and parson, as I may say. But I thought I ought to come and say you, and till you as I don't belave Moirton would do anything very bad, an' I'm shoore he'll be home afore the wake's out. I've soiphered it out by the Rule of Thray. As Moirton Goodwin wuz to his other throubles—comin' out all roight—so is Moirton Goodwin to his present diffi*c*ulties. If the first term and the third is the same, then the sicond and the fourth has got to be idintical. Perhaps I'm talkin' too larned; but you're an eddicated woman, Mrs. Goodwin, and you can say that me dimonsthration's entoirely corrict. Moirton 'll fetch the answer set down in the book ivery toime, without any remainder or mistake. Thair's no vulgar fractions about him."

"Fractious, did you say?" spoke in Job Goodwin, who had held his hand up to his best ear, to hear what Brady was saying. "No, I don't 'low he was fractious, fer the mos' part. But he's gone now, and he'll git killed like J•w did, and we'll all hev the fever, and then they'll be a war weth the Bridish, and the Injuns 'll be on us, and it 'pears like as if they wa'n't no eend of troubles a-comin'. Hey?"

At that very moment the latch was jerked up and

Henry came bursting into the room, gasping from excitement.

"What is it? Injuns?" asked Mr. Goodwin, getting to his feet.

But Henry gasped again.

"Spake!" said Brady. "Out wid it!"

"Mort's—a-puttin'—Dolly—in the stable!" said the breathless boy.

"Dolly's in the stable, did you say?" queried Job Goodwin, sitting down again hopelessly. "Then somebody—Injuns, robbers, or somebody—'s killed Mort, and she's found her way back!"

While Mr. Goodwin was speaking, Mrs. Wheeler slipped out of the open door, that she might not intrude upon the meeting; but Brady—oral newspaper that he was—waited, with the true journalistic spirit, for an interview. Hardly had Job Goodwin finished his doleful speech, when Morton himself crossed the threshold and reached out his hand to his mother, while she reached out both hands and — did what mothers have done for returning prodigals since the world was made. Her husband stood by bewildered, trying to collect his wits enough to understand how Morton could have been murdered by robbers or Indians and yet stand there. Not until the mother released him, and Morton turned and shook hands with his father, did the father get rid of the illusion that his son was certainly dead.

"Well, Moirton," said Brady, coming out of the shadow, "I'm roight glad to see ye back. I tould 'em ye'd bay home to-noight, maybe. I soiphered it out by the Single Rule of Thray that ye'd git back about this toime. One day fer sinnin', one day fer throyin' to run away from yersilf, one day for repintance, and the nixt the prodigal son falls on his mother's neck and confisses his sins."

Morton was glad to find Brady present; he was a safeguard against too much of a scene. And to avoid speaking of subjects more unpleasant, he plunged at once into an account of his adventure at Brewer's Hole, and of his arrest for stealing his own horse. Then he told how he had escaped by the good offices of Mr. Donaldson. Mrs. Goodwin was secretly delighted at this. It was a new bond between the young man and the minister, and now at last she should see Morton converted. The religious experience Morton reserved. He wanted to break it to his mother alone, and he wanted to be the first to speak of it to Patty. And so it happened that Brady, having gotten, as he supposed, a full account of Morton's adventures, and being eager to tell so choice and fresh a story, found himself unable to stay longer. But just as he reached the door, it occurred to him that if he did not tell Morton at once what had happened in his absence, some one else would anticipate him. He had sole possession of Morton's adventure anyhow; so he straightened himself up against the door and said:

"An' did ye hear what happened to Koike, the whoile ye was gone, Moirton?"

"Nothing bad, I hope," said Morton.

"Ye may belave it was bad, or ye may take it to be good, as ye plase. Ye know how Koike was bilin' over to shoot his uncle, afore ye went away in the fall. Will, on'y yisterday the Captin he jist met Koike in the road, and gives him some hard words fer sayin' what he did to him last Sunthay. An' fwat does Koike do but bowldly begins another exhortation, tellin' the Captin he was a sinner as desarved to go to hill, an' that he'd git there if he didn't whale about and take the other thrack. An' fwat does the Captin do but up wid the flat of his hand and boxes Koike's jaw. An' I thought Koike would 'a' sarved him as Magruder did Jake Sniger. But not a bit of it! He fired up rid, and thin got pale immajiately. Thin he turned round t'other soide of his face, and, wid a thremblin' voice, axed the Captin if he didn't want to slap that chake too? An' the Captin swore at him fer a hypocrite, and thin put out for home wid the jerks; an' he's been a-lookin' loike a sintince that couldn' be parsed iver sence."

"I wonder Kike bore it. I don't think I could," said Morton, meditatively.

"Av coorse ye couldn't. Ye're not a convarted Mithodist. But I must be goin'. I'm a-boardin' at the Captin's now."

CHAPTER XIX.

PATTY'S whole education tended to foster her pride, and in Patty's circumstances pride was conservative; it saved her from possible assimilation with the vulgarity about her. She was a lily among hollyhocks. Her mother had come of an "old family"—in truth, of two or three old families. All of them had considered that attachment to the Established Church was part and parcel of their gentility, and most of them had been staunch Tories in the Revolution. Patty had inherited from her mother refinement, pride, and a certain lofty inflexibility of disposition. In this congenial soil Mrs. Lumsden had planted traditional prejudices. Patty read her Prayer-book, and wished that she might once attend the stately Episcopal service; she disliked the *lowness* of all the sects: the sing-song of the Baptist preacher and the rant of the Methodist itinerant were equally distasteful. She had never seen a clergyman in robes, but she tried, from her mother's descriptions, to form a mental picture of the long-drawn dignity of the service in an Old Virginia country church. Patty was imaginative, like most girls of her age; but her ideals were ruled by the pride in which she had been cradled.

For the Methodists she entertained a peculiar aversion. Methodism was new, and, like everything new, lacked traditions, picturesqueness, mustiness, and all the other essentials of gentility in religious matters. The converts were rude, vulgar, and poor; the preachers were illiterate, and often rough in voice and speech; they made war on dancing and jewelry, and dancing and jewelry appertained to good-breeding. Ever since her father had been taken with that strange disorder called "the jerks," she had hated the Methodists worse than ever. They had made a direct attack on her pride.

The story of Morton's gambling had duly reached the ears of Patty. The thoughtful unkindness of her father could not leave her without so delectable a morsel of news. He felt sure that Patty's pride would be outraged by conduct so reckless, and he omitted nothing from the tale—the loss of horse and gun, the offer to stake his hat and coat, the proposal to commit suicide, the flight upon the forfeited horse— such were the items of Captain Lumsden's story. He told it at the table in order to mortify Patty as much as possible in the presence of her brothers and sisters and the hired men. But the effect was quite different from his expectations. With that inconsistency characteristic of the most sensible women when they are in love, Patty only pitied Morton's misfortunes. She saw him, in her imagination, a hapless and homeless wanderer. She would not abandon him in his misfortunes. He should have one friend at least. She was sorry he had gambled, but gambling was not inconsistent with gentlemanliness. She had often

heard that her mother would have inherited a planta-
tion if her grandfather had been able to let cards
alone. Gambling was the vice of gentlemen, a generous and impulsive weakness. Then, too, she laid
the blame on her favorite scape-goat. If it had not
been for Kike's exciting exhortation and the incon-
siderate violence of the Methodist revival, Morton's
misfortune would not have befallen him. Patty forgave in advance. Love condones all sins except sins
against love.

It was with more than his usual enjoyment of
gossip that the school-master hurried home to the
Captain's that evening to tell the story of Morton's
return, and to boast that he had already soiphered it
out by the single Rule of Thray that Moirton would
come out roight. The Captain, as he ate his waffles
with country molasses, slurred the whole thing, and
wanted to know if he was going to refuse to pay a
debt of honor and keep the mare, when he had fairly
lost her gambling with Burchard. But Patty inly
resolved to show her lover more affection than ever.
She would make him feel that her love would be
constant when the friendship of others failed. She
liked to flatter herself, as other young women have to
their cost, that her love would reform her lover.

Patty knew he would come. She went about her
work next morning, humming some trifling air, that
she might seem nonchalant. But after awhile she
happened to think that her humming was an indica-
tion of pre-occupation. So she ceased to hum. Then
she remembered that people would certainly interpret

silence as indicative of meditation; she immediately fell a-talking with might and main, until one of the younger girls asked : "What does make Patty talk so much ?" Upon which, Patty ceased to talk and went to work harder than ever; but, being afraid that the eagerness with which she worked would betray her, she tried to work more slowly until that was observed. The very devices by which we seek to hide mental pre-occupation generally reveal it.

At last Patty was fain to betake herself to the loom-room, where she could think without having her thoughts guessed at. Here, too, she would be alone when Morton should come.

Poor Morton, having told his mother of his religious change, found it hard indeed to tell Patty. But he counted certainly that she would censure him for gambling, which would make it so much easier for him to explain to her that the only way for him to escape from vice was to join the Methodists, and thus give up all to a better life. He shaped some sentences founded upon this supposition. But after all his effort at courage, and all his praying for grace to help him to "confess Christ before men," he found the cross exceedingly hard to bear; and when he set his foot upon the threshold of the loom-room, his heart was in his mouth and his face was suffused with guilty blushes. Ah, weak nature! He was not blushing for his sins, but for his repentance!

Patty, seeing his confusion, determined to make him feel how full of forgiveness love was. She saw nobleness in his very shame, and she generously resolved that she would not ask, that she would not allow, a confession. She extended her hand cordially and beamed upon him, and told him how glad she was that he had come back, and—and—well—; she couldn't find anything else to say, but she urged him to sit down and handed him a splint-bottom chair, and tried for the life of her to think of something to say—the silence was so embarrassing. But talking for talk's sake is always hard. One talks as one breathes —best when volition has nothing to do with it.

The silence was embarrassing to Morton, but not half so much so as Patty's talk. For he had not expected this sort of an opening. If she had accused him of gambling, if she had spurned him, the road would have been plain. But now that she loved him and forgave him of her own sweet generosity, how should he smite her pride in the face by telling her that he had joined himself to the illiterate, vulgar fanatical sect of ranting Methodists, whom she utterly despised? Truly the Enemy had set an unexpected snare for his unwary feet. He had resolved to confess his religious devotion with heroic courage, but he had not expected to be disarmed in this fashion. He talked about everything else, he temporized, he allowed her to turn the conversation as she would, hoping vainly that she would allude to his gambling. But she did not. Could it be that she had not heard of it? Must he then reveal that to her also?

While he was debating the question in his mind, Patty, imagining that he was reproaching himself for the sin and folly of gambling, began to talk of what had happened in the neighborhood—how Jake Sniger "fell with the power" on Sunday and got drunk on Tuesday: "that's all this Methodist fuss amounts to, you know," she said. Morton thought it ungracious to blurt out at this moment that he was a Methodist: there would be an air of contradiction in the avowal; so he sat still while Patty turned all the sobbing and sighing, and shouting and loud praying of the meetings into ridicule. And Morton became conscious that it was getting every minute more and more difficult for him to confess his conversion. He thought it better to return to his gambling for a starting point.

"Did you hear what a bad boy I've been, Patty?"

"Oh! yes. I'm sorry you got into such a bad scrape; but don't say any more about it, Morton. You're too good for me with all your faults, and you won't do it any more."

"But I want to tell you all about it, and what happened while I was gone. I'm afraid you'll think too hard of me—"

"But I don't think hard of you at all, and I don't want to hear about it because it is n't pleasant. It'll all come out right at last: I'd a great deal rather have you a little wild at first than a hard Methodist, like Kike, for instance."

"But—"

"I tell you, Morton, I won't hear a word. Not one word. I want you to feel that whatever anybody else may say, I know you're all right."

You think Morton very weak. But, do you know how exceedingly sweet is confidence from one you love, when there is only censure, and suspicion, and dark predictions of evil from everybody else? Poor Morton could not refuse to bask in the sunshine for a moment after so much of storm. It is not the north wind, but the southern breezes that are fatal to the ice-berg's voyage into sunny climes.

At last he rose to go. He felt himself a Peter. He had denied the Master!

"Patty," he said, with resolution, "I have not been honest with you. I meant to tell you something when I first came, and I didn't. It is hard to have to give up your love. But I'm afraid you won't care for me when I tell you—"

The severity of Morton's penitence only touched Patty the more deeply.

"Morton," she said, interrupting, "if you've done anything naughty, I forgive you without knowing it. But I don't want to hear any more about it, I tell you." And with that the blushing Patty held her cheek up for her betrothed to kiss, and when Morton, trembling with conflicting emotions, had kissed her for the first time, she slipped away quickly to prevent his making any painful confessions.

For a moment Morton stood charmed with her goodness. When he believed himself to have conquered, he found himself vanquished.

In a dazed sort of way he walked the greater part of the distance home. He might write to her about it. He might let her hear it from others. But he rejected both as unworthy of a man. The memory of the kiss thrilled him, and he was tempted to throw

away his Methodism and rejoice in the love of Patty,
now so assured. But suddenly he seemed to himself
to be another Judas. He had not denied the Lord—
he had betrayed him ; and with a kiss !

Horrified by this thought, Morton hastened back
toward Captain Lumsden's. He entered the loom-
room, but it was vacant. He went into the living-
room, and there he saw not Patty alone, but the whole
family. Captain Lumsden had at that moment entered
by the opposite door. Patty was carding wool with
hand-cards, and she looked up, startled at this re-
appearance of her lover when she thought him happily
dismissed.

"Patty," said Morton, determined not to fall into
any devil's snare by delay, and to atone for his great
sin by making his profession as public as possible,
"Patty, what I wanted to say was, that I have determined to be a Christian, and I have joined—the—
Methodist—Church."

Morton's sense of inner conflict gave this utterance
an unfortunate sound of defiance, and it aroused all
Patty's combativeness. It was in fact a death wound
to her pride. She had feared sometimes that Morton
would be drawn into Methodism, but that he should
join the despised sect without so much as consulting
her was more than she could bear. This, then, was the
way in which her forbearance and forgiveness were
rewarded ! There stood her father, sneering like a
Mephistopheles. She would resent the indignity, and
at the same time show her power over her lover.

"Morton, if you are a Methodist, I never want to

see you again," she said, with lofty pride, and a solemn awfulness of passion more terrible than an oath.

"Don't say that, Patty!" stammered Morton, stretching his hands out in eager, despairing entreaty. But this only gave Patty the greater assurance that a little decision on her part would make him give up his Methodism.

THE CHOICE.

"I do say it, Morton, and I will *never* take it back." There was a sternness in the white face and a fire in the black eyes that left Morton no hope.

But he straightened himself up now to his full six feet, and said, with manly stubbornness: " Then, Patty, since you make me choose, I shall not give up the Lord, even for you. But," he added, with a broken voice, as he turned away, " may God help me to bear it."

Ah, Matilda Maria! if Morton were a knight in armor giving up his ladye love for the sake of monastic religiousness, how admirable he would be! But even in his homespun he is a man making the greatest of sacrifices. It is not the garb or the age that makes sublime a soul's offering of heart and hope to duty. When Morton was gone Lumsden chuckled not a little, and undertook to praise Patty for her courage; but I have understood that she resented his compliments, and poured upon him some severe denunciation, in which the Captain heard more truth than even Kike had ventured to utter. Such are the inconsistencies of a woman when her heart is wounded.

It seems a trifle to tell just here, when Morton and Patty are in trouble—but you will want to know about Brady. He was at Colonel Wheeler's that evening, eagerly telling of Morton's escape from lynching, when Mrs. Wheeler expressed her gratification that Morton had ceased to gamble and become a Methodist

" Mithodist ? He's no Mithodist."

" Yes, he is." responded Mrs. Wheeler, " his mother

told me so; and what's more, she said she was glad of it." Then, seeing Brady's discomfiture, she added: " You didn't get all the news that time, Mr. Brady."

" Well, me dair madam, when I'm admithed to a family intervoo, it's not proper fer me to tell all I heerd. I didn't know the fact was made public yit, and so I had to denoy it. It's the honor of a Oirish gintleman, ye know."

What a journalist he would have made !

CHAPTER XX.

MORE than two years have passed since Morton made his great sacrifice. You may see him now riding up to the Hickory Ridge Church—a "hewed-log" country meeting-house. He is dressed in homespun clothes. At the risk of compromising him forever, I must confess that his coat is straight-breasted—shad-bellied as the profane call it—and his best hat a white one with a broad brim. The face is still fresh, despite the conflicts and hardships of one year's travel in the mountains of Eastern Kentucky, and the sickness and exposure of another year in the malarious cane-brakes of Western Tennessee. Perils of Indians, perils of floods, perils of alligators, perils of bad food, perils of cold beds, perils of robbers, perils of rowdies, perils of fevers, and the weariness of five thousand miles of horseback riding in a year, with five or six hundred preachings in the same time, and the care of numberless scattered churches in the wilderness have conspired to give sedateness to his countenance. And yet there is a youthfulness about the sun-browned cheeks, and a lingering expression of that sort of humor which Western people call "mischief" about the eyes, that match but grotesquely with white hat and shad-bellied coat.

He has been a preacher almost ever since he became a Methodist. How did he get his theological

GOING TO CONFERENCE.

education? It used to be said that Methodist preach-ers were educated by the old ones telling the young ones all they knew; but besides this oral instruction Morton carried in his saddle-bags John Wesley's simple, solid sermons, Charles Wesley's hymns, and a Bible. Having little of the theory and system of theology, he was free to take lessons in the larger school of life and practical observation. For the rest, the free criticism to which he was subject from other preachers, and the contact with a few families of refinement, had obliterated his dialect. Naturally a gentleman at heart, he had, from the few stately gentlemen that he met, quickly learned to be a gentleman in manners. He is regarded as a young man of great promise by the older brethren; his clear voice is very charming, his strong and manly speech and his tender feeling are very inspiring, and on his two circuits he has reported extraordinary revivals. Some of the old men sagely predict that "he's got bishop-timber in him," but no such ambitious dreams disturb his sleep. He has not "gone into a decline" on account of Patty. A healthy nature will bear heavy blows. But there is a pain, somewhere—everywhere—in his being, when he thinks of the girl who stood just above him in the spelling-class, and who looked so divine when she was spinning her two dozen cuts a day. He does not like this regretful feeling. He prays to be forgiven for it. He acknowledges in class-meeting and in love-feast that he is too much like Lot's wife—he finds his heart prone to look back toward the objects he once loved. Often in riding through the stillness of a deep forest —and the primeval forest is to him the peculiar abode of the Almighty—his noble voice rings out fervently and even pathetically with that stanza :

> " The dearest idol I have known,
>   Whate'er that idol be,
>   Help me to tear it from thy throne
>   And worship only Thee !"

No man can enjoy a joke with more zest than he, and none can tell a story more effectively in a generation of preachers who are all good story-tellers. He loves his work; its dangers and difficulties satisfy the ambition of his boyhood; and he has had no misgivings, except when once or twice he has revisited his parents in the Hissawachee Bottom. Then the longing to see Patty has seized him and he has been fain to hurry away, praying to be delivered from every snare of the enemy.

He is not the only man in a straight-breasted coat who is approaching the country meeting-house. It is conference-time, and the greetings are hearty and familiar. Everybody is glad to see everybody, and, after a year of separation, nobody can afford to stand on ceremony with anybody else. Morton has hardly alighted before half a dozen preachers have rushed up to him and taken him by the hand. A tall brother, with a grotesque twitch in his face, cries out:

"How do you do, Brother Goodwin? Glad to see the alligators haven't finished you!"

To which Morton returns a laughing reply; but suddenly he sees, standing back of the rest and waiting his turn, a young man with a solemn, sallow face, pinched by sickness and exposure, and bordered by the straight black hair that falls on each side of it. He wears over his clothes a blanket with arm-holes cut through, and seems to be perpetually awaiting an ague-chill. Seeing him, Morton pushes the rest aside, and catches the wan hand in both of his own with a cry: "Kike, God bless you! How are you, dear old fellow? You look sick."

Kike smiled faintly, and Morton threw his arm over his shoulder and looked in his face. "I am sick, Mort. Cast down, but not destroyed, you know. I hope I am ready to be offered up."

"Not a bit of it. You've got to get better. Offered up? Why, you aren't fit to offer to an alligator. Where are you staying?"

"Out there." Kike pointed to the tents of a camp-meeting barely visible through the trees. The people in the neighborhood of the Hickory Ridge Church, being unable to entertain the Conference in their homes, had resorted to the device of getting up a camp-meeting. It was easier to take care of the preachers out of doors than in. Morton shook his head as he walked with Kike to the thin canvas tent under which he had been assigned to sleep. The white spot on the end of Kike's nose and the blue lines under his finger-nails told plainly of the on-coming chill, and Morton hurried away to find some better shelter for him than under this thin sheet. But this was hard to do. The few brethren in the neighborhood had already filled their cabins full of guests, mostly in infirm health, and Kike, being one of the younger men, renowned only for his piety and his revivals, had not been thought of for a place elsewhere than on the camp-ground. Finding it impossible to get a more comfortable resting place for his friend, Morton turned to seek for a physician. The only doctor in the neighborhood was a Presbyterian minister, retired from the ministry on account of his impaired health. To him Morton went to ask for medicine for Kike.

"Dr. Morgan, there is a preacher sick down at the camp-ground," said Morton, "and—"

"And you want me to see him," said the doctor, in an alert, anticipative fashion, seizing his "pill-bags" and donning his hat.

When the two rode up to the tent in which Kike was lodged they found a prayer-meeting of a very exciting kind going on in the tent adjoining. There were cries and groans and amens and hallelujahs commingled in a way quite intelligible to the experienced ear of Morton, but quite unendurable to the orderly doctor.

"A bad place for a sick man, sir," he said to Morton, with great positiveness.

"I know it is, doctor," said Morton; "and I've done my best to get him out of it, but I cannot. See how thin this tent-cover is."

"And the malaria of these woods is awful. Camp-meetings, sir, are always bad. And this *fuss* is enough to drive a patient crazy."

Morton thought the doctor prejudiced, but he said nothing. They had now reached the corner of the tent where Kike lay on a straw pallet, holding his hands to his head. The noise from the prayer-meeting was more than his weary brain would bear.

"Can you sit on my horse?" said the doctor, promptly proceeding to lift Kike without even explaining to him who he was, or where he proposed to take him.

Morton helped to place Kike in the saddle, but the poor fellow was shaking so that he could not sit there. Morton then brought out Dolly—she was all his own now—and took the slight form of Kike in his arms, he riding on the croup, and the sick man in the saddle.

"Where shall I ride to, doctor?"

"To my house," said the doctor, mounting his own horse and spurring off to have a bed made ready for Kike.

As Morton rode up to the doctor's gate, the shaking Kike roused a little and said, "She's the same fine old Dolly, Mort."

"A little more sober. The long rides in the cane-brakes, and the responsibility of the Methodist itinerancy, have given her the gravity that belongs to the ministry."

Such a bed as Kike found in Dr. Morgan's house! After the rude bear-skins upon which he had languished in the backwoods cabins, after the musty feather-beds in freezing lofts, and the pallets of leaves upon which he had shivered and scorched and fought fleas and musquitoes, this clean white bed was like a foretaste of heaven. But Kike was almost too sick to be grateful. The poor frame had been kept up by will so long, that now that he was in a good bed and had Morton he felt that he could afford to be sick. What had been ague settled into that wearisome disease called bilious fever. Morton staid by him nearly all of the time, looking into the conference now and then to see the venerable Asbury in the chair, listening to a grand speech from McKendree, attending on the third day of the session, when, with the others who had been preaching two years on probation, he was called forward to answer the "Questions" always propounded to "Candidates for admission to the conference." Kike only was missing from the list of those who were to have heard the bishop's exhortations, full of martial fire, and to have answered his questions in regard to their spiritual state. For above all gifts of speech or depths of learning, or acuteness of reasoning, the early Methodists esteemed devout affections; and no man was of account for the ministry who was not "groaning to be made perfect in this life." The question stands in the discipline yet, but very many young men who assent to it groan after nothing so much as a city church with full galleries.

The strange mystery in which appointments were involved could not but pique curiosity. Morton having had one year of mountains, and one year of cane-brakes, had come to wish for one year of a little more comfort, and a little better support. There is a romance about going threadbare and tattered in a good cause, but even the romance gets threadbare and tattered if it last too long, and one wishes for a little sober reality of warm clothes to relieve a romance, charming enough in itself, but dull when it grows monotonous.

The awful hour of appointments came on at last. The brave-hearted men sat down before the bishop, and before God, not knowing what was to be their fate. Morton could not guess where he was going. A miasmatic cane-brake, or a deadly cypress swamp, might be his doom, or he might—but no, he would not hope that his lot might fall in Ohio. He was a young man, and a young man must take his chances. Morton found himself more anxious about Kike than about himself. Where would the bishop send the invalid? With Kike it might be a matter of life and death, and Kike would not hear to being left without work. He meant, he said, to cease at once to work and live.

The brethren, still in sublime ignorance of their destiny, sang fervently that fiery hymn of Charles Wesley's:

> "Jesus, the name high over all,
>   In hell or earth or sky,
> Angels and men before him fall,
>   And devils fear and fly.
>
> "O that the world might taste and see,
>   The riches of his grace,
> The arms of love that compass me
>   Would all mankind embrace."

And when they reached the last stanzas there was the ring of soldiers ready for battle in their martial voices. That some of them would die from exposure, malaria, or accident during the next year was probable. Tears came to their eyes, and they involuntarily began to grasp the hands of those who stood next them as they approached the climax of the hymn, which the bishop read impressively, two lines at a time, for them to sing:

> "His only righteousness I show,
>   His saving truth proclaim,
> 'Tis all my business here below
>   To cry, 'Behold the Lamb!'

"Happy if with my latest breath
I may but gasp his name,
Preach him to all and cry in death,
'Behold, behold the Lamb!'"

Then, with suffused eyes, they resumed their seats, and
the venerable Asbury, with calmness and with a voice
faltering with age, made them a brief address; tender
and sympathetic at first, earnest as he proceeded, and
full of ardor and courage at the close.

"When the British Admiralty," he said, "wanted
some man to take Quebec, they began with the oldest
General first, asking him: 'General, will you go and
take Quebec?' To which he made reply, 'It is a very
difficult enterprise.' 'You may stand aside,' they said.
One after another the Generals answered that they
would, in some more or less indefinite manner, until
the youngest man on the list was reached. 'General
Wolfe,' they said, 'will you go and take Quebec?'
'I'll do it or die,' he replied." Here the bishop
paused, looked round about upon them, and added,
with a voice full of emotion, "He went, and did both.
We send you first to take the country allotted to you.
We want only men who are determined to do it or
die! Some of you, dear brethren, will do both. If
you fall, let us hear that you fell like Methodist
preachers at your post, face to the foe, and the shout
of victory on your lips."

The effect of this speech was beyond description.
There were sobs, and cries of "Amen," "God grant
it," "Halleluiah!" from every part of the old log
church. Every man was ready for the hardest place,

if he must.   Gravely, as one who trembles at his responsibility, the bishop brought out his list.   No man looked any more upon his fellow.   Every one kept his eyes fixed upon the paper from which the bishop read the appointments, until his own name was reached. Some showed pleasure when their names were called, some could not conceal a look of pain.   When the reading had proceeded half way down the list, Morton heard, with a little start, the words slowly enounced as the bishop's eyes fell on him:

"Jenkinsville Circuit—Morton Goodwin."

Well, at least Jenkinsville was in Ohio.   But it was in the wickedest part of Ohio.   Morton half suspected that he was indebted to his muscle, his courage, and his quick wit for the appointment.   The rowdies of Jenkinsville Circuit were worse than the alligators of Mississippi.   But he was young, hopeful and brave, and rather relished a difficult field than otherwise.   He listened now for Kike's name.   It came at the bottom of the list:

"Pottawottomie Creek — W. T. Smith, Hezekiah Lumsden."

The bishop had not dared to entrust a circuit to a man so sick as Kike was.   He had, therefore, sent him as "second man" or "junior preacher" on a circuit in the wilderness of Michigan.

The last appointment having been announced, a simple benediction closed the services, and the brethren who had foregone houses and homes and fathers and mothers and wives and children for the kingdom of heaven's sake saddled their horses, called, one by one, at

Dr. Morgan's to say a brotherly " God bless you !" to the sick Kike, and rode away, each in his own direction, and all with a self-immolation to the cause rarely seen since the Middle-Age.

They rode away, all but Kike. languishing yet with fever, and Morton, watching by his side.

CHAPTER XXI.

CONVALESCENCE.

AT last Kike is getting better, and Morton can be spared. There is no longer any reason why the rowdies on Jenkinsville Circuit should pine for the muscular young preacher whom they have vowed to "lick as soon as they lay eyes on to him." Dolly's legs are aching for a gallop. Morton and Dr. Morgan have exhausted their several systems of theology in discussion. So, at last, the impatient Morton mounts the impatient Dolly, and gallops away to preach to the impatient brethren and face the impatient ruffians of Jenkinsville Circuit. Kike is left yet in his quiet harbor to recover. The doctor has taken a strange fancy to the zealous young prophet, and looks forward with sadness to the time when he will leave.

Ah, happiest experience of life, when the flood tide sets back through the veins! You have no longer any pain; you are not well enough to feel any responsibility; you cannot work; there is no obligation resting on you but one—that is rest. Such perfect passivity Kike had never known before. He could walk but little. He sat the livelong day by the open window, as listless as the grass that waved before the wind. All the sense of dire responsibility, all those feelings of the awfulness of life, and the fearfulness of his work, and the dreadfulness of his accountability, were in abeyance. To eat, to drink, to sleep, to wake and breathe, to suffer as a passive instrument the play of whatever feeling might chance to come, was Kike's life.

In this state the severity of his character was laid aside. He listened to the quick and eager conversation of Dr. Morgan with a gentle pleasure; he answered the motherly questions of Mrs. Morgan with quiet gratitude; he admired the goodness of Miss Jane Morgan, their eldest and most exemplary daughter, as a far off spectator. There were but two things that had a real interest for him. He felt a keen delight in watching the wayward flight of the barn swallows as they went chattering out from under the eaves— their airy vagabondage was so restful. And he liked to watch the quick, careless tread of Henrietta Morgan, the youngest of the doctor's daughters, who went on forever talking and laughing with as little reck as the swallows themselves. Though she was eighteen, there was in her full child-like cheeks, in her contagious laugh—a laugh most unprovoked, coming of itself—in her playful way of performing even her duties, a something that so contrasted with and relieved the habitual austerity of Kike's temper, and that so fell in with his present lassitude and happy carelessness, that he allowed his head, resting weakly upon a pillow, to turn from side to side, that his eyes might follow her. So diverting were her merry replies, that he soon came to talk with her for the sake of hearing them. He was not forgetful of the solemn injunctions Mr. Wesley had left for the prudent behavior of young ministers in the presence of women. With Miss Jane he was very careful lest he should in any way compromise himself, or awaken her affections. Jane was the kind of a girl he would want to marry, if he were to marry. But Nettie was a child—a cheerful butterfly—as refreshing to his weary mind as a drink of cold water to a fever-patient. When she was out of the room, Kike was impatient; when she returned, he was glad. When she sewed, he drew the large chair in which he rested in front of her, and talked in his grave fashion, while she, in turn, amused him with a hundred fancies. She seemed to shine all about him like sunlight. Poor Kike could not refuse to enjoy a fellowship so delightful, and Nettie Morgan's reverence for young Lumsden's saintliness, and pity for his sickness, grew apace into a love for him.

Long before Kike discovered or Nettie suspected this, the doctor had penetrated it. Kike's wholehearted devotion to his work had charmed the ex-minister, who moved about in his alert fashion, talking with eager rapidity, anticipating Kike's grave sentences before he was half through — seeing and hearing everything while he seemed to note nothing. He was not averse to this attachment between the two. Provided always, that Kike should give up traveling. It was all but impossible, indeed, for a man to be a Methodist preacher in that day and "lead about a wife." A very few managed to combine the ministry with marriage, but in most cases marriage rendered "location" or secularization imperative.

Kike sat one day talking in the half-listless way that is characteristic of convalescence, watching Nettie

CONVALESCENCE.

Morgan as she sewed and laughed, when Dr. Morgan came in, put his pill-bags upon the high bureau, glanced quickly at the two, and said:

"Nettie, I think you'd better help your mother. The double-and-twisting is hard work."

Nettie laid her sewing down. Kike watched her until she had disappeared through the door; then he listened until the more vigorous spinning indicated to him that younger hands had taken the wheel. His heart sank a little—it might be hours before Nettie could return.

Dr. Morgan busied himself, or pretended to busy himself, with his medicines, but he was observing how the young preacher's eyes followed his daughter, how his countenance relapsed into its habitual melancholy when she was gone. He thought he could not be mistaken in his diagnosis.

"Mr. Lumsden," he said, kindly, "I don't know what we shall do when you get well. I can't bear to have you go away."

"You have been too good, doctor. I am afraid you have spoiled me." The thought of going to Pottawottomie Creek was growing more and more painful to Kike. He had put all thoughts of the sort out of his mind, because the doctor wished him to keep his mind quiet. Now, for some reason, Doctor Morgan seemed to force the disagreeable future upon him. Why was it unpleasant? Why had he lost his relish for his work? Had he indeed backslidden?

While the doctor fumbled over his bottles, and for the fourth time held a large phial, marked *Sulph. de Quin.*, up to the light, as though he were counting the grains, the young preacher was instituting an inquiry into his own religious state. Why did he shrink from Pottawottomie Creek circuit? He had braved much harder toil and greater danger. On Pottawottomie Creek he would have a senior colleague upon whom all administrative responsibilities would devolve, and the year promised to be an easy one in comparison with the preceding. On inquiring of himself he found that there was no circuit that would be attractive to him in his present state of mind, except the one that lay all around Dr. Morgan's house. At first Kike Lumsden, playing hide-and-seek with his own motives, as other men do under like circumstances, gave himself much credit for his grateful attachment to the family. Surely gratitude is a generous quality, and had not Dr. Morgan, though of another denomination, taken him under his roof and given him professional attention free of charge? And Mrs. Morgan and Jane and Nettie, had they not cared for him as though he were a brother? What could be more commendable than that he should find himself loth to leave people who were so good?

But Kike had not been in the habit of cheating himself. He had always dealt hardly with Kike Lumsden. He could not rest now in this subterfuge; he would not give himself credit that he did not deserve. So while the doctor walked to the window and senselessly examined the contents of one of his bottles marked "*Hydrarg.*," Kike took another and closer look at his own mind and saw that the one person whose loss would be painful to him was not Dr. Morgan, nor his excellent wife, nor the admirable Jane, but the volatile Nettie, the cadence of whose spinning wheel he was even then hearkening to. The consciousness that he was in love came to him suddenly—a consciousness not without pleasure, but with a plentiful admixture of pain.

Doctor Morgan's eyes, glancing with characteristic alertness, caught the expression of a new self-knowledge

and of an anxious pain upon the forehead of Lumsden. Then the physician seemed all at once satisfied
with his medicines. The bottle labelled "*Hydrarg.*"
and the "*Sulph. de Quin.*" were now replaced in the
saddle bags.

At this moment Nettie herself came into the room
on some errand. Kike had heard her wheel stop—
had looked toward the door—had caught her glance
as she came in, and had, in that moment, become
aware that he was not the only person in love. Was
it, then, that the doctor wished to prevent the attachment going further that he had delicately reminded
his guest of the approach of the time when he must
leave? These thoughts aroused Kike from the lassitude of his slow convalescence. Nettie went back to
her wheel, and set it humming louder than ever, but
Kike heard now in its tones some note of anxiety
that disturbed him. The doctor came and sat down
by him and felt his pulse, ostensibly to see if he had
fever, really to add yet another link to the chain of
evidence that his surmise was correct.

"Mr. Lumsden," said he, "a constitution so much
impaired as yours cannot recuperate in a few days."

"I know that, sir," said Kike, "and I am anxious
to get to my mother's for a rest there, that I may not
burden you any longer, and——"

"You misunderstand me, my dear fellow, if you
think I want to be rid of you. I wish you would
stay with me always; I do indeed."

For a moment Kike looked out of the window. To
stay with the doctor always would, it seemed to him,

be a heaven upon earth. But had he not renounced all thought of a heaven on earth? Had he not said plainly that here he had no abiding place? Having put his hand to the plow, should he look back?

"But I ought not to give up my work."

It was not in this tone that Kike would have spurned such a temptation awhile before.

"Mr. Lumsden," said the doctor, "you see that I am useful here. I cannot preach a great deal, but I think that I have never done so much good as since I began to practice medicine. I need somebody to help me. I cannot take care of the farm and my practice too. You could look after the farm, and preach every Sunday in the country twenty miles round. You might even study medicine after awhile, and take the practice as I grow older. You will die, if you go on with your circuit-riding. Come and live with me, and be my——assistant." The doctor had almost said "my son." It was in his mind, and Kike divined it.

"Think about it," said Dr. Morgan, as he rose to go, "and remember that nobody is obliged to kill himself."

And all day long Kike thought and prayed, and tried to see the right; and all day long Nettie found occasion to come in on little errands, and as often as she came in did it seem clear to Kike that he would be justified in accepting Dr. Morgan's offer; and as often as she went out did he tremble lest he were about to betray the trust committed to him.

CHAPTER XXII.

THE DECISION.

THE austerity of Kike's conscience had slumbered during his convalescence. It was wide awake now. He sat that evening in his room trying to see the right way. According to old Methodist custom he looked for some inward movement of the spirit—some "impression"—that should guide him.

During the great religious excitement of the early part of this century, Western pietists referred everything to God in prayer, and the belief in immmediate divine direction was often carried to a ludicrous extent. It is related that one man retired to the hills and prayed a week that he might know how he should be baptized, and that at last he came rushing out of the woods, shouting "Hallelujah! Immersion!" Various devices were invented for obtaining divine direction—devices not unworthy the ancient augurs. Lorenzo Dow used to suffer his horse to take his own course at each divergence of the road. It seems to have been a favorite delusion of pietism, in all ages, that God could direct an inanimate object, guide a dumb brute, or impress a blind impulse upon the human mind, but could not enlighten or guide the judgment itself. The opening of a Bible at random for a directing text became so common during the Wesleyan

movement in England, that Dr. Adam Clarke thought
it necessary to utter a stout Irish philippic against
what he called "Bible sortilege."

These devout divinings, these vanes set to catch
the direction of heavenly breezes, could not but impress so earnest a nature as Kike's. Now in his
distress he prayed with eagerness and opened his
Bible at random to find his eye lighting, not on any
intelligible or remotely applicable passage, but upon a
bead-roll of unpronounceable names in one of the
early chapters of the Book of Chronicles. This
disappointment he accepted as a trial of his faith.
Faith like Kike's is not to be dashed by disappointment. He prayed again for direction, and opened
at last at the text: "Simon, son of Jonas, lovest
thou me more than these?" The marked trait in
Kike's piety was an enthusiastic personal loyalty to
the Lord Jesus Christ. This question seemed directed
to him, as it had been to Peter, in reproach. He
would hesitate no longer. Love, and life itself, should
be sacrificed for the Christ who died for him. Then he
prayed once more, and there came to his mind the
memory of that saying about leaving houses and homes
and lands and wives, for Christ's sake. It came to him,
doubtless, by a perfectly natural law of mental association. But what did Kike know of the association of
ideas, or of any other law of mental action? Wesley's
sermons and Benson's Life of Fletcher constituted his
library. To him it seemed certain that this text of
scripture was "suggested." It was a call from Christ
to give up all for him. And in the spirit of the

sublimest self-sacrifice, he said: "Lord, I will keep back nothing!"

But emotions and resolutions that are at high tide in the evening often ebb before morning. Kike thought himself strong enough to begin again to rise at four o'clock, as Wesley had ordained in those "rules for a preacher's conduct" which every Methodist preacher even yet *promises* to keep. Following the same rules, he proceeded to set apart the first hour for prayer and meditation. The night before all had seemed clear; but now that morning had come and he must soon proceed to execute his stern resolve, he found himself full of doubt and irresolution. Such vacillation was not characteristic of Kike, but it marked the depth of his feeling for Nettie. Doubtless, too, the enervation of convalescence had to do with it. Certainly in that raw and foggy dawn the forsaking of the paradise of rest and love in which he had lingered seemed to require more courage than he could muster. After all, why should he leave? Might he not be mistaken in regard to his duty? Was he obliged to sacrifice his life?

He conducted his devotions in a state of great mental distraction. Seeing a copy of Baxter's Reformed Pastor which belonged to Dr. Morgan lying on the window-seat, he took it up, hoping to get some light from its stimulating pages. He remembered that Wesley spoke well of Baxter; but he could not fix his mind upon the book. He kept listlessly turning the leaves until his eye lighted upon a sentence in Latin. Kike knew not a single word of Latin, and for that

very reason his attention was the more readily attracted by the sentence in an unknown tongue. He read
it, "*Nec propter vitam, vivendi perdere causas.*" He
found written in the margin a free rendering: "Let us
not, for the sake of life, sacrifice the only things worth
living for." He knelt down now and gave thanks for
what seemed to him Divine direction. He had been
delivered from a temptation to sacrifice the great end
of living for the sake of saving his life.

It cost him a pang to bid adieu to Dr. Morgan
and his motherly wife and the excellent Jane. It
cost him a great pang to say good-bye to Nettie
Morgan. Her mobile face could ill conceal her feeling.
She did not venture to come to the door. Kike
found her alone in the little porch at the back of the
house, trying to look unconcerned. Afraid to trust
himself he bade her farewell dryly, taking her hand
coldly for a moment. But the sight of her pain-
stricken face touched him to the quick: he seized her
hand again, and, with eyes full of tears, said huskily:
"Good-bye, Nettie! God bless you, and keep you forever." and then turned suddenly away, bidding the
rest a hasty adieu and riding off eagerly, almost
afraid to look back. He was more severe than ever
in the watch he kept over himself after this. He
could never again trust his treacherous heart.

Kike rode to his old home in the Hissawachee
Settlement. "The Forks" had now come to be quite
a village; the valley was filling with people borne on
that great wave of migration that swept over the
Alleghanies in the first dozen years of the century.

The cabin in which his mother lived was very little different from what it was when he left it. The old stick chimney showed signs of decrepitude; the barrel which served for chimney-pot was canted a little on one side, giving to the cabin, as Kike thought, an unpleasant air, as of a man a little exhilarated with whiskey, who has tipped his hat upon the side of his head to leer at you saucily. The mother received him joyously, and wiped her eyes with her apron when she saw how sick he had been. Brady was at the widow's cabin, and though he stood by the fire-place when Kike entered, the two splint-bottomed chairs sat suspiciously close together. Brady had long thought of changing his state, but both Brady and the widow were in mortal fear of Kike, whose severity of judgment and sternness of reproof appalled them. "If it wasn't for Koike," said Brady to himself, "I'd propose to the widdy. But what would the lad say to sich follies at my toime of loife? And the widdy's more afeard of him than I am. Did iver anybody say the loikes of a b'y that skeers his schoolmasther out of courtin his mother, and his mother out of resavin the attintions of a larnt grammairian loike mesilf? The misfortin' is that Koike don't have no wakenisses himsilf. I wish he had jist one, and thin I wouldn't keer. If I could only foind that he'd iver looked jist a little swate loike at iny young girl, I wouldn't moind his cinsure. But, somehow, I kape a-thinkin' what would Koike say, loike a ould coward that I am."

Kike had come home to have his tattered wardrobe

improved, and the thoughtful mother had already made
him a warm, though not very shapely, suit of jeans.
It cost Kike a struggle to leave her again. She did
not think him fit to go. But she did not dare to say
so. How should she venture to advise one who
seemed to her wondering heart to live in the very
secrets of the Almighty? God had laid hands on
him—the child was hers no longer. But still she
looked her heart-breaking apprehensions as he set
out from home, leaving her standing disconsolate in
the doorway wiping her eyes with her apron.

And Brady, seeing Kike as he rode by the school-
house, ventured to give him advice—partly by way of
finding out whether Kike had any "wakeniss" or not.

"Now, Koike, me son, as your ould taycher, I
thrust you'll bear with me if I give you some advoice,
though ye have got to be sich a praycher. Ye'll not
take offinse, me lad?"

"O no; certainly not, Mr. Brady," said Kike,
smiling sadly.

"Will, thin, ye're of a delicate constitooshun as
shure as ye're born, and it's me own opinion as ye
ought to git a good wife to nurse ye, and thin you
could git a home and maybe do more good than ye
do now."

Kike's face settled into more than its wonted
severity. The remembrance of his recent vacillation
and the sense of his present weakness were fresh in
his mind. He would not again give place to the
devil.

"Mr. Brady, there's something more important

than our own ease or happiness. We were not made to seek comfort, but to give ourselves to the work of Christ. And see! your head is already blossoming for eternity, and yet you talk as if this world were all."

Saying this, Kike shook hands with the master solemnly and rode away, and Mr. Brady was more appalled than ever.

"The lad haint got a wakeniss," he said, disconsolately. "Not a wakeniss," he repeated, as he walked gloomily into the school-house, took down a switch and proceeded to punish Pete Sniger, who, as the worst boy in the school, and a sort of evil genius, often suffered on general principles when the master was out of humor.

Was Kike unhappy when he made his way to the distant Pottawottomie Creek circuit?

Do you think the Jesuit missionaries, who traversed the wilds of America at the call of duty as they heard it, were unhappy men? The highest happiness comes not from the satisfaction of our desires, but from the denial of them for the sake of a high purpose. I doubt not the happiest man that ever sailed through Levantine seas, or climbed Cappadocian mountains, was Paul of Tarsus. Do you think that he envied the voluptuaries of Cyprus, or the rich merchants of Corinth? Can you believe that one of the idlers in the Epicurean gardens, or one of the Stoic loafers in the covered sidewalks of Athens, could imagine the joy that tided the soul of Paul over all tribulations? For there is a sort of awful delight in self-sacrifice, and Kike defied the storms of a northern winter, and all the difficulties and dangers of the wilderness, and all the hardships of his lonely lot, with one saying often on his lips: "O Lord, I have kept back nothing!"

I have heard that about this time young Lumsden was accustomed to electrify his audiences by his fervent preaching upon the Christian duty of Glorying in Tribulation, and that shrewd old country women would nod their heads one to another as they went home afterward, and say: "He's seed a mighty sight o' trouble in his time, I 'low, fer a young man." "Yes; but he's got the victory; and how powerful sweet he talks about it! I never heerd the beat in all my born days."

K

CHAPTER XXIII.

TWO years have ripened Patty from the girl to the woman. If Kike is happy in his self-abnegation, Patty is not happy in hers. Pride has no balm in it. However powerful it may be as a stimulant, it is poor food. And Patty has little but pride to feed upon. The invalid mother has now been dead a year, and Patty is almost without companionship, though not without suitors. Land brings lovers—land-lovers, if nothing more—and the estate of Patty's father is not her only attraction. She is a young woman of a certain nobility of figure and carriage; she is not large, but her bearing makes her seem quite commanding. Even her father respects her, and all the more does he wish to torment her whenever he finds opportunity. Patty is thrifty, and in the early West no attraction outweighed this wifely ordering of a household. But Patty will not marry any of the suitors who calculate the infirm health of her father and the probable division of his estate, and who mentally transfer to their future homes the thrift and orderliness they see in Captain Lumsden's. By refusing them all she has won the name of a proud girl. There are times when out of sight of everybody she weeps, hardly knowing why. And since her mother's death she reads the prayer-book more than ever, finding in the severe confessions therein framed for us miserable sinners, and the plaintive cries of the litany, a voice for her innermost soul.

Captain Lumsden fears she will marry and leave him, and yet it angers him that she refuses to marry. His hatred of Methodists has assumed the intensity of a monomania since he was defeated for the legis- lature partly by Methodist opposition. All his love of power has turned to bitterest resentment, and every thought that there may be yet the remotest possibility of Patty's marrying Morton afflicts him beyond measure. He cannot fathom the reason for her obsti- nate rejection of all lovers; he dislikes her growing seriousness and her fondness for the prayer-book. Even the prayer-book's earnestness has something Methodistic about it. But Patty has never yet been in a Methodist meeting, and with this fact he com- forts himself. He has taken pains to buy her jewelry and "artificials" in abundance, that he may, by dressing her finely, remove her as far as possible from temptations to become a Methodist. For in that time, when fine dressing was not common and country neighborhoods were polarized by the advent of Method- ism in its most aggressive form, every artificial flower and every earring was a banner of antagonism to the new sect; a well-dressed woman in a congregation was almost a defiance to the preacher. It seemed to Lumsden, therefore, that Patty had prophylactic orna- ments enough to save her from Methodism. And to all of these he added covert threats that if any child of his should ever join these crazy Methodist loons, he would turn him out of doors and never see him again. This threat was always indirect—a remark dropped incidentally; the pronoun which represented the unknown quantity of a Methodist Lumsden was always masculine, but Patty did not fail to comprehend.

One day there came to Captain Lumsden's door that out-cast of New England — a tin-peddler. Western people had never heard of Yale College or any other glory of Connecticut or New England. To them it was but a land that bred pestilent peripatetic peddlers of tin-ware and wooden clocks. Western rogues would cheat you out of your horse or your farm

THE CONNECTICUT PEDDLER.

if a good chance offered, but this vile vender of Yankee tins, who called a bucket a "pail," and said "noo" for new, and talked nasally, would work an hour to cheat you out of a "fipenny bit." The tin-peddler, one Munson, thrust his sharpened visage in at Lumsden's door and "made bold" to *in*quire if he

could git a night's lodging, which the Captain, like
other settlers, granted without charge. Having unload-
ed his stock of "tins" and "put up" his horse, the
Connecticut peddler "made bold" to ask many leading questions about the family and personal history
of the Lumsdens, collectively and individually. Having thus taken the first steps toward acquaintance by
this display of an aggravating interest in the welfare
of his new friends, he proceeded to give elaborate
and truthful accounts—with variations—of his own
recent adventures, to the boundless amusement of the
younger Lumsdens, who laughed more heartily at the
Connecticut man's words and pronunciation than at
his stories. He said, among other things, that he had
ben to Jinkinsville t'other day to what the Methodis'
called a "basket meetin'." But when he had proceeded so far with his narrative, he prudently stopped
and made bold to *in*quire what the Captain thought
of these Methodists. The Captain was not slow to
express his opinion, and the man of tins, having thus
reassured himself by taking soundings, proceeded to
tell that they was a dreffle craoud of folks to that
meetin'. And he, hevin' a sharp eye to business, hed
went forrard to the mourner's bench to be prayed fer.
Didn't do no pertik'ler harm to hev folks pray fer ye,
ye know. Well, ye see, the Methodis' they wanted to
*in*courage a seeker, and so they all bought some tins.
Purty nigh tuck the hull load offen his hands! (And
here the peddler winked one eye at the Captain and
then the other at Patty.) Fer they was sech a dreffle
lot of folks there. Come to hear a young preacher

as is 'mazin' elo'kent—Parson Goodwin by name, anf
he was a *good one* to preach, sartain.

This startled Patty and the Captain.

"Goodwin?" said the Captain; "Morton Goodwin?"

"The identikle," said the peddler.

"Raised only half a mile from here," said Lumsden, "and we don't think much of him."

"Neither did I," said the peddler, trimming his
sails to Lumsden's breezes. "I calkilate I could
preach e'en a'most as well as he does, myself, and I
wa'n't brought up to preachin', nother. But he's got
a good v'ice fer singin'—sich a ring to't, ye see, and
he's got a smart way thet comes the sympathies over the
women folks and weak-eyed men, and sets 'em cryin'
at a desp'ate rate. Was brought up here, was he?
Du tell! He's powerful pop'lar." Then, catching the
Captain's eye, he added: "Among the women, I
mean."

"He'll marry some shouting girl, I suppose," said
the Captain, with a chuckle.

"That's jist what he's going to do," said the peddler, pleased to have some information to give. Seeing
that the Captain and his daughter were interested in
his communication, the peddler paused a moment. A
bit of gossip is too good a possession for one to part
with too quickly.

"You guessed good, that time," said the tinware
man. "I heerd say as he was a goin' to splice with a
gal that could pray like a angel afire. An' I heerd
her pray. She nearly peeled the shingles off the skewl-
haouse Sich another *ex*citement as she perjuced, I

never did see. An' I went up to her after meetin'
and axed a interest in her prayers. Don't do no
harm, ye know, to git sich lightnin' on yer own side!
An' I took keer to git a good look at her face, for
preachers ginerally marry purty faces. Preachers is a
good deal like other folks, ef they do purtend to be
better, hey? Well, naow, that Ann Elizer Meacham *is*
purty, sartain. An' everybody says he's goin' to marry
her; an' somebody said the presidin' elder mout tie
'em up next Sunday at Quartily Meetin', maybe. Then
they'll divide the work in the middle and go halves.
She'll pray and he'll preach." At this the peddler
broke into a sinister laugh, sure that he had conciliated
both the Captain and Patty by his news. He now
proposed to sell some tinware, thinking he had worked
his audience up to the right state of mind.

Patty did not know why she should feel vexed at
hearing this bit of intelligence from Jenkinsville. What
was Morton Goodwin to her? She went around the
house as usual this evening, trying to hide all appearance of feeling. She even persuaded her father to
buy half-a-dozen tin cups and some milk-buckets—she
smiled at the peddler for calling them *pails*. She was
not willing to gratify the Captain by showing him how
much she disliked the scoffing "Yankee." But when
she was alone that evening, even the prayer-book had
lost its power to soothe. She was mortified, vexed,
humiliated on every hand. She felt hard and bitter,
above all, toward the sect that had first made a division between Morton and herself, and cordially blamed
the Methodists for all her misfortunes.

It happened that upon the very next Sunday Russell Bigelow was to preach. Far and wide over the West had traveled the fame of this great preacher, who, though born in Vermont, was wholly Western in his impassioned manner. "An orator is to be judged not by his printed discourses, but by the memory of the effect he has produced," says a French writer; and if we may judge of Russell Bigelow by the fame that fills Ohio and Indiana even to this day, he was surely an orator of the highest order. He is known as the "indescribable." The news that he was to preach had set the Hissawachee Settlement afire with eager curiosity to hear him. Even Patty declared her intention of going, much to the Captain's regret. The meeting was not to be held at Wheeler's, but in the woods, and she could go for this time without entering the house of her father's foe. She had no other motive than a vague hope of hearing something that would divert her; life had grown so heavy that she craved excitement of any kind. She would take a back seat and hear the famous Methodist for herself. But Patty put on all of her gold and costly apparel. She was determined that nobody should suspect her of any intention of "joining the church." Her mood was one of curiosity on the surface, and of proud hatred and quiet defiance below.

No religious meeting is ever so delightful as a meeting held in the forest; no forest is so satisfying as a forest of beech; the wide-spreading boughs— drooping when they start from the trunk, but well sustained at the last — stretch out regularly and with a steady horizontalness, the last year's leaves form a carpet like a cushion, while the dense foliage shuts out the sun. To this meeting in the beech woods Patty chose to walk, since it was less than a mile away.* As she passed through a little cove, she saw a man lying flat on his face in prayer. It was the preacher. Awe-stricken, Patty hurried on to the meeting. She had fully intended to take a seat in the rear of the congregation, but being a little confused and absent-minded she did not observe at first where the stand had been erected, and that she was entering the congregation at the side nearest to the pulpit. When she discovered her mistake it was too late to withdraw, the aisle beyond her was already full of standing people; there was nothing for her but to take the only vacant seat in sight. This put her in the very midst of the members, and in this position she was quite conspicuous; even strangers from other settlements saw with astonishment a woman elegantly dressed, for that time, sitting in the very midst of the devout sisters—for the men and women sat apart. All around Patty there was not a single "artificial," or piece of jewelry. Indeed, most of the women wore calico sunbonnets. The Hissawachee people who knew her were astounded to see Patty at meeting at all. They remembered her treatment of Morton, and they looked upon Captain Lumsden as Gog and Magog incarnated in one. This sense of the conspicuousness

---

* I give the local tradition of Bigelow's text, sermon, and the accompanying incident.

of her position was painful to Patty, but she presently forgot herself in listening to the singing. There never was such a chorus as a backwoods Methodist congregation, and here among the trees they sang hymn after hymn, now with the tenderest pathos, now with triumphant joy, now with solemn earnestness. They sang "Children of the Heavenly King," and "Come let us anew," and "Blow ye the trumpet, blow," and "Arise my soul, arise," and "How happy every child of grace!" While they were singing this last, the celebrated preacher entered the pulpit, and there ran through the audience a movement of wonder, almost of disappointment. His clothes were of that sort of cheap cotton cloth known as "blue drilling," and did not fit him. He was rather short, and inexpressibly awkward. His hair hung unkempt over the best portion of his face—the broad projecting forehead. His eyebrows were overhanging; his nose, cheek-bones and chin large. His mouth was wide and with a sorrowful depression at the corners, his nostrils thin, his eyes keen, and his face perfectly mobile. He took for his text the words of Eleazar to Laban,— "Seeking a bride for his master," and, according to the custom of the time, he first expounded the incident, and then proceeded to "spiritualize" it, by applying it to the soul's marriage to Christ. Notwithstanding the ungainliness of his frame and the awkwardness of his postures, there was a gentlemanliness about his address that indicated a man not unaccustomed to good society. His words were well-chosen; his pronunciation always correct; his speech grammatical. In all of these regards Patty was disappointed.

But the sermon. Who shall describe " the indescribable "? As the servant, he proceeded to set forth the character of the Master. What struck Patty was not the nobleness of his speech, nor the force of his argument; she seemed to see in the countenance that every divine trait which he described had reflected itself in the life of the preacher himself. For none but the manliest of men can ever speak worthily of Jesus Christ. As Bigelow proceeded he won her famished heart to Christ. For such a Master she could live or die; in such a life there was what Patty needed most—a purpose; in such a life there was a friend; in such a life she would escape that sense of the ignobleness of her own pursuits, and the unworthiness of her own pride. All that he said of Christ's love and condescension filled her with a sense of sinfulness and meanness, and she wept bitterly. There were a hundred others as much affected, but the eyes of all her neighbors were upon her. If Patty should be converted, what a victory!

And as the preacher proceeded to describe the joy of a soul wedded forever to Chirst—living nobly after the pattern of His life—Patty resolved that she would devote herself to this life and this Saviour, and rejoiced in sympathy with the rising note of triumph in the sermon. Then Bigelow, last of all, appealed to courage and to pride—to pride in its best sense. Who would be ashamed of such a Bridegroom? And as he depicted the trials that some must pass through in accepting Him, Patty saw her own situation, and mentally made the sacrifice. As he described the glory of renouncing the world, she thought of her jewelry and the spirit of defiance in which she had put it on. There, in the midst of that congregation, she took out her earrings, and stripped the flowers from the bonnet. We may smile at the unnecessary sacrifice to an overstrained literalism, but to Patty it was the solemn renunciation of the world—the whole-hearted espousal of herself, for all eternity, to Him who stands for all that is noblest in life. Of course this action was visible to most of the congregation—most of all to the preacher himself. To the Methodists it was the greatest of triumphs, this public conversion of Captain Lumsden's daughter, and they showed their joy in many pious ejaculations. Patty did not seek concealment. She scorned to creep into the kingdom of heaven. It seemed to her that she owed this publicity. For a moment all eyes were turned away from the orator. He paused in his discourse until Patty had removed the emblems of her pride and antagonism. Then, turning with tearful eyes to the audience, the preacher, with simple-hearted sincerity and inconceivable effect, burst out with, "Hallelujah! I have found a bride for my Master!"

CHAPTER XXIV

DRAWING THE LATCH-STRING IN.

U P to this point Captain Lumsden had been a spectator—having decided to risk a new attack of the
jerks that he might stand guard over Patty. But Patty
was so far forward that he could not see her, except
now and then as he stretched his small frame to peep
over the shoulders of some taller man standing in
front. It was only when Bigelow uttered these exulting
words that he gathered from the whispers about him
that Patty was the center of excitement. He instantly
began to swear and to push through the crowd, declar-
ing that he would take Patty home and teach her to
behave herself. The excitement which he produced
presently attracted the attention of the preacher and of
the audience. But Patty was too much occupied with
the solemn emotions that engaged her heart, to give
any attention to it.

"She is my daughter, and she's *got* to learn to
obey," said Lumsden in his quick, rasping voice, push-
ing energetically toward the heart of the dense assemblage with the purpose of carrying Patty off by force.
Patty heard this last threat, and turned round just at
the moment when her father had forced his way through
the fringe of standing people that bordered the densely

packed congregation, and was essaying, in his headlong anger, to reach her and drag her forth.

The Methodists of that day generally took pains to put themselves under the protection of the law in order to avoid disturbance from the chronic rowdyism of a portion of the people. There was a magistrate and a constable on the ground, and Lumsden, in pene- trating the cordon of standing men, had come directly upon the country justice, who, though not a Methodist, had been greatly moved by Bigelow's oratory, and who, furthermore, was prone, as country justices sometimes are, to exaggerate the dignity of his office. At any rate, he was not a little proud of the fact that this great orator and this assemblage of people had in some sense put themselves under the protection of the Majesty of the Law as represented in his own im- portant self. And for Captain Lumsden to come swearing and fuming right against his sacred person was not only a breach of the law, it was—what the justice considered much worse—a contempt of court. Hence ensued a dialogue :

The Court—Captain Lumsden, I am a magistrate. In interrupting the worship of Almighty God by this peaceful assemblage you are violating the law. I do not want to arrest a citizen of your standing; but if you do not cease your disturbance I shall be obliged to vindicate the majesty of the law by ordering the constable to arrest you for a breach of the peace, as against this assembly. (J. P. here draws himself up to his full stature, in the endeavor to represent the dignity of the law.)

Outraged Father—Squire, I'll have you know that Patty Lumsden's my daughter, and I have a right to control her; and you'd better mind your own business.

Justice of the Peace (lowering his voice to a solemn and very judicial bass)—Is she under eighteen years of age?

By-stander (who does n't like Lumsden) — She's twenty.

Justice—If your daughter is past eighteen, she is of age. If you lay hands on her I'll have to take you up for a salt and battery. If you carry her off I'll take her back on a writ of replevin. Now, Captain, I could arrest you here and fine you for this disturbance; and if you don't leave the meeting at once I'll do it.

Here Captain Lumsden grew angrier than ever, but a stalwart class-leader from another settlement, provoked by the interruption of the eloquent sermon and out of patience with "the law's delay," laid off his coat and spat on his hands preparatory to ejecting Lumsden, neck and heels, on his own account. At the same moment an old sister near at hand began to pray aloud, vehemently: "O Lord, convert him! Strike him down, Lord, right where he stands, like Saul of Tarsus. O Lord, smite the stiff-necked persecutor by almighty power!"

This last was too much for the Captain. He might have risked arrest, he might have faced the herculean class-leader, but he had already felt the jerks and was quite superstitious about them. This prayer agitated him. He was not ambitious to emulate Paul,

and he began to believe that if he stood still a min
ute longer he would surely be smitten to the ground
at the request of the sister with a relish for dramatic
conversions. Casting one terrified glance at the old
sister, whose confident eyes were turned toward heaven,
Lumsden broke through the surrounding crowd and
started toward home at a most undignified pace.

Patty's devout feelings were sadly interrupted during the remainder of the sermon by forebodings.
But she had a will as inflexible as her father's, and
now that her will was backed by convictions of duty
it was more firmly set than ever. Bigelow announced
that he would " open the door of the church," and
the excited congregation made the forest ring with
that hymn of Watts' which has always been the re-
cruiting song of Methodism. The application to Patty's
case produced great emotion when the singing reached
the stanzas:

> " Must I be carried to the skies
>   On flowery beds of ease,
> While others fought to win the prize
>   And sailed through bloody seas?
>
> " Are there no foes for me to face?
>   Must I not stem the flood?
> Is this vile world a friend to grace
>   To help me on to God?"

At this point Patty slowly rose from the place
where she had been sitting weeping, and marched
resolutely through the excited crowd until she reached
the preacher, to whom she extended her hand in
token of her desire to become a church-member

While she came forward, the congregation sang with great fervor, and not a little sensation:

> "Since I must fight if I would reign,
> Increase my courage, Lord;
> I'll bear the toil, endure the pain,
> Supported by thy word."

After many had followed Patty's example the meeting closed. Every Methodist shook hands with the new converts, particularly with Patty, uttering words of sympathy and encouragement. Some offered to go home with her to keep her in countenance in the inevitable conflict with her father, but, with a true delicacy and filial dutifulness, Patty insisted on going alone. There are battles which are fought better without allies.

That ten minutes' walk was a time of agony and suspense. As she came up to the house she saw her father sitting on the door-step, riding-whip in hand. Though she knew his nervous habit of carrying his raw-hide whip long after he had dismounted—a habit having its root in a domineering disposition—she was not without apprehension that he would use personal violence. But he was quiet now, from extreme anger.

"Patty," he said, "either you will promise me on the spot to give up this infernal Methodism, or you can't come in here to bring your praying and groaning into my ears. Are you going to give it up?"

"Don't turn me off, father," pleaded Patty. "You need me. I can stand it, but what will you do when your rheumatism comes on next winter? Do let me stay and take care of you. I won't bother you about my religion."

" I won't have this blubbering, shouting nonsense in my house," screamed the father, frantically. He would have said more, but he choked. "You've disgraced, the family," he gasped, after a minute.

Patty stood still, and said no more.

"Will you give up your nonsense about being religious ? "

Patty shook her head.

" Then, clear out ! " cried the Captain, and with an oath he went into the house and pulled the latch-string in. The latch-string was the symbol of hospitality. To say that "the latch-string was out" was to open your door to a friend ; to pull it in was the most significant and inhospitable act Lumsden could perform. For when the latch-string is in, the door is locked. The daughter was not only to be a daughter no longer, she was now an enemy at whose approach the latch-string was withdrawn.

Patty was full of natural affection. She turned away to seek a home. Where ? She walked aimlessly down the road at first. She had but one thought as she receded from the old house that had been her home from infancy——

The latch-string was drawn in.

CHAPTER XXV.

ANN ELIZA.

HOW shall I make you understand this book, reader of mine, who never knew the influences that surrounded a Methodist of the old sort. Up to this point I have walked by faith; I could not see how the present generation could be made to comprehend the earnestness of their grandfathers. But I have hoped that, none the less, they might dimly perceive the possibility of a religious fervor that was as a fire in the bones.

But now?

You have never been a young Methodist preacher of the olden time. You never had over you a presiding elder who held your fate in his hands; who, more than that, was the man appointed by the church to be your godly counsellor. In the olden time especially, presiding elders were generally leaders of men, the best and greatest men that the early Methodist ministry afforded; greatest in the qualities most prized in ecclesiastical organization — practical shrewdness, executive force, and a piety of unction and lustre. How shall I make you understand the weight which the words of such a man had when he thought it needful to counsel or admonish a young preacher?

Our old friend Magruder, having shown his value as an organizer, had been made an "elder," and just now he thought it his duty to have a solemn conversation with the "preacher-in-charge" of Jenkinsville circuit, upon matters of great delicacy. Magruder was not a man of nice perceptions, and he was dimly conscious of his own unfitness for the task before him. It was on the Saturday of a quarterly meeting. He had said to the "preacher-in-charge" that he would like to have a word with him, and they were walking side by side through the woods. Neither of them looked at the other. The "elder" was trying in vain to think of a point at which to begin; the young preacher was wondering what the elder would say.

"Let us sit down here on this lind log, brother," said Magruder, desperately.

When they had sat down there was a pause.

"Have you ever thought of marrying, brother Goodwin?" he broke out abruptly at last.

"I have, brother Magruder," said Morton, curtly, not disposed to help the presiding elder out of his difficulty. Then he added: "But not thinking it a profitable subject for meditation, I have turned my thoughts to other things."

"Ahem! But have you not taken some steps toward matrimony without consulting with your brethren, as the discipline prescribes?"

"No, sir."

"But, Brother Goodwin, I understand that you have done a great wrong to a defenceless girl, who is a stranger in a strange land."

"Do you mean Sister Ann Eliza Meacham?" asked Morton, startled by the solemnity with which the presiding elder spoke.

"I am glad to see that you feel enough in the matter to guess who the person is. You have encouraged her to think that you meant to marry her. If I am correctly informed, you even advised  Holston, who was her lover, not to annoy her any more, and you assumed to defend her rights in the lawsuit about a piece of land. Whether you meant to marry her or not, you have at least compromised her. And in such circumstances there is but one course open to a Christian or a gentleman." The

ANN ELIZA. elder spoke severely.

"Brother Magruder, I will tell you the plain truth," said Morton, rising and speaking with vehemence. "I have been very much struck with the eloquence of Sister Ann Eliza when she leads in prayer or speaks in love-feast. I did not mean to marry anybody. I have always defended the poor and the helpless. She told me her history one day, and I felt sorry for her. I determined to befriend her." Here Morton paused in some embarrassment, not knowing just how to proceed.

"Befriend a woman! That is the most imprudent thing in the world for a minister to do, my dear brother. You cannot befriend a woman without doing harm."

"Well, she wanted help, and I could not refuse to give it to her. She told me that she had refused Bob Holston five times, and that he kept troubling her. I met Bob alone one day, and I remonstrated with him pretty earnestly, and he went all round the country and said that I told him I was engaged to Ann Eliza, and would whip him if he didn't let her alone. What I did tell him was, that I was Ann Eliza's friend, because she had no other, and that I thought, as a gentleman, he ought to take five refusals as sufficient, and not wait till he was knocked down by refusals."

"Why, my brother," said the elder, "when you take up a woman's cause that way, you have got to marry her or ruin her and yourself, too. If you were not a minister you might have a female friend or two; and you might help a woman in distress. But you are a sheep in the midst of—of—wolves. Half the girls on this circuit would like to marry you, and if you were to help one of them over the fence, or hold her bridle-rein for her while she gets on the horse, or talk five minutes with her about the turnip crop, she would consider herself next thing to engaged. Now, as to Sister Ann Eliza, you have given occasion to gossip over the whole circuit."

"Who told you so?" asked Morton, with rising indignation.

" Why, everybody. I hadn't more than touched the circuit at Boggs' Corners till I heard that you were to be married at this very Quarterly Meeting. And I felt a little grieved that you should go so far without any consultation with me. I stopped at Sister Sims's—she's Ann Eliza's aunt I believe—and told her that I supposed you and Sister Ann Eliza were going to require my aid pretty soon, and she burst into tears. She said that if there had been anything between you and Ann Eliza, it must be broken off, for you hadn't stopped there at all on your last round. Now tell me the plain truth, brother. Did you not at one time entertain a thought of marrying Sister Ann Eliza Meacham?"

" I have thought about it. She is good-looking and I could not be with her without liking her. Then, too, everybody said that she was cut out for a preacher's wife. But I never paid her any attention that could be called courtship. I stopped going there because somebody had bantered me about her. I was afraid of talk. I will not deny that I was a little taken with her, at first, but when I thought of marrying her I found that I did not love her as one ought to love a wife—as much as I had once loved somebody else. And then, too, you know that nine out of every ten who marry have to locate sooner or later, and I don't want to give up the ministry. I think it's hard if a man cannot help a girl in distress without being forced to marry her."

" Well, Brother Goodwin, we'll not discuss the matter further," said the elder, who was more than ever convinced by Morton's admissions that he had acted reprehensibly. " I have confidence in you. You have done a great wrong, whether you meant it or not. There is only one way of making the thing right. It's a bad thing for a preacher to have a broken heart laid at his door. Now I tell you that I don't know anybody who would make a better preacher's wife than Sister Meacham. If the case stands as it does now I may have to object to the passage of your character at the next conference."

This last was an awful threat. In that time when the preachers lived far apart, the word of a presiding elder was almost enough to ruin a man. But instead of terrifying Morton, the threat made him sullenly stubborn. If the elder and the conference could be so unjust he would bear the consequences, but would never submit.

The congregation was too large to sit in the school-house, and the presiding elder accordingly preached in the grove. All the time of his preaching Morton Goodwin was scanning the audience to see if the zeal-ous Ann Eliza were there. But no Ann Eliza appeared. Nothing but grief could thus keep her away from the meeting. The more Morton meditated upon it, the more guilty did he feel. He had acted from the highest motives. He did not know that Ann Eliza's aunt— the weak-looking Sister Sims—had adroitly intrigued to give his kindness the appearance of courtship. How could he suspect Sister Sims or Ann Eliza of any design ? Old ministers know better than to trust im-plicitly to the goodness and truthfulness of all pious people. There are people, pious in their way, in whose natures intrigue and fraud are so indigenous that they grow all unsuspected by themselves. Intrigue is one of the Diabolonians of whom Bunyan speaks—a small but very wicked devil that creeps into the city of Mansoul under an alias.

A susceptible nature like Morton's takes color from other people. He was conscious that Magruder's confidence in him was weakened, and it seemed to him that all the brethren and sisters looked at him askance. When he came to make the concluding prayer he had a sense of hollowness in his devotions, and he really began to suspect that he might be a hypocrite.

In the afternoon the Quarterly Conference met, and in the presence of class-leaders, stewards, local preachers and exhorters from different parts of the circuit, the once popular preacher felt that he had somehow lost caste. He received fifteen dollars of the twenty which the circuit owed him, according to the discipline, for three months of labor; and small as was the amount, the scrupulous and now morbid Morton doubted whether he were fairly entitled to it. Sometimes he thought seriously of satisfying his doubting conscience by marrying Ann Eliza with or without love. But his whole proud, courageous nature rebelled against submitting to marry under compulsion of Magruder's threat.

At the evening service Goodwin had to preach, and he got on but poorly. He looked in vain for Miss Ann Eliza Meacham. She was not there to go through the audience and with winning voice persuade those who were smitten with conviction to come to the mourner's

bench for prayer. She was not there to pray audibly
until every heart should be shaken. Morton was not
the only person who missed her. So famous a "working Christian " could not but be a general favorite;
and the people were not slow to divine the cause
of her absence. Brother Goodwin found the faces
of his brethren averted, and the grasp of their
hands less cordial. But this only made him sulky and
stubborn. He had never meant to excite Sister Meacham's expectations, and he would not be driven to
marry her.

The early Sunday morning of that Quarterly Meeting saw all the roads crowded with people. Everybody was on horseback, and almost every horse carried
"double." At half-past eight o'clock the love-feast
began in the large school-house. No one was admitted
who did not hold a ticket, and even of those who had
tickets some were turned away on account of their
naughty curls, their sinful " artificials," or their wicked
ear-rings. At the moment when the love-feast began
the door was locked, and no tardy member gained
admission. Plates, with bread cut into half-inch cubes,
were passed round, and after these glasses of water,
from which each sipped in turn—this meagre provision
standing ideally for a feast. Then the speaking was
opened by some of the older brethren, who were particularly careful as to dates, announcing, for instance,
that it would be just thirty-seven years ago the twenty-
first day of next November since the Lord " spoke
peace to my never-dying soul while I was kneeling at
the mourner's bench in Logan's school-house on the

banks of the South Fork of the Roanoke River in Old Virginny." This statement the brethren had heard for many years, with a proper variation in date as the time advanced, but now, as in duty bound, they greeted it again with pious ejaculations of thanksgiving. There was a sameness in the perorations of these little speeches. Most of the old men wound up by asking an interest in the prayers of the brethren, that their "last days might be their best days," and that their "path might grow brighter and brighter unto the perfect day." Soon the elder sisters began to speak of their trials and victories, of their "ups and downs," their "many crooked paths," and the religion that "happifies the soul." With their pathetic voices the fire spread, until the whole meeting was at a white-heat, and cries of "Hallelujah!" "Amen!" "Bless the Lord!" "Glory to God!" and so on expressed the fervor of feeling. Of course, you, sitting out of the atmosphere of it and judging coldly, laugh at this indecorous fervor. Perhaps it is just as well to laugh, but for my part I cannot. I know too well how deep and vital were the emotions out of which came these utterances of simple and earnest hearts. I find it hard to get over an early prejudice that piety is of more consequence than propriety.

Morton was looking in vain for Ann Eliza. If she were present he could hardly tell it. Make the bonnets of women cover their faces and make them all alike, and set them in meeting with faces resting forward upon their hands, and then dress them in a uniform of homespun cotton, and there is not much

individuality left. If Ann Eliza Meacham were present she would, according to custom, speak early; and
all that this love-feast lacked was one of her rapt and
eloquent utterances. So when the speaking and singing
had gone on for an hour, and the voice of Sister
Meacham was not heard, Morton sadly concluded that
she must have remained at home, heart-broken on
account of disappointment at his neglect. In this he
was wrong. Just at that moment a sister rose in the
further corner of the room and began to speak in a
low and plaintive voice. It was Ann Eliza. But how
changed!

She proceeded to say that she had passed through
many fiery trials in her life. Of late she had been led
through deep waters of temptation, and the floods of
affliction had gone over her soul. (Here some of the
brethren sighed, and some of the sisters looked at
Brother Goodwin.) The devil had tempted her to stay
at home. He had tempted her to sit silent this morning, telling her that her voice would only discourage
others. But at last she had got the victory and
received strength to bear her cross. With this, her
voice rose and she spoke in tones of plaintive triumph
to the end. Morton was greatly affected, not because her
affliction was universally laid at his door, but because
he now began to feel, as he had not felt before, that
he had indeed wrought her a great injury. As she
stood there, sorrowful and eloquent, he almost loved
her. He pitied her; and Pity lives on the next floor
below Love.

As for Ann Eliza, I would not have the reader

think too meanly of her. She had resolved to "catch" Rev. Morton Goodwin from the moment she saw him. But one of the oldest and most incontestable of the rights which the highest civilization accords to woman is that of "bringing down" the chosen man if she can. Ann Eliza was not consciously hypocritical. Her deep religious feeling was genuine. She had a native genius for devotion—and a genius for devotion is as much a natural gift as a genius for poetry. Notwithstanding her eloquence and her rare talent for devotion, her gifts in the direction of honesty and truthfulness were few and feeble. A phrenologist would have described such a character as possessing "Spirituality and Veneration very large; Conscientiousness small." You have seen such people, and the world is ever prone to rank them at first as saints, afterwards as hypocrites; for the world classifies people in gross—it has no nice distinctions. Ann Eliza, like most people of the oratorical temperament, was not over-scrupulous in her way of producing effects. She could sway her own mind as easily as she could that of others. In the case of Morton, she managed to believe herself the victim of misplaced confidence. She saw nothing reprehensible either in her own or her aunt's manœuvering. She only knew that she had been bitterly disappointed, and characteristically blamed him through whom the disappointment had come.

Morton was accustomed to judge by the standards of his time. Such genuine fervor was, in his estimation, evidence of a high state of piety. One "who lived so near the throne of grace," in Methodist phrase, must be honest and pure and good. So Morton reasoned. He had wounded such an one. He owed reparation. In marrying Ann Eliza he would be acting generously, honestly and wisely, according to the opinion of the presiding elder, the highest authority he knew. For in Ann Eliza Meacham he would get the most saintly of wives, the most zealous of Christians, the most useful of women. So when Mr. Magruder exhorted the brethren at the close of the service to put away every sin out of their hearts before they ventured to take the communion, Morton, with many tears, resolved to atone for all the harm he had unwittingly done to Sister Ann Eliza Meacham, and to marry her—if the Lord should open the way.

But neither could he remain firm in this conclusion. His high spirit resented the threat of the presiding elder. He would not be driven into marriage. In this uncomfortable frame of mind he passed the night. But Magruder being a shrewd man, guessed the state of Morton's feelings, and perceived his own mistake. As he mounted his horse on Monday morning, Morton stood with averted eyes, ready to bid an official farewell to his presiding elder, but not ready to give his usual cordial adieu to Brother Magruder.

"Goodwin," said Magruder, looking at Morton with sincere pity, "forgive me; I ought not to have spoken as I did. I know you will do right, and I had no right to threaten you. Be a man; that is all. Live above reproach and act like a Christian. I am sorry you have involved yourself. It is better not to marry, maybe, though I have always maintained that a married man *can* live in the ministry if he is careful and has a good wife. Besides, Sister Meacham has some land."

So saying, he shook hands and rode away a little distance. Then he turned back and said:

"You heard that Brother Jones was dead?"

"Yes."

"Well, I'm going to send word to Brother Lumsden to take his place on Peterborough circuit till Conference. I suppose some young exhorter can be found to take Lumsden's place as second man on Pottawottomie Creek, and Peterborough is too important a place to be left vacant."

"I'm afraid Kike won't stand it," said Morton, coldly.

"Oh! I hope he will. Peterborough isn't much more unhealthy than Pottawottomie Creek. A little more intermittent fever, maybe. But it is the best I can do. The work is everything. The men are the Lord's. Lumsden is a good man, and I should hate to lose him, though. He'll stop and see you as he comes through, I suppose. I think I'd better give you the plan of his circuit, which I got the other day." After adieux, a little more friendly than the first, the two preachers parted again.

Morton mounted Dolly. The day was far advanced, and he had an appointment to preach that very evening at the Salt Fork school-house. He had never yet failed to suffer from a disturbance of some sort when

he had preached in this rude neighborhood; and
having spoken very boldly in his last round, he was
sure of a perilous encounter. But now the prospect of
fighting with the wild beasts of Salt Fork was almost
enchanting. It would divert him from graver apprehensions.

CHAPTER XXVI.

ENGAGEMENT.

YOU do not like Morton in his vacillating state of
mind as he rides toward Salt Fork, weighing
considerations of right and wrong, of duty and disin-
clination, in the balance. He is not an epic hero, for
epic heroes act straightforwardly, they either know by
intuition just what is right, or they are like Milton's
Satan, unencumbered with a sense of duty. But Morton was neither infallible nor a devil. A man of sensitive conscience cannot, even by accident, break a
woman's heart without compunction.

When Goodwin approached Salt Fork he was met
by Burchard, now sheriff of the county, and warned
that he would be attacked. Burchard begged him to
turn back. Morton might have scoffed at the cowardice and time-serving of the sheriff, if he had not been
under such obligations to him, and had not been
touched by this new evidence of his friendship. But
Goodwin had never turned back from peril in his life.

"I have a right to preach at Salt Fork, Burchard,"
he said, "and I will do it or die."

Even in the struggle at Salt Fork Morton could
not get rid of his love affair. He was touched to find
lying on the desk in the school-house a little unsigned

billet in Ann Eliza's handwriting, uttering a warning similar to that just given by Burchard.

It was with some tremor that he looked round, in the dim light of two candles, upon the turbulent faces between him and the door. His prayer and singing were a little faint. But when once he began to preach, his combative courage returned, and his ringing voice rose above all the shuffling sounds of disorder. The interruptions, however, soon became so distinct that he dared not any longer ignore them. Then he paused in his discourse and looked at the rioters steadily.

"You think you will scare me. It is my business to rebuke sin. I tell you that you are a set of ungodly ruffians and law breakers. I tell your neighbors here that they are miserable cowards. They let lawless men trample on them. I say, shame on them! They ought to organize and arrest you if it cost their lives."

Here a click was heard as of some one cocking a horse-pistol. Morton turned pale; but something in his warm, Irish blood impelled him to proceed. "I called you ruffians awhile ago," he said, huskily. "Now I tell you that you are cut-throats. If you kill me here to-night, I will show your neighbors that it is better to die like a man than to live like a coward. The law will yet be put in force whether you kill me or not. There are some of you that would belong to Micajah Harp's gang of robbers if you dared. But you are afraid; and so you only give information and help to those who are no worse, only a little braver than you are."

Goodwin had let his impetuous temper carry him too far. He now saw that his denunciation had degenerated into a taunt, and this taunt had provoked his enemies beyond measure. He had been foolhardy; for what good could it do for him to throw away his life

in a row? There was murder in the eyes of the ruffians. Half-a-dozen pistols were cocked in quick succession and he caught the glitter of

FACING A MOB.

knives. A hasty consultation was taking place in the back part of the room, and the few Methodists near him huddled together like sheep. If he intended to save his

life there was no time to spare. The address and presence of mind for which he had been noted in boyhood
did not fail him now. It would not do to seem to quail
Without lowering his fiercely indignant tone, he raised
his right hand and demanded that honest citizens
should rally to his support and put down the riot.
His descending hand knocked one of the two candles
from the pulpit in the most accidental way in the
world. Starting back suddenly, he managed to upset
and extinguish the other just at the instant when the
infuriated roughs were making a combined rush upon
him. The room was thus made totally dark. Morton
plunged into the on-coming crowd. Twice he was
seized and interrogated, but he changed his voice and
avoided detection. When at last the crowd gave up
the search and began to leave the house, he drifted
with them into the outer darkness and rain. Once
upon Dolly he was safe from any pursuit.

When the swift-footed mare had put him beyond
danger, Morton was in better spirits than at any time
since the elder's solemn talk on the preceding Saturday.
He had the exhilaration of a sense of danger and of
a sense of triumph. So bold a speech, and so masterly
an escape as he had made could not but demoralize
men like the Salt Forkers. He laughed a little at
himself for talking about dying and then running away,
but he inly determined to take the earliest opportunity
to urge upon Burchard the duty of a total suppression
of these lawless gangs. He would himself head a party
against them if necessary.

This cheerful mood gradually subsided into depression as his mind reverted to the note in Ann Eliza's writing. How thoughtful in her to send it ! How delicate she was in not signing it ! How forgiving must her temper be ! What a stupid wretch he was to attract her affection, and now what a perverse soul he was to break her devoted heart !

This was the light in which Morton saw the situation. A more suspicious man might have reasoned that Ann Eliza probably knew no more of Goodwin's peril at Salt Fork than was known in all the neighboring country, and that her note was a gratuitous thrusting of herself on his attention. A suspicious person would have reasoned that her delicacy in not signing the note was only a pretense, since Morton had become familiar with her peculiar handwriting in the affair of the lawsuit in which he had assisted her. But Morton was not suspicious. How could he be suspicious of one upon whom the Lord had so manifestly poured out his Spirit ? Besides, the suspicious view would not have been wholly correct, since Ann Eliza did love Morton almost to distraction, and had entertained the liveliest apprehensions of his peril at Salt Fork.

But with however much gratitude he might regard Ann Eliza's action, Morton Goodwin could not quite bring himself to decide on marriage. He could not help thinking of the morning when negro Bob had discovered him talking to Patty by the spring-house, nor could he help contrasting that strong love with the feebleness of the best affection he could muster for the handsome, pious, and effusive Ann Eliza Meacham.

But as he proceeded round the circuit it became more and more evident to Morton that he had suffered in reputation by his cool treatment of Miss Meacham. Elderly people love romance, and they could not forgive him for not bringing the story out in the way they wished. They felt that nothing could be so appropriate as the marriage of a popular preacher with so zealous a woman. It was a shock to their sense of poetic completeness that he should thus destroy the only fitting denouement. So that between people who were disappointed at the come-out, and young men who were jealous of the general popularity of the youthful preacher, Morton's acceptability had visibly declined. Nevertheless there was quite a party of young women who approved of his course. He had found the minx out at last!

One of the results of the Methodist circuit system, with its great quarterly meetings, was the bringing of people scattered over a wide region into a sort of organic unity and a community of feeling. It widened the horizon. It was a curious and, doubtless, also a beneficial thing, that over the whole vast extent of half-civilized territory called Jenkinsville circuit there was now a common topic for gossip and discussion. When Morton reached the very northernmost of his forty-nine preaching places, he had not yet escaped from the excitement.

" Brother Goodwin," said Sister Sharp, as they sat at breakfast, " whatever folks may say, I am sure you had a perfect right to give up Sister Meacham. A man ain't bound to marry a girl when he finds her out. *I* don't think it would take a smart man like you long to find out that Sister Meacham isn't all she pretends to be. I have heard some things about her standing in Pennsylvania. I guess you found them out."

"I never meant to marry Sister Meacham," said Morton, as soon as he could recover from the shock, and interrupt the stream of Sister Sharp's talk.

"Everybody thought you did."

"Everybody was wrong, then; and as for finding out anything, I can tell you that Sister Meacham is, I believe, one of the best and most useful Christians in the world."

"That's what everybody thought," replied the other, maliciously, "until you quit off going with her so suddenly. People have thought different since."

This shot took effect. Morton could bear that people should slander him. But, behold! a crop of slanders on Ann Eliza herself was likely to grow out of his mistake. In the midst of a most unheroic and, as it seemed to him, contemptible vacillation and perplexity, he came at last to Mount Zion meeting-house. It was here that Ann Eliza belonged, and here he must decide whether he would still leave her to suffer reproach while he also endured the loss of his own good name, or make a marriage which, to those wiser than he, seemed in every way advisable. Ann Eliza was not at meeting on this day. When once the benediction was pronounced, Goodwin resolved to free himself from remorse and obloquy by the only honorable course. He would ride over to

Sister Sims's, and end the matter by engaging himself to Ann Eliza.

Was it some latent, half - perception of Sister Meacham's true character that made him hesitate? Or was it that a pure-hearted man always shrinks from marriage without love? He reined his horse at the road-fork, and at last took the other path and claimed the hospitality of the old class-leader of Mount Zion class, instead of receiving Sister Sims's welcome. He intended by this means to postpone his decision till afternoon.

Out of the frying-pan into the fire! The leader took Brother Goodwin aside and informed him that Sister Ann Eliza was very ill. She might never recover. It was understood that she was slowly dying of a broken heart.

Morton could bear no more. To have made so faithful a person, who had even interfered to save his life, suffer in her spirit was bad enough; to have brought reproach upon her, worse; to kill her outright was ingratitude and murder. He wondered at his own stupidity and wickedness. He rode in haste to Sister Sims's. Ann Eliza, in fact, was not dangerously ill, and was ill more of a malarious fever than of a broken heart; though her chagrin and disappointment had much to do with it. Morton, convinced that he was the author of her woes, felt more tenderness to her in her emaciation than he had ever felt toward her in her beauty. He could not profess a great deal of love, so he contented himself with expressing his gratitude for the Salt Fork warning. Explanations about the past were awkward, but fortunately Ann Eliza was ill and ought not to talk much on exciting subjects. Besides, she did not seem to be very exacting. Morton's offer of marriage was accepted with a readiness that annoyed him. When he rode away to his next appointment, he did not feel so much relieved by having done his duty as he had expected to. He could not get rid of a thought that the high-spirited Patty would have resented an offer of marriage under these circumstances, and on such terms as Ann Eliza had accepted. And yet, one must not expect all qualities in one person. What could be finer than Ann Eliza's lustrous piety? She was another Hester Ann Rogers, a second Mrs. Fletcher, maybe. And how much she must love him to pine away thus! And how forgiving she was!

CHAPTER XXVII.

THE CAMP MEETING.

THE incessant activity of a traveling preacher's life did not allow Morton much opportunity for the society of the convalescent Ann Eliza. Fortunately. For when he was with her out of meeting he found her rather dull. To all expression of religious sentiment and emotion she responded sincerely and with unction; to Morton's highest aspirations for a life of real self-sacrifice she only answered with a look of perplexity. She could not understand him. He was " so queer," she said.

But people whose lives are joined ought to make the best of each other. Ann Eliza loved Morton, and because she loved him she could endure what seemed to her an unaccountable eccentricity. If Goodwin found himself tempted to think her lacking in some of the highest qualities, he comforted himself with reflecting that all women were probably deficient in these regards. For men generalize about women, not from many but from one. And men, being egotists, suffer a woman's love for themselves to hide a multitude of sins. And then Morton took refuge in other people's opinions. Everybody thought that Sister Meacham was just the wife for him. It is pleasant to have the opinion of all the world on your side where your own heart is doubtful.

Sometimes, alas! the ghost of an old love flitted through the mind of Morton Goodwin and gave him a moment of fright. But Patty was one of the things of this world which he had solemnly given up. Of her conversion he had not heard. Mails were few and postage cost a silver quarter on every letter; with poor people, correspondence was an extravagance not to be thought of except on the occasion of a death or wedding. At farthest, one letter a year was all that might be afforded. As it was, Morton was neither very happy nor very miserable as he rode up to the New Canaan camp-ground on a pleasant midsummer afternoon with Ann Eliza by his side.

Sister Meacham did not lack hospitable entertainment. So earnest and gifted a Christian as she was always welcome; and now that she held a mortgage on the popular preacher every tent on the ground would have been honored by her presence. Morton found a lodging in the preacher's tent, where one bed, larger, transversely, than that of the giant Og, was provided for the collective repose of the preachers, of whom there were half-a-dozen present. It was always a solemn mystery to me, by what ingenious over-lapping of sheets, blankets and blue-coverlets the sisters who made this bed gave a cross-wise continuity to the bed-clothing.

This meeting was held just six weeks after the quarterly meeting spoken of in the last chapter. Goodwin's circuit lay on the west bank of the Big Wiaki

River, and this camp-meeting was held on the east bank of that stream.

It was customary for all the neighboring preachers to leave their circuits and lend their help in a camp-meeting. All detached parties were drawn in to make ready for a pitched battle. Morton had, in his ringing voice, earnest delivery, unfaltering courage and quick wit, rare qualifications for the rude campaign, and, as the nearest preacher, he was, of course, expected to help.

The presiding elder's order to Kike to repair to Jonesville circuit had gone after the zealous itinerant like " an arrow after a wild goose," and he had only received it in season to close his affairs on Pottawottomie Creek circuit and reach this camp-meeting on his way to his new work. His emaciated face smote Morton's heart with terror. The old comrade thought that the death which Kike all but longed for could not be very far away. And even now the zealous and austere young man was so eager to reach his circuit of Peterborough that he would only consent to tarry long enough to preach on the first evening. His voice was weak, and his appeals were often drowned in the uproar of a mob that had come determined to make an end of the meeting.

So violent was the opposition of the rowdies from Jenkinsville and Salt Fork that the brethren were demoralized. After the close of the service they gathered in groups debating whether or not they should give up the meeting. But two invincible men stood in the pulpit looking out over the scene. Without a

thought of surrendering, Magruder and Morton Goodwin were consulting in regard to police arrangements,

"Brother Goodwin," said Magruder, "we shall have
the sheriff here in the morning. I am afraid he hasn't
got back-bone enough to handle these fellows. Do
you know him?"

"Burchard? Yes; I've known him two or three
years."

Morton could not help liking the man who had so
generously forgiven his gambling debt, but he had
reason to believe that a sheriff who went to Brewer's
Hole to get votes would find his hands tied by his
political alliances.

"Goodwin," said Magruder, "I don't know how to
spare you from preaching and exhorting, but you must
take charge of the police and keep order."

"You had better not trust me," said Goodwin.

"Why?"

"If I am in command there'll be a fight. I don't
believe in letting rowdies run over you. If you put
me in authority, and give me the law to back me,
somebody 'll be hurt before morning. The rowdies
hate me and I am not fond of them. I've wanted
such a chance at these Jenkinsville and Salt Fork fellows ever since I've been on the circuit."

"I wish you *would* clean them out," said the sturdy
old elder, the martial fire shining from under his
shaggy brows.

Morton soon had the brethren organized into a
police. Every man was to carry a heavy club; some
were armed with pistols to be used in an emergency.

Part of the force was mounted, part marched afoot. Goodwin said that his father had fought King George, and he would not be ruled by a mob. By such fannings of the embers of revolutionary patriotism he managed to infuse into them some of his own courage.

At midnight Morton Goodwin sat in the pulpit and sent out scouts. Platforms of poles, six feet high and covered with earth, stood on each side of the stand or pulpit. On these were bright fires which threw their light over the whole space within the circle of tents. Outside the circle were a multitude of wagons covered with cotton cloth, in which slept people from a distance who had no other shelter. In this outer darkness Morton, as military dictator, had ordered other platforms erected, and on these fires were now kindling.

The returning scouts reported at midnight that the ruffians, seeing the completeness of the preparations, had left the camp-ground. Goodwin was the only man who was indisposed to trust this treacherous truce. He immediately posted his mounted scouts farther away than before on every road leading to the ground, with instructions to let him know instantly, if any body of men should be seen approaching.

From Morton's previous knowledge of the people, he was convinced that in the mob were some men more than suspected of belonging to Micajah Harp's gang of thieves. Others were allies of the gang—of that class which hesitates between a lawless disposition and a wholesome fear of the law, but whose protection and assistance is the right foot upon which every form of brigandage stands. Besides these there were the reckless young men who persecuted a camp-meeting from a love of mischief for its own sake; men who were not yet thieves, but from whose ranks the bands of thieves were recruited. With these last Morton's history gave him a certain sympathy. As the classes represented by the mob held the balance of power in the politics of the county, Morton knew that he had not much to hope from a trimmer such as Burchard.

About four o'clock in the morning one of the mounted sentinels who had been posted far down the road came riding in at full speed, with intelligence that the rowdies were coming in force from the direction of Jenkinsville. Goodwin had anticipated this, and he immediately awakened his whole reserve, concentrating the scattered squads and setting them in ambush on either side of the wagon track that led to the campground. With a dozen mounted men well armed with clubs, he took his own stand at a narrow place where the foliage on either side was thickest, prepared to dispute the passage to the camp. The men in ambush had orders to fall upon the enemy's flanks as soon as the fight should begin in front. It was a simple piece of strategy learned of the Indians.

The marauders rode on two by two until the leaders, coming round a curve, caught sight of Morton and his right hand man. Then there was a surprised reining up on the one hand, and a sudden dashing charge on the other. At the first blow Goodwin felled his man, and the riderless horse ran backward through the ranks. The mob was taken by surprise, and before the ruffians could rally Morton uttered a cry to his men in the bushes, which brought an attack upon both flanks. The rowdies fought hard, but from the beginning the victory of the guard was assured by the advantage of ambush and surprise. The only question to be settled was that of capture, for Morton had ordered the arrest of every man that the guard could bring in. But so sturdy was the fight that only three were taken. One of the guard received a bad flesh wound from a pistol shot. Goodwin did not give up pursuing the retreating enemy until he saw them dash into the river opposite Jenkinsville. He then rode back, and as it was getting light threw himself upon one side of the great bunk in the preachers' tent, and slept until he was awakened by the horn blown in the pulpit for the eight o'clock preaching.

When Sheriff Burchard arrived on the ground that day he was evidently frightened at the earnestness of Morton's defence. Burchard was one of those politicians who would have endeavored to patch up a compromise with a typhoon. He was in a strait between his fear of the animosity of the mob and his anxiety to please the Methodists. Goodwin, taking advantage of this latter feeling, got himself appointed a deputy-sheriff, and, going before a magistrate, he secured the issuing of writs for the arrest of those whom he knew to be leaders. Then he summoned his guard as a posse, and, having thus put law on his side, he announced that if the ruffians came again the guard must follow him until they were entirely subdued.

Burchard took him aside, and warned him solemnly that such extreme measures would cost his life.
Some of these men belonged to Harp's band, and he
would not be safe anywhere if he made enemies of
the gang. "Don't throw away your life," entreated
Burchard.

"That's what life is for," said Morton. "If a
man's life is too good to throw away in fighting the
devil, it isn't worth having." Goodwin said this in a
way that made Burchard ashamed of his own cowardice. But Kike, who stood by ready to depart, could
not help thinking that if Patty were in place of Ann
Eliza, Morton might think life good for something
else than to be thrown away in a fight with rowdies.

As there was every sign of an approaching riot
during the evening service, and as no man could
manage the tempest so well as Brother Goodwin,
he was appointed to preach. A young theologian of
the present day would have drifted helpless on the
waves of such a mob. When one has a congregation
that listens because it ought to listen, one can afford
to be prosy; but an audience that will only listen
when it is compelled to listen is the best discipline in
the world for an orator. It will teach him methods of
homiletic arrangement which learned writers on Sacred
Rhetoric have never dreamed of.

The disorder had already begun when Morton Goodwin's tall figure appeared in the stand. Frontier-men
are very susceptible to physical effects, and there was
a clarion-like sound to Morton's voice well calculated
to impress them. Goodwin enjoyed battle; every power

M

of his mind and body was at its best in the presence
of a storm. He knew better than to take a text. He
must surprise the mob into curiosity.

"There is a man standing back in the crowd
there," he began, pointing his finger in a certain
direction where there was much disorder, and pausing
until everybody was still, "who reminds me of a funny
story I once heard." At this point the turbulent sons
of Belial, who loved nothing so much as a funny
story, concluded to postpone their riot until they
should have their laugh. Laugh they did, first at one
funny story, and then at another—stories with no
moral in particular, except the moral there is in a
laugh. Brother Mellen, who sat behind Morton, and
who had never more than half forgiven him for not
coming to a bad end as the result of disturbing a
meeting, was greatly shocked at Morton's levity in the
pulpit, but Magruder, the presiding elder, was delighted. He laughed at each story, and laughed loud
enough for Goodwin to hear and appreciate the
senior's approval of his drollery. But somehow—the
crowd did not know how,—at some time in his discourse—the Salt Fork rowdies did not observe when,—
Morton managed to cease his drollery without detection, and to tell stories that brought tears instead of
laughter. The mob was demoralized, and, by keeping
their curiosity perpetually excited, Goodwin did not
give them time to rally at all. Whenever an interruption was attempted, the preacher would turn the
ridicule of the audience upon the interlocutor, and so
gain the sympathy of the rough crowd who were

habituated to laugh on the side of the winner in all
rude tournaments of body or mind. Knowing perfectly well that he would have to fight before the
night was over, Morton's mind was stimulated to its
utmost. If only he could get the religious interest
agoing, he might save some of these men instead of
punishing them. His soul yearned over the people.
His oratory at last swept out triumphant over everything; there was weeping and sobbing; some fell in
uttering cries of anguish; others ran away in terror.
Even Burchard shivered with emotion when Morton
described how, step by step, a young man was led
from bad to worse, and then recited his own experience. At last there was the utmost excitement. As
soon as this hurricane of feeling had reached the
point of confusion, the rioters broke the spell of Morton's speech and began their disturbance. Goodwin
immediately invited the penitents into the enclosed
pen-like place called the altar, and the whole space
was filled with kneeling mourners, whose cries and
groans made the woods resound. But at the same
moment the rioters increased their noisy demonstra-
tions, and Morton, finding Burchard inefficient to quell
them, descended from the pulpit and took command
of his camp-meeting police.

Perhaps the mob would not have secured headway
enough to have necessitated the severest measures if
it had not been for Mr. Mellen. As soon as he
detected the rising storm he felt impelled to try the
effect of his stentorian voice in quelling it. He did
not ask permission of the presiding elder, as he was in

duty bound to do, but as soon as there was a pause in the singing he began to exhort. His style was violently aggressive, and only served to provoke the mob. He began with the true old Homeric epithets of early Methodism, exploding them like bomb-shells. "You are hair-hung and breeze-shaken over hell," he cried.

"You don't say!" responded one of the rioters, to the infinite amusement of the rest.

For five minutes Mellen proceeded to drop this kind of religious aqua fortis upon the turbulent crowd, which grew more and more turbulent under his inflammatory treatment. Finding himself likely to be defeated, he turned toward Goodwin and demanded that the camp-meeting police should enforce order. But Morton was contemplating a masterstroke that should

"HAIR-HUNG AND BREEZE-SHAKEN."

annihilate the disorder in one battle, and he was not to be hurried into too precipitate an attack.

Brother Mellen resumed his exhortation, and, as small doses of nitric-acid had not allayed the irritation, he thought it necessary to administer stronger ones. "You'll go to hell," he cried, "and when you get there your ribs will be nothing but a gridiron to roast your souls in!"

"Hurrah for the gridiron!" cried the unappalled ruffians, and Brother Mellen gave up the fight, reproaching Morton hotly for not suppressing the mob. "I thought you was a man," he said.

"They'll get enough of it before daylight," said Goodwin, savagely. "Do you get a club and ride by my side to-night, Brother Mellen; I am sure you are a man."

Mellen went for his horse and club, grumbling all the while at Morton's tardiness.

"Where's Burchard?" cried Morton.

But Burchard could not be found, and Morton felt internal maledictions at Burchard's cowardice.

Goodwin had given orders that his scouts should report to him the first attempt at concentration on the part of the rowdies. He had not been deceived by their feints in different parts of the camp, but had drawn his men together. He knew that there was some directing head to the mob, and that the only effectual way to beat it was to beat it in solid form.

At last a young man came running to where Goodwin stood, saying: "They're tearing down a tent."

"The fight will be there," said Morton, mounting deliberately. "Catch all you can, boys. Don't shoot if you can help it. Keep close together. We have got to ride all night."

He had increased his guard by mustering in every able-bodied man, except such as were needed to conduct the meetings. Most of these men were Methodists, but they were all frontiermen who knew that peace and civilization have often to be won by breaking heads. By the time this guard started the camp was in extreme confusion; women were running in every direction, children were crying and men were stoutly denouncing Goodwin for his tardiness.

Dividing his mounted guard of thirty men into two parts, he sent one half round the outside of the camp-ground in one direction, while he rode with the other to attack the mob on the other side. The foot-police were sent through the circle to attack them in a third direction.

As Morton anticipated, his delay tended to throw the mob off their guard. They had demolished one tent and, in great exultation, had begun on another, when Morton's cavalry rode in upon them on two sides, dealing heavy and almost deadly blows with their iron-wood and hickory clubs. Then the footmen charged them in front, and the mob were forced to scatter and mount their horses as best they could. As Morton had captured some of them, the rest rallied on horseback and attempted a rescue. For two or three minutes the fight was a severe one. The roughs made several rushes upon Morton, and nothing but the savage blows that Mellen laid about him saved the leader from falling into their hands. At last, however, after firing several shots, and wounding one of the guard, they retreated, Goodwin vigorously persuading his men to continue the charge. When the rowdies had been driven a short distance, Morton saw by the light of a platform torch, the same strangely dressed man who had taken

the money from his hand that day near Brewer's Hole.
This man, in his disguise of long beard and wolf-skin
cap, was trying to get past Mellen and into the camp
by creeping through the bushes.

"Knock him over," shouted Goodwin to Mellen.
"I know him—he's a thief."

No sooner said than Mellen's club had felled him,
and but for the intervening brush-wood, which broke
the force of the blow, it might have killed him.

"Carry him back and lock him up," said Morton
to his men; but the other side now made a strong
rush and bore off the fallen highwayman.

Then they fled, and this time, letting the less
guilty rowdies escape, Morton pursued the well-
known thieves and their allies into and through Jenkinsville, and on through the country, until the hunted
fellows abandoned their horses and fled to the woods
on foot. For two days more Morton harried them,
arresting one of them now and then until he had captured eight or ten. He chased one of these into
Brewer's Hole itself. The shoes had been torn from
his feet by briers in his rough flight, and he left
tracks of blood upon the floor. The orderly citizens
of the county were so much heartened by this boldness
and severity on Morton's part that they combined
against the roughs and took the work into their own
hands, driving some of the thieves away and terrifying
the rest into a sullen submission. The camp-meeting
went on in great triumph.

Burchard had disappeared — how, nobody knew.
Weeks afterward a stranger passing through Jenkins-

ville reported that he had seen such a man on a keelboat leaving Cincinnati for the lower Mississippi, and it soon came to be accepted that Burchard had found a home in New Orleans, that refuge of broken adventurers. Why he had fled no one could guess.

CHAPTER XXVIII.

PATTY AND HER PATIENT.

WE left Patty standing irresolute in the road. The latch-string of her father's house was drawn in; she must find another home. Every Methodist cabin would be open to her, of course; Colonel Wheeler would be only too glad to receive her. But Colonel Wheeler and all the Methodist people were openly hostile to her father, and delicacy forbade her allying herself so closely with her father's foes. She did not want to foreclose every door to a reconciliation. Mrs. Goodwin's was not to be thought of. There was but one place, and that was with Kike's mother, the widow Lumsden, who, as a relative, was naturally her first resort in exile.

Here she found a cordial welcome, and here she found the schoolmaster, still attentive to the widow, though neither he nor she dared think of marriage with Kike's awful displeasure in the back-ground.

"Well, well," said Brady, when the homeless Patty had received permission to stay in the cabin of her aunt-in-law : "Well, well, how sthrange things comes to pass, Miss Lumsden. You turned Moirton off yersilf fer bein' a Mithodis' and now ye're the one that gits sint adrift." Then, half musingly, he added : "I wish

Moirton noo, now don't oi ? Revinge is swate, and this sort of revinge would be swater on many accounts."

The helpless Patty could say nothing, and Brady looked out of the window and continued, in a sort of soliloquy : " Moirton would be *that* glad. Ha ! ha ! He'd say the divil niver sarved him a better thrick than by promptin' the Captin to turn ye out. It'll simplify matters fer Moirton. A sum's aisier to do when its simplified, loike. An' now it'll be as aisy to Moirton when he hears about it, as twice one is two— as si ple as puttin' two halves togither to make a urit. Here the master rubbed his hands in glee. He was pleased with the success of his illustration. Then he muttered : " They'll agree in ginder, number and parson ! "

" Mr. Brady, I don't think you ought to make fun of me."

" Make fun of ye ! Bliss yer dair little heart, it aint in yer ould schoolmasther to make fun of ye, whin ye've done yer dooty. I was only throyin' to congratilate ye on how aisy Moirton would conjugate the whole thing whin he hears about it."

" Now, Mr. Brady," said Patty, drawing herself up with her old pride, " I know there will be those who will say that I joined the church to get Morton back. I want you to say that Morton is to be married—was probably married to-day—and that I knew of it some days ago."

Brady's countenance fell. " Things niver come out roight," he said, as he absently put on his hat. " They talk about spicial providinces." he soliloquized, as he walked away, "and I thought as I had caught one at last. But it does same sometoimes as if a bluntherin Oirishman loike mesilf could turn the univarse better if he had aholt of the stairin' oar. But, psha! Oi've only got one or two pets of me own to look afther. God has to git husbands fer ivery woman ixcipt the old maids. An' some women has to have two, of which I hope is the Widdy Lumsden! But Mithodism upsets iverything. Koike's so religious that he can't love anybody but God, and he don't know how to pity thim that does. And Koike's made us both mortally afeard of his goodness. I wish he'd fall dead in love himself once; thin he'd know how it fales!"

Patty soon found that her father could not brook her presence in the neighborhood, and that the widow's hospitality to her was resented as an act of hostility to him. She accordingly set herself to find some means of getting away from the neighborhood, and at the same time of earning her living.

Happily, at this moment came presiding elder Magruder to a quarterly meeting on the circuit to which Hissawachee belonged, and, hearing of Patty's case, he proposed to get her employment as a teacher. He had heard that a teacher was wanted in the neighborhood of the Hickory Ridge church, where the conference had met. So Patty was settled as a teacher. For ten hours a day she showed children how to "do sums, heard their lessons in Lindley Murray, listened to them droning through the moralizing poems in the "Didactic" department of the old English Reader, and taught

them spelling from the "a-b abs" to "in-com-pre-hen
si-bil-i-ty" and its octopedal companions. And she
boarded round, but Dr. Morgan, the Presbyterian
ex-minister, when he learned that she was Kike's
cousin, and a sufferer for her religion, insisted that

THE SCHOOL-MISTRESS OF HICKORY RIDGE.

her Sundays should be passed in his house. And
being almost as much a pastor as a doctor among the
people, he soon found Patty a rare helper in his labors
among the poor and the sick. Something of good

breeding and refinement there was in her manner that
made her seem a being above the poor North Caro-
linans who had moved into the hollows, and her
kindness was all the more grateful on account of her
dignity. She was "a grand lady," they declared, and
besides was "a kinder sorter angel, like, ye know, in
her way of tendin' folks what's sick." They loved to
tell how "she nussed Bill Turner's wife through the
awfulest spell of the yaller janders you ever seed;
an' toted *Miss* Cole's baby roun' all night the night
her ole man was fotch home shot through the arm
with his own good-fer-nothin' keerlessness. She's better'n forty doctors, root *or* calomile."

One day Doctor Morgan called at the school-house
door just as the long spelling-class had broken up,
and Patty was getting ready to send the children home.
The doctor sat on his horse while each of the boys,
with hat in one hand and dinner-basket in the other,
walked to the door, and, after the fashion of those good
old days, turned round and bowed awkwardly at the
teacher. Some bobbed their heads forward on their
breasts; some jerked them sidewise; some, more re-
spectful, bent their bodies into crescents. Each
seemed alike glad when he was through with this
abominable bit of ceremony, the only bit of ceremony
in the whole round of their lives. The girls, in short
linsey dresses, with copperas-dyed cotton pantalettes,
came after, dropping "curcheys" in a style that would
have bewildered a dancing-master.

"Miss Lumsden," said the doctor, when the teacher
appeared, "I am sorry to see you so tired. I want

you to go home with me. I have some work for you to do to-morrow."

There were no buggies in that day. The roads were mostly bridle-paths, and those that would admit wagons would have shaken a buggy to pieces. Patty climbed upon a fence-corner, and the doctor rode as close as possible to the fence where she stood. Then she dropped upon the horse behind him, and the two rode off together.

Doctor Morgan explained to Patty that a strange man was lying wounded at the house of a family named Barkins, on Higgins's Run. The man refused to give his name, and the family would not tell what they knew about him. As Barkins bore a bad reputation, it was quite likely that the stranger belonged to some band of thieves who lived by horse-stealing and plundering emigrants. He seemed to be in great mental anguish, but evidently distrusted the doctor. The doctor therefore wished Patty to spend Saturday at Barkins's, and do what she could for the patient. "It is our business to do the man good," said Doctor Morgan, "not to have him arrested. Gospel is always better than Law."

On Saturday morning the doctor had a horse saddled with a side-saddle for Patty, and he and she rode to Higgins's Hollow, a desolate, rocky glen, where once lived a noted outlaw from whom the hollow took its name, and where now resided a man who was suspected of giving much indirect assistance to the gangs of thieves that infested the country, though he was too lame to be actively engaged in any bold enterprises.

Barkins nodded his head in a surly fashion at Patty as she crossed the threshold, and Mrs. Barkins, a square-shouldered, raw-boned woman, looked half inclined to dispute the passage of any woman over her door-sill. Patty felt a shudder of fear go through her frame at the thought of staying in such a place all day; but Doctor Morgan had an authoritative way with such people. When called to attend a patient. he put the whole house under martial law.

"Mrs. Barkins, I hope our patient's better. He needs a good deal done for him to-day, and I brought the school-mistress to help you, knowing you had a houseful of children and plenty of work."

"I've got a powerful sight to do, Doctor Morgan, but you had orter know'd better'n to fetch a school-miss in to spy out a body's housekeepin' 'thout givin' folks half a chance to bresh up a little. I 'low she haint never lived in no holler, in no log-house weth ten of the *wust* childern you ever seed and a decreppled ole man." She sulkily brushed off a stool with her apron and offered it to Patty. But Patty, with quick tact, laid her sunbonnet on the bed, and, while the doctor went into the only other room of the house to see the patient, she seized upon the woman's dish-towel and went to wiping the yellow crockery as Mrs. Barkins washed it, and to prevent the crabbed remonstrance which that lady had ready, she began to tell how she had tried to wipe dishes when she was little, and how she had upset the table and spilt everything on the floor. She looked into Mrs. Barkins's face with so much friendly confidence, her laugh had so much assurance of Mrs. Barkins's concurrence in it, that the square visage relaxed a little, and the woman proceeded to show her increasing friendliness by boxing " Jane Marier " for " stan'in' too closte to the lady and starrin at her that a-way."

Just then the doctor opened the squeaky door and beckoned to Patty.

" I've brought you the only medicine that will do you any good," he said, rapidly, to the sick man. " This is Miss Lumsden, our school-mistress, and the best hand in sickness you ever saw. She will stay with you an hour."

The patient turned his wan face over and looked wearily at Patty. He seemed to be a man of forty, but suffering and his unshorn beard had given him a haggard look, and he might be ten years younger. He had evidently some gentlemanly instincts, for he looked about the room for a seat for Patty. " I'll take care of myself," said Patty, cheerfully—seeing his anxious desire to be polite.

" I will write down some directions for you," said Dr. Morgan, taking out pencil and paper. When he handed the directions to Patty they read:

" I leave you a lamb among wolves. But the Shepherd is here! It is the only chance to save the poor fellow's life or his soul. I will send Nettie over in an hour with jelly, and if you want to come home with her you can do so. I will stop at noon."

With that he bade her good-bye and was gone. Patty put the room in order, wiped off the sick man's temples, and he soon fell into a sleep. When he awoke she again wiped his face with cold water. "My mother used to do that," he said.

"Is she dead?" asked Patty, reverently.

"I think not. I have been a bad man, and it is a wonder that I didn't break her heart. I would like to see her!"

"Where is she?" asked Patty.

The patient looked at her suspiciously: "What's the use of bringing my disgrace home to her door?" he said.

"But I think she would bear your disgrace and everything else for the sake of wiping your face as I do."

"I believe she would," said the wounded man, tremulously. "I would like to go to her, and ever since I came away I have meant to go as soon as I could get in the way of doing better. But I get worse all the time. I'll soon be dead now, and I don't care how soon. The sooner the better;" and he sighed wearily.

Patty had the tact not to contradict him.

"Did your mother ever read to you?" she asked.

"Yes; she used to read the Bible on Sundays and I used to run away to keep from hearing it. I'd give everything to hear her read now."

"Shall I read to you?"

"If you please."

"Shall I read your mother's favorite chapter?" said Patty.

"How do you know which that is?—I don't!"

"Don't you think one woman knows how another

woman feels?" asked Patty. And she sat by the little four-light window and took out her pocket Testament and read the three immortal parables in the fifteenth of Luke. The man's curiosity was now wide awake; he listened to the story of the sheep lost and found, but when Patty glanced at his face, it was unsatisfied; he hearkened to the story of the coin that was lost and found, and still he looked at her with faint eagerness, as if trying to guess why she should call that his mother's favorite chapter. Then she read slowly, and with sincere emotion, that truest of fictions, the tale of the prodigal son and his hunger, and his good resolution, and his tattered return, and the old father's joy. And when she looked up, his eyes tightly closed could not hide his tears.

"Do you think that is her favorite chapter?" he asked.

"Of course it must be," said Patty, conclusively. "And you'll notice that this prodigal son didn't wait to make himself better, or even until he could get a new suit of clothes."

The sick man said nothing.

The raw-boned Mrs Barkins came to the door at that moment and said:

"The doctor's gal's out yer and want's to see you."

"You wont go away yet?" asked the patient, anxiously.

"I'll stay," said Patty, as she left the room.

Nettie, with her fresh face and dimpled cheeks, was standing timidly at the outside door. Patty took the jelly from her hand and sent a note to the Doctor:

"The patient is doing well every way, and I am in the safest place in the world—doing my duty."

And when the doctor read it he said, in his nervously abrupt fashion: "Perfect angel!"

CHAPTER XXIX.

PATTY'S JOURNEY.

EVEN wounds and bruises heal more rapidly when the heart is cheered, and as Patty, after spending Saturday and Sunday with the patient, found time to come in and give him his breakfast every morning before she went to school, he grew more and more cheerful, and the doctor announced in his sudden style that he'd "get along." In all her interviews Patty was not only a woman but a Methodist. She read the Bible and talked to the man about repentance; and she would not have been a Methodist of that day had she neglected to pray with him. She could not penetrate his reserve. She could not guess whether what she said had any influence on him or not. Once she was startled and lost faith in any good result of her labors when she happened, in arranging things about the room, to come upon a hideous wolf-skin cap and some heavy false-whiskers. She had more than suspected all along that her patient was a highwayman, but upon seeing the very disguises in which his crimes had been committed, she shuddered, and asked herself whether a man so hardened that he was capable of theft—perhaps of murder—could ever be any better. She found herself, after that, trying to imagine how the wounded man would look in so fierce a mask. But she soon remembered all that she had learned of the Methodist faith in the power of the Divine Spirit working in the worst of sinners, and she got her testament and read aloud to the highwayman the story of the crucified thief.

It was on Thursday morning, as she helped him take his breakfast—he was sitting propped up in bed —that he startled her most effectually. Lifting his eyes, and looking straight at her with the sort of stare that comes of feebleness, he asked:

"Did you ever know a young Methodist circuit rider named Goodwin?"

Patty thought that he was penetrating her secret. She turned away to hide her face, and said:

"I used to go to school with him when we were children."

"I heard him preach a sermon awhile ago," said the patient, "that made me tremble all over. He's a great preacher. I wish I was as good as he is."

Patty made some remark about his having been a good boy.

"Well, I don't know," said the patient; "I used to hear that he had been a little hard—swore and drank and gambled, to say nothing of dancing and betting on horses. But they said some girl jilted him in that day. I suppose he got into bad habits because she jilted him, or else she jilted him because he was bad. Do you know anything about it?"

"Yes."

"She's a heartless thing, I suppose?"

Patty reddened, but the sick man did not see it She was going to defend herself—he must know that she was the person—but how? Then she remembered that he was only repeating what had been a matter of common gossip, and some feeling of mischievousness led her to answer:

"She acted badly—turned him off because he be-came a Methodist."

"But there was trouble before that, I thought. When he gambled away his coat and hat one night."

"Trouble with her father, I think," said Patty, casting about in her own mind how she might change the conversation.

"Is she alive yet?" he asked.

"Yes."

"Give her head to marry Goodwin now, I'll bet," said the man.

Patty now plead that she must hasten to school. She omitted reading the Bible and prayer with the patient for that morning. It was just as well. There are states of mind not favorable to any but the most private devotions.

On Friday evening Patty intended to go by the cabin a moment, but on coming near she saw horses tied in front of it, and her heart failed her. She reasoned that these horses belonged to members of the gang and she could not bring herself to plunge into their midst in the dusk of the evening. But on Satur-day morning she found the strangers not yet gone, and heard them speak of the sick man as "Pinkey." "Too soft! too soft! altogether," said one. "We ought to have shipped him——" Here the conversation was broken off.

The sick man, whom the others called Pinkey, she found very uneasy. He was glad to see her, and told her she must stay by him. He seemed anxious for the men to go away, which at last they did. Then he listened until Mrs. Barkins and her children became sufficiently uproarious to warrant him in talking.

"I want you to save a man's life."

"Whose?"

"Preacher Goodwin's."

Patty turned pale. She had not the heart to ask a question.

"Promise me that you will not betray me and I'll tell you all about it."

Patty promised.

"He's to be killed as he goes through Wild Cat Woods on Sunday afternoon. He preaches in Jenkinsville at eleven, and at Salt Fork at three. Between the two he will be killed. You must go yourself. They'll never suspect you of such a ride. If any man goes out of this settlement, and there's a warning given, he'll be shot. You must go through the woods to-night. If you go in the daytime, you and I will both be killed, maybe. Will you do it?"

Patty had her full share of timidity. But in a moment she saw a vision of Morton Goodwin slain.

"I will go."

"You must not tell the doctor a word about where you're going; you must not tell Goodwin how you got the information."

"He may not believe me."

"Anybody would believe you."

"But he will think that I have been deceived, and he cannot bear to look like a coward."

"That's true," said Pinkey. "Give me a piece of paper. I will write a word that will convince him."

He took a little piece of paper, wrote one word and folded it. "I can trust you; you must not open this paper," he said.

"I will not," said Patty.

"And now you must leave and not come back here until Monday or Tuesday. Do not leave the settlement until five o'clock. Barkins will watch you when you leave here. Don't go to Dr. Morgan's till afternoon and you will get rid of all suspicion. Take the east road when you start, and then if anybody is watching they will think that you are going to the lower settlement. Turn round at Wright's corner. It will be dark by the time you reach the Long Bottom, but there is only one trail through the woods. You must ride through to-night or you cannot reach Jenkinsville to-morrow. God will help *you*, I suppose, if He ever helps anybody, which I don't more than half believe."

Patty went away bewildered. The journey did not seem so dreadful as the long waiting. She had to appear unconcerned to the people with whom she boarded. Toward evening she told them she was going away until Monday, and at five o'clock she was at the doctor's door, trembling lest some mishap should prevent her getting a horse.

"Patty, howdy?" said the doctor, eyeing her agitated face sharply. "I didn't find you at Barkins's as I expected when I got there this morning. Sick man did not say much. Anything wrong? What scared you away?"

"Doctor, I want to ask a favor."

"You shall have anything you ask."

"But I want you to let me have it on trust, and ask me no questions and make no objections."

"I will trust you."

"I must have a horse at once for a journey."

"This evening?"

"This evening."

"But, Patty, I said I would trust you; but to go away so late, unless it is a matter of life and death——"

"It is a matter of life and death."

"And you can't trust me?"

"It is not my secret. I promised not to tell you."

"Now, Patty, I *must* break my promise and ask questions. Are you certain you are not deceived? May n't there be some plot? May n't I go with you? Is it likely that a robber should take any interest in saving the life of the person you speak of?"

Patty looked a little startled. "I may be deceived, but I feel so sure that I ought to go that I will try to go on foot, if I cannot get a horse."

"Patty, I don't like this. But I can only trust your judgment. You ought not to have been bound not to tell me."

"It is a matter of life and death that I shall go.

N

It is a matter of life and death to another that it shall not be known that I went. It is a matter of life and death to you and me both that you shall not go with me."

"Is the life you are going to save worth risking your own for? Is it only the life of a robber?"

"It is a life worth more than mine. Ask me no more questions, but have Bob saddled for me." Patty spoke as one not to be refused.

The horse was brought out, and Patty mounted, half eagerly and half timidly.

"When will you come back?"

"In time for school, Monday."

"Patty, think again before you start," called the doctor.

"There's no time to think," said Patty, as she rode away.

"I ought to have forbidden it," the doctor muttered to himself half a hundred times in the next forty-eight hours.

When she had ridden a mile on the road that led to the "lower settlement" she turned an acute angle, and came back on the hypothenuse of a right-angled triangle, if I may speak so geometrically. She thus went more than two miles to strike the main trail toward Jenkinsville, at a point only a mile away from her starting-place. She reached the woods in Long Bottom just as Pinkey told her she would, at dark. She was appalled at the thought of riding sixteen miles through a dense forest of beech trees in the night over a bridle-path. She reined up her horse, folded her hands, and offered a fervent prayer for courage and help, and then rode into the blackness ahead.

There is a local tradition yet lingering in this very valley in Ohio in regard to this dark ride of Patty's. I know it will be thought incredible, but in that day marvelous things were not yet out of date. This legend, which reaches me from the very neighborhood of the occurrence, is that, when Patty had nerved herself for her lonely and perilous ride by prayer, there came to her, out of the darkness of the forest, two beautiful dogs. One of them started ahead of her horse and one of them became her rear-guard. Protected and comforted by her dumb companions, Patty rode all those lonesome hours in that wilderness bridlepath. She came, at midnight, to a settler's house on the farther verge of the unbroken forest and found lodging. The dogs lay in the yard. In the early morning the settler's wife came out and spoke to them but they gave her no recognition at all. Patty came a few moments later, when they arose and greeted her with all the eloquence of dumb friends, and then, having seen her safely through the woods and through the night, the two beautiful dogs, wagging a friendly farewell, plunged again into the forest and went—no man knows whither.

Such is the legend of Patty's Ride as it came to me well avouched. Doubtless Mr. John Fiske or Mr. M. D. Conway could explain it all away and show how there was only one dog, and that he was not beautiful, but a stray bull-dog with a stumpy tail. Or that the whole thing is but a "solar myth." The middle-ages have not a more pleasant story than this of angels sent in the form of dogs to convoy a brave lady on a noble mission through a dangerous forest. At any rate, Patty believed that the dumb guardians were answers to her prayer. She bade them good-by as they disappeared in the mystery whence they came, and rode on, rejoicing in so signal a mark of God's favor to her enterprise. Sometimes her heart was sorely troubled at the thought of Morton's being already the husband of another, and all that Sunday morning she took lessons in that hardest part of Christian living— the uttering of the little petition which gives all the inevitable over into God's hands and submits to the accomplishment of His will.

She reached Jenkinsville at half-past eleven. Meeting had already begun. She knew the Methodist church by its general air of square ugliness, and near it she hitched old Bob.

When she entered the church Morton was preaching. Her long sun-bonnet was a sufficient disguise, and she sat upon the back seat listening to the voice whose music was once all her own. Morton was preaching on self-denial, and he made some allusions to his own trials when he became a Christian which deeply touched the audience, but which moved none so much as Patty.

The congregation was dismissed but the members remained to " class," which was always led by the preacher when he was present. Most of the members sat near the pulpit, but when the "outsiders" had gone Patty sat lonesomely on the back seat, with a large space between her and the rest. Morton asked each one to speak, exhorting each in turn. At last, when all the rest had spoken, he walked back to where Patty sat, with her face hidden in her sun-bonnet, and thus addressed her:

"My strange sister, will you tell us how it is with you to-day? Do you feel that you have an interest in the Savior?"

Very earnestly, simply, and with a tinge of melancholy Patty spoke. There was that in her superior diction and in her delicacy of expression that won upon the listeners, so that, as she ceased, the brethren and sisters uttered cordial ejaculations of "The Lord bless our strange sister," and so on. But Morton? From the first word he was thrilled with the familiar sound of the voice. It could not be Patty, for why should Patty be in Jenkinsville? And above all, why should she be in class-meeting? Of her conversion he had not heard. But though it seemed to him impossible that it could be Patty, there was yet a something in voice and manner and choice of words that had almost overcome him; and though he was noted for the freshness of the counsels that he gave in class-meeting, he was so embarrassed by the sense of having known the speaker, that he could not think of anything to say. He fell hopelessly into that trite exhortation with which the old leaders were wont to cover their inanity.

"Sister," he said, "you know the way—walk in it."

Then the brethren and sisters sang:

"O brethren will you meet me

And the meeting was dismissed.

The members thought themselves bound to speak to the strange sister. She evaded their kindly questions as they each shook hands with her, only answering that she wished to speak with Brother Goodwin. The preacher was eager and curious to converse with her, but one of the old brethren had button-holed him to complain that Brother Hawkins had 'tended a barbecue the week before, and he thought that he had ought to be "read out" if he didn't make confession. When the old brother had finished his complaint and had left the church, Morton was glad to see the strange sister lingering at the door. He offered his hand and said:

"A stranger here, I suppose?"

"Not quite a stranger, Morton."

"Patty, is this you?" Morton exclaimed

Patty for her part was pleased and silent.

"Are you a Methodist then?"

"I am."

"And what brought you to Jenkinsville?" he said, greatly agitated.

"To save your life. I am glad I can make you some amend for the way I treated you the last time I saw you."

"To save my life! How?"

"I came to tell you that if you go to Salt Fork this afternoon you will be killed on the way."

"How do you know?"

"You must not ask any questions. I cannot tell you anything more."

"I am afraid, Patty, you have believed somebody who wanted to scare me."

Patty here remembered the mysterious piece of paper which Pinkey had given her. She handed it to Morton, saying:

"I don't know what is in this, but the person who sent the message said that you would understand."

Morton opened the paper and started. "Where is he?" he asked.

"You must not ask questions," said Patty, smiling faintly.

"And you rode all the way from Hissawachee to tell me?"

"Not at all. When I joined the church Father pulled the latch-string in. I am teaching school at Hickory Ridge."

"Come, Patty, you must have some dinner." Morton led her horse to the house of one of the members, introduced her as an old schoolmate, who had brought him an important warning, and asked that she receive some dinner.

He then asked Patty to let him go back with her or send an escort, both of which she firmly refused. He left the house and in a minute sat on his Dolly before the gate. At sight of Dolly Patty could have wept. He called her to the gate.

"If you won't let me go with you I must go to Salt Fork. These men must understand that I am not afraid. I shall ride ten miles farther round and they will never know how I did it. Dolly can do it, though. How shall I thank you for risking your life for me'

Patty, if I can ever serve you let me know, and I'll die for you. I would rather die for you than not."

"Thank you, Morton. You are married, I hear."

"Not married, but I am to be married." He spoke half bitterly, but Patty was too busy suppressing her own emotion to observe his tone.

"I hope you'll be happy." She had determined to say so much.

"Patty, I tell you I am wretched, and will be till I die. I am marrying one I never chose. I am utterly miserable. Why did n't you leave me to be waylaid and killed? My life is n't worth the saving. But God bless you, Patty."

So saying, he touched Dolly with the spurs and was soon gone away around the Wolf Creek road—a long hard ride, with no dinner, and a sermon to preach at three o'clock.

And all the hour that Patty ate and rested in Jenkinsville, her hostess entertained her with accounts of Sister Ann Eliza Meacham, whom Brother Goodwin was to marry. She heard how eloquent was Sister Meacham in prayer, how earnest in Christian labor, and what a model preacher's wife she would be. But the good sister added slyly that she did n't more than half believe Brother Goodwin wanted to marry at all. He'd tried his best to give Ann Eliza up once, but could n't do it.

When Patty rode out of the village that afternoon she did her best, as a good Christian, to feel sorry that Morton could not love the one he was to marry. In an intellectual way she did regret it, but in her heart she was a woman.

CHAPTER XXX.

THE SCHOOLMASTER AND THE WIDOW.

WHEN Kike had appeared at the camp meeting, as we related, it was not difficult to forecast his fate. Everybody saw that he was going into a consumption. One year, two years at farthest, he might manage to live, but not longer. Nobody knew this so well as Kike himself. He rejoiced in it. He was one of those rare spirits to whom the invisible world is not a dream but a reality, and to whom religious duty is a voice never neglected. That he had sacrificed his own life to his zeal he understood perfectly well, and he had no regrets except that he had not been more zealous. What was life if he could save even one soul?

"But," said Morton to him one day, "you are wrong, Kike. If you had taken care of yourself you might have lived to save so many more."

"Morton, if your eye were fastened on one man drowning," replied Kike, "and you thought you could save him at the risk of your health, you wouldn't stop to calculate that by avoiding that peril you might live long enough to save many others. When God puts a soul before me I save that one if it costs my life. When I am gone God will find others. It is glorious to work for God, but it is awful. What if by some neglect of mine a soul should drop into hell? O! Morton, I am oppressed with responsibility! I will be glad when God shall say, It is enough."

Few of the preachers remonstrated with Kike. He was but fulfilling the Methodist ideal; they admired him while most of them could not quite emulate him. Read the minutes of the old conferences and you will see everywhere among the brief obituaries, headstones in memory of young men who laid down their lives as Kike was doing. Men were nothing—the work was everything. Methodism let the dead bury their dead; it could hardly stop to plant a spear of grass over the grave of one of its own heroes.

But Pottawottomie Creek circuit was poor and wild, and it had paid Kike only five dollars for his whole nine months' work. Two of this he had spent for horse-shoes, and two he had given away. The other one had gone for quinine. Now he had no clothes that would long hold together. He would ride to Hissawachee and get what his mother had carded and spun, and woven, and cut, and sewed for the son whom she loved all the more that he seemed no longer to be entirely hers. He could come back in three days. Two days more would suffice to reach Peterborough circuit. So he sent on to the circuit, in advance, his appointments to preach, and rode off to Hissawachee. But he did not get back to camp-meeting. An attack of fever held him at home for several weeks.

At last he was better and had set the day for his departure from home. His mother saw what everybody saw, that if Kike ever lived to return to his home it would only be to die. And as this was, perhaps, his last visit, Mrs. Lumsden felt in duty bound to tell him of her intention to marry Brady. While Brady thought to do the handsome thing by secretly getting a marriage license, intending, whenever the widow should mention the subject to Kike, to immediately propose that Kike should perform the ceremony of marriage. It was quite contrary to the custom of that day for a minister to officiate at a wedding of one of his own family; Brady defied custom, however. But whenever Mrs. Lumsden tried to approach Kike on the subject, her heart failed her. He was so wrapped up in heavenly subjects, so full of exhortations and aspirations, that she despaired beforehand of making him understand her feelings. Once she began by alluding to her loneliness, upon which Kike assured her that if she put her trust in the Lord he would be with her. What was she to do? How make a rapt seer like Kike understand the wants of ordinary mortals? And that, too, when he was already bidding adieu to this world?

The last morning had come, and Brady was urging on the weeping widow that she must go into the room where Kike was stuffing his small wardrobe into his saddle-bags, and tell him what was in their hearts.

"Oh, I can't bear to," said she. "I won't never see him any more and I might hurt him, and —— "

"Will," said Brady, "thin I'll hev to do it mesilf."

"If you only would!" said she, imploringly.

"But it's so much more appropriate for you to do it, Mrs. Lumsden. If I do it, it'll same jist loike axin' the b'y's consint to marry his mother."

"But I can't noways do it," said the widow. "If you love me you might take that load offen me."

"I'll do it if it kills me, sthraight," and Brady marched into the sitting-room, where Kike, exhausted by his slight exertion, was resting in the shuck-bottom rocking-chair. Brady took a seat opposite to him on a chair made out of a transformed barrel, and roached up his iron gray hair uneasily. To his surprise Kike began the conversation.

"Mr. Brady, you and mother a'n't acting very wisely, I think," said Kike.

"Ye've noticed us, thin," said Brady, in terror.

"To be sure I have."

"Will, now, Koike, I'll till you fwat I'm thinkin'. Ye're pecooliar loike; ye don't know how to sympathoize with other folks because ye're livin' roight up in hiven all the toime."

"Why don't you live more in heaven?"

"Will, I think I'd throy if I had somebody to help me," said Brady, adroitly. "But I'm one of the koind that's lonesome, and in doire nade of company. I was jilted whin I was young, and I thought I'd niver be a fool agin. But ye see ye ain't niver been in love in all yer loife, and how kin ye fale fer others?"

"Maybe I have been in love, too," said Kike, a strange softness coming into his voice.

"Did ye iver! Who'd a thought it?" And Brady made large eyes at him. "Thin ye ought to fale fer the infarmities of others," he added with some exultation.

"I do. That's why I said you and mother were very foolish."

"Fwy, now; there it is agin. Fwat do ye mane?"

"Why this. When I was here before I saw that you and mother had taken a liking to each other. I thought by this time you'd have been married. And I didn't see any reason why you shouldn't. But you're as far away as ever. Here's mother's land that needs somebody to take care of it. I am going away never to come back. If I could see you married the only earthly care I have would be gone, and I could die in peace, whenever and wherever the Lord calls me."

"God bliss ye, Koike," said Brady, wiping his eyes. "Fwy didn't you say that before? Ye're a prophet and a angel, I belave. I wish I was half as good, or a quarther. God bliss ye, me boy. I wish—I wish ye would thry to live afwoile. I've been athrying' and your mother's been athryin' to muster up courage to spake to ye about this, and ye samed so hively we thought ye would be displaced. Now, will ye marry us before ye go?"

"I haven't got any license."

"Here 'tis, in me pocket."

"Where's a witness or two?"

"I hear some women-folks come to say good-bye to ye in the other room."

"I'd like to marry you now," said Kike. "I must get away in an hour."

And he married them. They wept over him, and he made no concealment that he was going away for the last time. He rode out from Hissawachee never to come back. Not sad, but exultant, that he had sacrificed everything for Christ and was soon to enter into the life everlasting. For, faithless as we are in this day, let us never hide from ourselves the fact that the faith of a martyr is indeed a hundred fold more a source of joy than houses and lands, and wife and children.

CHAPTER XXXI.

KIKE.

TO reach Peterborough Kike had to go through Morton's great diocese of Jenkinsville Circuit. He could not ride far. Even so intemperate a zealot as Kike admitted so much economy of force into his calculations. He must save his strength in journeying or he could not reach his circuit, much less preach when he got there. At the close of his second day he inquired for a Methodist house at which to stop, and was directed to the double-cabin of a "located" preacher—one who had been a "travelling" preacher, but, having married, was under the necessity of entangling himself with the things of this world that he might get bread for his children. As he rode up to the house Kike gladly noted the horses hitched to the fence as an evidence that there must be a meeting in progress. He was in Morton's circuit; who could tell that he should not meet him here?

When Kike entered the house, Morton stood in the door between the two rooms preaching, with the back of a "split-bottomed" chair for a pulpit. For a moment the pale face of Kike, so evidently smitten with death, appalled him; then it inspired him, and Morton never spoke better on that favorite theme of the early

Methodist evangelist—the rest in heaven—than while drawing his inspiration from the pallid countenance of his comrade.

"Ah! Kike!" he said, when the meeting was dismissed, "I wish you had my body."

"What do you want to keep me out of heaven for, Mort? Let God have his way," said Kike, smiling contentedly.

But long after Kike slept that night Morton lay awake. He could not let the poor fellow go off alone. So in the morning he arranged with the located brother to take his appointments for awhile and let him ride one day with Kike.

"Ride ten or twenty if you want to," said the ex-preacher. "The corn's laid by and I've got nothing to do, and I'm spoiling for a preach."

Peterborough circuit lay off to the southeast of Hickory Ridge, and Morton, persuaded that Kike was unfit to preach, endeavored to induce him to turn aside and rest at Dr. Morgan's, only ten miles out of his road.

"I tell you, Morton, I've got very little strength left. I cannot spend it better than in trying to save souls. There's Peterborough vacant three months since Brother Jones was first taken sick. I want to make one or two rounds at least, preaching with all the heart I have. Then I'll cease at once to work and live, and who knows but that I may slay more in my death than in my life?"

But Morton feared that he would not be able to make one round. He thought he had an overestimate of his strength, and that the final break-down might come at any moment. So, on the morning of the second day he refused to yield to Kike's entreaties to return. He would see him safe among the members on Peterborough circuit, anyhow.

Now it happened that they missed the trail and wandered far out of their way. It rained all the afternoon, and Kike got drenched in crossing a stream. Then a chill came on, and Morton sought shelter. He stopped at a cabin.

"Come in, come in, brethren," said the settler, as soon as he saw them. "I 'low ye're preachers. Brother Goodwin I know. Heerd him down at camp-meetin' last fall,—time conference met on the Ridge. And this brother looks mis'rable. Got the shakes, I 'low? Your name, brother, is—

"Brother Lumsden," said Morton.

"Lumsden? Wy, that air's the very name of our school-miss, and she's stayin' here jes' now. I kinder recolleck that you was sick up at Dr. Morgan's, conference time. Hey?"

Morton looked bewildered.

"How far is Dr. Morgan's from here?"

"Nigh onto three quarter 'round the road, I 'low. Ain't it, Sister Lumsden?" This last to Patty, who at that moment appeared from the bedroom, and without answering the question, greeted Morton and Kike with a cry of joy. Patty was "boarding round," and it was her time to stay here.

"How did we get here? We aimed at Lanham's Ferry," said Morton, bewildered.

"Tuck the wrong trail ten mile back, I 'low. You should've gone by Hanks's Mills."

Despite all protestations from the Methodist brother, Morton was determined to take Kike to Dr. Morgan's. Kike was just sick enough to be passive, and he suf-

THE REUNION.

fered himself to be put back into the saddle to ride to the doctor's. Patty, meanwhile, ran across the fields and gave warning, so that Kike was summarily stowed away in the bed he had occupied before. Thus do

men try to run away from fate, and rush into her arms
in spite of themselves.

It did not require very great medical skill to understand what must be the result of Kike's sickness.

"What is the matter with him, Doctor?" asked
Morton, next morning.

"Absolute physical bankruptcy, sir," answered the
physician, in his abrupt manner. "There's not water
enough left in the branch to run the mill seven days.
Wasted life, sir, wasted life. It is a pity but you
Methodists had a little moderation in your zeal."

Kike uneasily watched the door, hoping every
minute that he might see Nettie come in. But she did
not come. He had wished to avoid her father's house
for fear of seeing her, but he could not bear to
be thus near her and not see her. Toward evening
he called Patty to him.

"Lean down here!" he said.

Patty put her ear down that nobody might hear.

"Where's Nettie?" asked Kike.

"About the house, somewhere," said Patty.

"Why don't she come in to see me?"

"Not because she doesn't care for you," said Patty;
"she seems to be crying half the time."

Kike watched the door uneasily all that evening.
But Nettie did not come. To have come into Kike's
room would have been to have revealed her love for
one who had never declared his love for her. The
mobile face of Nettie disclosed every emotion. No
wonder she was fain to keep away. And yet the desire
to see him almost overcame her fear of seeing him.

When the doctor came in to see Kike after breakfast the next morning, the patient looked at him wistfully.

"Doctor Morgan, tell me the truth. Will I ever get up?"

"You can never get up, my dear boy," said the physician, huskily.

A smile of relief spread over Kike's face. At that word the awful burden of his morbid sense of responsibility for the world's salvation, the awful burden of a self-sacrifice that was terrible and that must be life-long, slipped from his weary soul. There was then nothing more to be done but to wait for the Master's release. He shut his eyes, murmured a "Thank God!" and lay for minutes, motionless. As the doctor made a movement to leave him, Kike opened his eyes and looked at him eagerly.

"What is it, my boy?" said Morgan, stroking the straight black hair off Kike's forehead, and petting him as though he were a child. "What do you want?"

"Doctor —— " said Kike, and then closed his eyes again.

"Don't be afraid to tell me what is in your heart, dear boy." The tears were in the doctor's eyes.

"If you think it best—if you think it best, mind—I would like to see Nettie."

"Of course it is best. I am glad you mentioned it. It will do her good, poor soul."

"If you think it best —— "

"Well?" said the doctor, seeing that Kike hesitated. "Speak out."

"All alone."

"Yes, you shall see her alone. That is best." The doctor's utterance was choked as he hastened out.

Kike lay with eyes fixed on the door. It seemed a long time after the doctor went before Nettie came in. It was only three minutes—three minutes in which Nettie vainly strove to wipe away tears that flowed faster than she could remove them. At last her hand was on the latch. She gained a momentary self-control. But when she opened the door and saw his emaciated face, and his black eyes looking so eagerly for her, it was too much for the poor little heart. The next moment she was on her knees by his bed, sobbing violently. And Kike put out his feeble hands and drew the golden head up close to his bosom, and spoke tenderer words than he had ever heard spoken in his life. And then he closed his eyes, and for a long time nothing was said. It came about after Nettie's tears were spent that they talked of all that they had felt; of the life past and of the immortal life to come. Hours went by and none intruded upon this betrothal for eternity. Patty had waited without, expecting to be called to take her place again by her cousin's bedside. But she did not like to remain in conversation with Morton. It could bring nothing but pain to them both. It occurred to her that she had not seen her patient in Higgins's Hollow since Kike came. She started immediately, glad to escape from the regrets excited by the presence of Morton, and touched with remorse that she had so long neglected a man on whose heart she thought she had been able to make some religious impression.

CHAPTER XXXII.

PINKEY was grum. He didn't like to be neglected, if he was a highwayman. He had gotten out of bed and drawn on his boots.

"So you could n't come to see me because there was a young preacher sick at the doctor's?" he said, when Patty entered.

"The young preacher is my cousin," said Patty, "and he is going to die."

"Your cousin," said Pinkey, softened a little. "But Goodwin is there, too. I hope you didn't tell him anything about me?"

"Not a word."

"He ought to be grateful to you for saving his life."

"He seems to be."

"And people that are grateful are very likely to have other feelings after awhile." There was a significance in Pinkey's manner that Patty greatly disliked.

"You should not talk in that way. Mr. Goodwin is engaged to be married."

"Is he? Do you mind telling me her name?"

"To a lady named Meacham, I believe."

"What?—Who?—To Ann Eliza? How did it happen that I have never heard of that? To Ann Eliza! Confound her; what a witch that girl is! I wish I could spoil her game this time. Goodwin 's too good for her and she sha'n't have him." Then he sat still as if in meditation. After a moment he resumed: "Now, Miss Lumsden, you've done one good turn for him, you must do another. I want to send a note to this Ann Eliza."

"*I* cannot take it," said Patty, trembling.

"You saved his life, and now you are unwilling to save him from a worse evil. You ought not to refuse."

"You ought not to ask it. The circumstances of the case are peculiar. I will not take it."

"Will you take a note to Goodwin?"

"Not on this business."

Pinkey was startled at the emotion she showed, and looked at her inquiringly: "You were a schoolmate of Morton's—of Goodwin's, I mean—and a body would think that you might be the identical sweetheart that sent him adrift for joining the Methodists—and then joined the Methodists herself, eh?"

Patty said nothing, but turned away.

"By the holy Moses," said Pinkey, in a half-soliloquy, "if that's the case, I'll break the net of that fisherwoman this time or drown myself a-trying."

Patty had intended to read the Bible to her patient, but her mind was so disturbed that she thought best to say good-morning. Pinkey roused himself from a reverie to call her back.

"Will you answer me one question?" he asked.

" Does Goodwin want to marry this girl? Is he ╷appy about it, do you think?"

"I am sure he isn't," said Patty, reproaching herself in a moment that she had said so much.

Patty made some kindly remark to Mrs. Barkins as she went out, walked briskly to the fence, halted, looked off over the field a moment, turned round and came back. When she re-entered Pinkey's room he had put on his great false-whiskers and wolf-skin cap, and she trembled at the transformation. He started, but said: " Don't be afraid, Miss Lumsden, I am not meditating mischief. I will not hurt you, certainly, and you must not betray me. Now, what is it?"

' Don't do anything wrong in this matter," said Patty. " Don't do anything that'll lie heavy on your soul when you come to die.—I'm afraid you'll do something wrong for Mr. Goodwin's sake, or—mine."

"No. But if I was able to ride I'd do one thunderin' good thing. But I am too weak to do anything, plague on it!"

"I wish you would put these deceits in the fire and do right," she said, indicating his disguises. "I am disappointed to see that you are going back to your old ways."

He made no reply, but laid off his disguises and lay down on the bed, exhausted. And Patty departed, grieved that all her labors were in vain, while Pinkey only muttered to himself, "I'm too weak, confound it!"

CHAPTER XXXIII.

THE ALABASTER BOX BROKEN.

NOT until Dr. Morgan came in at noon did any one venture to open the door of Kike's room. He found the patient much better. But the improvement could not be permanent, the sedative of mental rest and the tonic of joy had come too late.

"Morton," said Kike, "I want Dolly to do me one more service. Nettie will explain to you what it is."

After a talk with Nettie, Morton rode Dolly away, leading Kike's horse with him. The doctor thought he could guess what Morton went for, but, even in melancholy circumstances, lovers, like children, are fond of having secrets, and he did not try to penetrate that which it gave Kike and Nettie pleasure to keep to themselves. At ten o'clock that night Morton came back without Kike's horse.

"Did you get it?" whispered Kike, who had grown visibly weaker.

Morton nodded.

"And you sent the message?"

"Yes."

Kike gave Nettie a look of pleasure, and then sank into a satisfied sleep, while Morton proceeded to relate to Doctor Morgan and Patty that he had seen in the

o

moonlight a notorious highwayman. "His nickname is Pinkey; nobody knows who he is or where he comes from or goes to. He got a hard blow in a fight with the police force of the camp meeting. It's a wonder it did n't break his head. I searched for him everywhere, but he had effectually disappeared. If I had been armed to-night I should have tried to arrest him, for he was alone."

Patty and the doctor exchanged looks.

"Our patient, Patty."

But Patty did not say a word.

"You must have got that information through him!" said Morton, with surprise.

But Patty only kept still.

"I won't ask you any questions, but what if I had killed my deliverer! Strange that he should be the bearer of a message to me, though. I should rather expect him to kill me than to save me."

Patty wondered that Pinkey had ventured away while yet so weak, and found in herself the flutterings of a hope for which she knew there was no satisfactory ground.

When Saturday morning came, Kike was sinking. "Doctor Morgan," he said, "do not leave me long. Nettie and I want to be married before I die."

"But the license?" said the doctor, affecting not to suspect Kike's secret.

"Morton got it the other day. And I am looking for my mother to-day. I don't want to be married till she comes. Morton took my horse and sent for her."

Saturday passed and Kike's mother had not arrived. On Sunday morning he was almost past speaking. Nettie had gone out of the room, and Kike was apparently asleep.

" Splendid life wasted," said the doctor, sadly, to Morton, pointing to the dying man.

"Yes, indeed. What a pity he had no care for himself," answered Morton.

" Patty," said Kike, opening his eyes, " the Bible." Patty got the Bible.

" Read in the twenty-sixth of Matthew, from the seventh verse to the thirteenth, inclusive," Kike spoke as if he were announcing a text.

Then, when Patty was about to read, he said: " Stop. Call Nettie."

When Nettie came he nodded to Patty, and she read all about the alabaster box of ointment, very precious, that was broken over the head of Jesus, and the complaint that it was wasted, with the Lord's reply.

" You are right, my dear boy," said Doctor Morgan, with effusion, "what is spent for love is never wasted. It is a very precious box of ointment that you have broken upon Christ's head, my son. The Lord will not forget it."

When Kike's mother and Brady rode up to the door on Sunday morning, the people had already begun to gather in crowds, drawn by the expectation that Morton would preach in the Hickory Ridge church. Hearing that Kike, whose piety was famous all the country over, was dying, they filled Doctor

Morgan's house and yard, sitting in sad, silent groups on the fences and door-steps, and standing in the shade of the yard trees. As the dying preacher's mother passed through, the crowd of country people fell back and looked reverently at her.

Kike was already far gone. He was barely able to greet his mother and the good-hearted Brady, whose demonstrative Irish grief knew no bounds. Then Kike and Nettie were married, amidst the tears of all. This sort of a wedding is more hopelessly melancholy than a funeral. After the marriage Nettie knelt by Kike's side, and he rallied for a moment and solemnly pronounced a benediction on her. Then he lifted up his hands, crying faintly, " O Lord! I have kept back nothing. Amen."

His hands dropped upon the head of Nettie. The people had crowded into the hall and stood at the windows. For awhile all thought him dead.

A white pigeon flew in at one of the windows and lighted upon the bed of the dying man. The early Western people believed in marvels, and Kike was to them a saint. At sight of the snow-white dove pluming itself upon his breast they all started back. Was it a heavenly visitant? Kike opened his eyes and gazed upon the dove a moment. Then he looked significantly at Nettie, then at the people. The dove plumed itself a moment longer, looked round on the people out of its mute and gentle eyes, then flitted out of the window again and disappeared in the sunlight. A smile overspread the dying man's face, he clasped his hands upon his bosom, and it was a full minute before any-

body discovered that the pure, heroic spirit of Hezekiah Lumsden had gone to its rest.

He had requested that no name should be placed
over his grave. "Let God have any glory that may
come from my labors, and let everybody but Nettie
forget me," he said. But Doctor Morgan had a slab
of the common blue limestone of the hills—marble was
not to be had—cut out for a headstone. The device
upon it was a dove, the only inscription : "An alabaster
box of very precious ointment."

Death is not always matter for grief. If you have
ever beheld a rich sunset from the summit of a
lofty mountain, you will remember how the world was
transfigured before you in the glory of resplendent
light, and how, long after the light had faded from
the cloud-drapery, and long after the hills had begun
to lose themselves in the abyss of darkness, there
lingered a glory in the western horizon — a joyous
memory of the splendid pomp of the evening. Even
so the glory of Kike's dying made all who saw it feel
like those who have witnessed a sublime spectacle,
which they may never see again. The memory of
it lingered with them like the long-lingering glow
behind the western mountains. Sorry that the suffering life had ended in peace, one could not be ; and
never did stormy day find more placid sunset than
his. Even Nettie had never felt that he belonged to
her. When he was gone she was as one whom an
angel of God had embraced. She regretted his absence,
but rejoiced in the memory of his love ; and she had
not entertained any hopes that could be disappointed.

The only commemoration his name received was in the conference minutes, where, like other such heroes, he was curtly embalmed in the usual four lines:

"Hezekiah Lumsden was a man of God, who freely gave up his life for his work. He was tireless in labor, patient in suffering, bold in rebuking sin, holy in life and conversation, and triumphant in death."

The early Methodists had no time for eulogies. A handful of earth, a few hurried words of tribute, and the bugle called to the battle. The man who died was at rest, the men who staid had the more work to do.

NOTE. In the striking incid tnt ot the dove lighting upon Kike's bed, I have followed strictly the statement of eye-witnesses.—E.E.

CHAPTER XXXIV.

PATTY had received, by the hand of Brady, a letter from her father, asking her to come home. Do not think that Captain Lumsden wrote penitently and asked Patty's forgiveness. Captain Lumsden never did anything otherwise than meanly. He wrote that he was now bedridden with rheumatism, and it seemed hard that he should be forsaken by his oldest daughter, who ought to be the stay of his declining years. He did not understand how Patty could pretend to be so religious and yet leave him to suffer without the comfort of her presence. The other children were young, and the house was in hopeless confusion. If the Methodists had not quite turned her heart away from her poor afflicted father, she would come at once and help him in his troubles. He was ready to forgive the past, and as for her religion, if she did not trouble him with it, she could do as she pleased. He did not think much of a religion that set a daughter against her father, though.

Patty was too much rejoiced at the open door that it set before her to feel the sting very keenly. There was another pain that had grown worse with every day she had spent with Morton. Beside her own sorrow she felt for him. There was a strange restlessness in his eyes, an eager and vacillating activity in what he was doing, that indicated how fearfully the tempest raged within. For Morton's old desperation was upon him, and Patty was in terror for the result. About the time of Kike's death the dove settled upon his soul also. He had mastered himself, and the restless wildness had given place to a look of constraint and suffering that was less alarming but hardly less distressing to Patty, who had also the agony of hiding her own agony. But the disappearance of Pinkey had awakened some hope in her. Not one jot of this trembling hopefulness did she dare impart to Morton, who for his part had but one consolation—he would throw away his life in the battle, as Kike had done before him.

So eager was Patty to leave her school now and hasten to her father, that she could not endure to stay the weeks that were necessary to complete her term. She had canvassed with Doctor Morgan the possibility of etting some one to take her place, and both had concluded that there was no one available, Miss Jane Morgan being too much out of health. But to their surprise Nettie offered her services. She had not been of much more use in the world than a humming-bird, she said, and now it seemed to her that Kike would be better pleased that she should make herself useful.

Thus released, Patty started home immediately, and Morton, who could not reach the distant part of his circuit, upon which his supply was now preaching, in time to resume his work at once, concluded to set out for Hissawachee also, that he might see how his parents fared. But he concealed his purpose from Patty, who departed in company with Brady and his wife. Morton would not trust himself in her society longer. He therefore rode round by a circuitous way, and, thanks to Dolly, reached Hissawachee before them.

I may not describe the enthusiasm with which Morton was received at home. Scarcely had he kissed his mother and shaken hands with his father, who was surprised that none of his dolorous predictions had been fulfilled, and greeted young Henry, now shooting up into manhood, when his mother whispered to him that his brother Lewis was alive and had come home.

"What! Lewis alive?" exclaimed Morton, "I thought he was killed in Pittsburg ten years ago."

"That was a false report. He had been doing badly, and he did not want to return, and so he let us believe him dead. But now he has come back and he is afraid you will not receive him kindly. I suppose he thinks because you are a preacher you will be hard on his evil ways. But you wont be too hard, will you?"

"I? God knows I have been too great a sinner myself for that. Where is Lew? I can just remember how he used to whittle boats for me when I was a little boy. I remember the morning he ran off, and how after that you always wanted to move West. Poor Lew! Where has he gone?"

His mother opened the door of the little bed-room and led out the brother.

"What! Burchard?" cried Morton. "What does this mean? Are you Lewis Goodwin?"

"I am!"

"That's why you gave me back my horse and gun when you found out who I was. That's how you

THE BROTHERS.

saved me that day at Brewer's Hole. And that's why you warned me at Salt Fork and sent me that other warning. Well, Lewis, I would be glad to see you anyhow, but I ought to be not only glad as a brother, but glad that I can thank you for saving my life."

"But I've been a worse man than you think, Mort.'

"What of that? God forgives, and I am sure that it is not for such a sinner as I am to condemn you. If you knew what desperate thoughts have tempted me in the last week you would know how much I am your brother."

Just here Brady knocked at the door and pushed it open, with a "Howdy, Misses Goodwin? Howdy, Mr. Goodwin? and, Moirton, howdy do?"

"This is my brother Lewis, Mr. Brady. We thought he was dead."

"Heigh-ho! The prodigal's come back agin, eh? Mrs. Goodwin, I congratilate ye."

And then Mrs. Brady was introduced to Lewis. Patty, who stood behind, came forward, and Morton said: "Miss Lumsden, my brother Lewis."

"You need n't introduce her," said Lewis. "She knows me already. If it had n't been for her I might have been dead, and in perdition, I suppose."

"Why, how 's that?" asked Morton, bewildered.

"She nursed me in sickness, and read the parable of the Prodigal Son, and told me that it was my mother's favorite chapter."

"So it is," said Mrs. Goodwin; "I 've read it every day for years. But how did you know that, Patty?"

"Why," said Lewis, "she said that one woman knew how another woman felt. But you don't know how good Miss Lumsden is. She did not know me as Lewis Goodwin or Burchard, but in quite a different character. I suppose I 'd as well make a clean breast

of it, Mort, at once.   Then there 'll be no surprises
afterward.   And if you hate me when you know it all,
I can't help it."   With that he stepped into the bed-
room and came forth with long beard and wolf-skin cap.

" What! Pinkey ? " said Morton, with horror.

" The Pinkey that you told that big preacher to
knock down, and then hunted all over the country to
find."

Seeing Morton's pained expression at this discovery
of his brother's bad character, Patty added adroitly:
" The Pinkey that saved your life, Morton."

Morton got up and stood before his brother.   " Give
me your hand again, Lewis.   I am so glad you came
home at last.   God bless you."

Lewis sat down and rested his head in his hands.
" I have been a very wicked man, Morton, but I never
committed a murder.   I am guilty of complicity.   I got
tangled in the net of Micajah Harp's band.   I helped
them because they had a hold on me, and I was too
weak to risk the consequences of breaking with them.
That complicity has spoiled all my life.   But the
crimes they laid on Pinkey were mostly committed by
others.   Pinkey was a sort of ghost at whose doors all
sins were laid."

" I must hurry home," said Patty.   " I only stopped
to shake hands," and she rose to go.

" Miss Lumsden," said Lewis, " you wanted me to
destroy these lies.   You shall have them to do what
you like with.   I wish you could take my sins, too."

Patty put the disguises into the fire.   " Only God
can take your sins," she said

"Even he can't make me forget them," said Lewis, with bitterness.

Patty went home in anxiety. Lewis Goodwin seemed to have forgotten the resolution he had made as Pinkey to save Morton from Ann Eliza.

But Patty went home bravely and let thoughts of present duty crowd out thoughts of possible happiness. She bore the peculiar paternal greetings of her father; she installed herself at once, and began, like a good genius, to evolve order out of chaos. By the time evening arrived the place had come to know its mistress again.

CHAPTER XXXV.

THAT evening, after dark, Morton and his Brother Lewis strolled into the woods together. It was not safe for Lewis to walk about in the day time. The law was on one side and the vengeance of Micajah Harp's band, perhaps, on the other. But in the twilight he told Morton something which interested the latter greatly, and which increased his gratitude to Lewis. That you may understand what this communication was, I must go back to an event that happened the week before—to the very last adventure that Lewis Goodwin had in his character of Pinkey.

Ann Eliza Meacham had been disappointed. She had ridden ten miles to Mount Tabor Church, one of Morton's principal appointments. No doubt Ann Eliza persuaded herself—she never had any trouble in persuading herself—that zeal for religious worship was the motive that impelled her to ride so far to church. But why, then, did she wish she had not come, when instead of the fine form and wavy locks of Brother Goodwin, she found in the pulpit only the located brother who was supplying his place in his absence at Kike's bedside? Why did she not go on to the afternoon appointment as she had intended? Certain

it is that when Ann Eliza left that little log church—
called *Mount* Tabor because it was built in a hollow,
perhaps—she felt unaccountably depressed. She considered it a spiritual struggle, a veritable hand to
hand conflict with Satan. She told the brethren and
sisters that she must return home, she even declined
to stay to dinner. She led the horse up to a log
and sprang into the saddle, riding away toward home
as rapidly as the awkward old natural pacer would
carry her. She was vexed that Morton should stay
away from his appointments on this part of his circuit to see anybody die. He might know that it
would be a disappointment to her. She satisfied herself, however, by picturing to her own imagination
the half-coldness with which she would treat Brother
Goodwin when she should meet him. She inly re-
hearsed the scene. But with most people there is a
more secret self, kept secret even from themselves.
And in her more secret self, Ann Eliza knew that
she would not dare treat Brother Goodwin coolly.
She had a sense of insecurity in her hold upon him.

Riding thus through the great forests of beech and
maple Ann Eliza had reached Cherry Run, only half
a mile from her aunt's house, and the old horse, scent-
ing the liberty and green grass of the pasture ahead
of him, had quickened his pace after crossing the
"run," when what should she see ahead but a man
in wolf-skin cap and long whiskers. She had heard of
Pinkey, the highwayman, and surely this must be he.
Her heart fluttered, she reined her horse, and the highwayman advanced.

"I haven't anything to give you. What do you want?"

"I don't want anything but to persuade you to do your duty," he said, seating himself by the side of the trail on a stump.

AN ACCUSING MEMORY.

"Let me go on," said Miss Meacham, frightened, starting her horse.

"Not yet," said Pinkey, seizing the bridle, "I want

to talk to you." And he sat down again, holding fast to her bridle-rein.

"What is it?" asked Ann Eliza, subdued by a sense of helplessness.

"Do you think, Sister Meacham," he said in a canting tone, "that you are doing just right? Is not there something in your life that is wrong? With all your praying, and singing, and shouting, you are a wicked woman."

Ann Eliza's resentment now took fire. "Who are you, that talk in this way? You are a robber, and you know it! If you don't repent you will be lost! Seek religion now. You will soon sin away your day of grace, and what an awful eternity—"

Miss Meacham had fallen into this hortatory vein, partly because it was habitual with her, and consequently easier in a moment of confusion than any other, and partly because it was her forte and she thought that these earnest and pathetic exhortations were her best weapons. But when she reached the words "awful eternity," Pinkey cried out sneeringly:

"Hold up, Ann Eliza! You don't run over me that way. I'm bad enough, God knows, and I'm afraid I shall find my way to hell some day. But if I do I expect to give you a civil good morning on my arrival, or welcome you if you get there after I do. You see I know all about you, and it's no use for you to glory-hallelujah me."

Ann Eliza did not think of anything appropriate to the occasion, and so she remained silent.

"I hear you have got young Goodwin on your

hooks, now, and that you mean to marry him against his will. Is that so?"

"No, it isn't. He proposed to me himself."

"O, yes! I suppose he did. You made him!"

"I didn't."

"I suppose not. You never did. Not even in Pennsylvania. How about young Harlow? Who made him?"

Ann Eliza changed color "Who are you?" she asked.

"And that fellow with dark hair, what's his name? The one you danced with down at Stevens's one night."

"What do you bring up all my old sins for?" asked Ann Eliza, weeping. "You know I have repented of all of them, and now that I am trying to lead a new life, and now that God has forgiven my sins and let me see the light of his reconciled countenance ——— "

"Stop, Ann Eliza," broke out Pinkey. "You sha'n't glory-hallelujah me in that style, confound you! Maybe God has forgiven you for driving Harlow to drink himself into tremens and the grave, and for sending that other fellow to the devil, and for that other thing, you know. You wouldn't like me to mention it. You've got a very pretty face, Ann Eliza,—you know you have. But Brother Goodwin don't love you. You entangled him; you know you did. Has God forgiven you for that, yet? Don't you think you'd better go to the mourners' bench next time yourself, instead of talking to the mourners as if you were an angel?

Come, Ann Eliza, look at yourself and see if you can sing glory-hallelujah. Hey?"

" Let me go," plead the young woman, in terror.

" Not yet, you angelic creature. Now that I come to think of it, piety suits your style of feature. Ann Eliza, I want to ask you one question before we part, to meet down below, perhaps. If you are so pious, why can't you be honest? Why can't you tell Preacher Goodwin what you left Pennsylvania for? Why the devil don't you let him know beforehand what sort of a horse he 's getting when he invests in you? Is it pious to cheat a man into marrying you, when you know he would n't do it if he knew the whole truth? Come now, you talk a good deal about the ' bar of God,' what do you think will become of such a swindle as you are, at the bar of God?"

" You are a wicked man," cried she, " to bring up the sins that I have put behind my back. Why should I talk with—with Brother Goodwin or anybody about them?"

For Ann Eliza always quieted her conscience by reasoning that God's forgiveness had made the unpleasant facts of her life as though they were not. It was very unpleasant, when she had put down her memory entirely upon certain points, to have it march up to her from without, wearing a wolf-skin cap and false whiskers, and speaking about the most disagree able subjects.

" Ann Eliza, I thought maybe you had a conscience, but you don't seem to have any. You are totally depraved, I believe, if you do love to sing and shout and pray. Now, when a preacher cannot get a man to be good by talking at his conscience, he talks damnation to him. But you think you have managed to get round on the blind side of God, and I don't suppose you are afraid of hell itself. So, as conscience and perdition won't touch you, I'll try something else. You are going to write a note to Preacher Goodwin and let him off. I am going to carry it."

"I won't write any such a note, if you shoot me!"

"You are n't afraid of gunpowder. You think you'd sail into heaven straight, by virtue of your experiences. I am not going to shoot you, but here is a pencil and a piece of paper. You may write to Goodwin, or I shall. If I write I will put down a truthful history of all Ann Eliza Meacham's life, and I shall be quite particular to tell him why you left Pennsylvania and came out here to evangelize the wilderness, and play the mischief with your heavenly blue eyes. But, if you write, I'll keep still."

"I'll write, then," she said, in trepidation.

"You'll write now, honey," replied her mysterious tormentor, leading the horse up to the stump.

Ann Eliza dismounted, sat down and took the pencil. Her ingenious mind immediately set itself to devising some way by which she might satisfy the man who was so strangely acquainted with her life, and yet keep a sort of hold upon the young preacher. But the man stood behind her and said, as she began, "Now write what I say. I don't care how you open. Call him any sweet name you please. But you'd better say 'Dear Sir.'"

Ann Eliza wrote: "Dear Sir."

"Now say: 'The engagement between us is broken off. It is my fault, not yours.'"

"I won't write that."

"Yes, you will, my pious friend. Now, Ann Eliza, you 've got a nice face; when a man once gets in love with you he can't quite get out. I suppose I will feel tender toward you when we meet to part no more, down below. I was in love with you once."

"Who are you?"

"O, that don't matter! I was going to say that if I had n't been in love with your blue eyes once I would n't have taken the trouble to come forty miles to get you to write this letter. I was only a mile away from Brother Goodwin, as you call him, when I heard that you had victimized him. I could have sent him a note. I came over here to save you from the ruin you deserve. I would have told him more than the people in Pennsylvania ever knew. Come, my dear, scribble away as I say, or I will tell him and everybody else what will take the music out of your love-feast speeches in all this country."

With a tremulous hand Ann Eliza wrote, reflecting that she could send another note after this and tell Brother Goodwin that a highwayman who entertained an insane love for her had met her in a lonely spot and extorted this from her. She handed the note to Pinkey.

"Now, Ann Eliza, you 'd better ask God to forgive this sin, too. You may pray and shout till you die. I 'll never say anything—unless you open communication with preacher Goodwin again. Do that, and I 'll blow you sky-high."

"You are cruel, and wicked, and mean, and—"

"Come, Ann Eliza, you used to call me sweeter names than that, and you don't look half so fascinating when you 're mad as when you are talking heavenly. Good by, Miss Meacham." And with that Pinkey went into a thicket and brought forth his own horse and rode away, not on the road but through the woods.

If Ann Eliza could have guessed which one of her many lovers this might be she would have set about forming some plan for circumventing him. But the mystery was too much for her. She sincerely loved Morton, and the bitter cup she had given to others had now come back to her own lips. And with it came a little humility. She could not again forget her early sins so totally. She looked to see them start out of the bushes by the wayside at her.

After this recital it is not necessary that I should tell you what Lewis Goodwin told his brother that night as they strolled in the woods.

At midnight Lewis left home, where he could not stay longer with safety. The war with Great Britain had broken out and he joined the army at Chillicothe under his own name, which was his best disguise. He was wounded at Lundy's Lane, and wrote home that he was trying to wipe the stain off his name. He afterward moved West and led an honest life, but the memory of his wild youth never ceased to give him pain. Indeed nothing is so dangerous to a reformed sinner as forgetfulness.

CHAPTER XXXVI.

GETTING THE ANSWER.

WHEN Patty went down to strain the milk on the morning after her return, the hope of some deliverance through Lewis Goodwin had well-nigh died out. If he had had anything to communicate, Morton would not have delayed so long to come to see her. But, standing there as of old, in the moss-covered spring-house, she was, in spite of herself, dreaming dreams of Morton, and wondering whether she could have misunderstood the hint that Lewis Goodwin, while he was yet Pinkey, had dropped. By the time the first crock was filled with milk and adjusted to its place in the cold current, she had recalled that morning of nearly three years before, when she had resolved to forsake father and mother and cleave to Morton; by the time the second crock had been neatly covered with its clean block she thought she could almost hear him, as she had heard him singing on that morning :

> " Ghaist nor bogle shalt thou fear,
> Thou 'rt to love and heaven sae dear,
> Nocht of ill may come thee near,
> My bonnie dearie."

Both she and Morton had long since, in accordance

with the Book of Discipline, given up "singing those songs that do not tend to the glory of God," but she felt a longing to hear Morton's voice again, assuring her of his strong protection, as it had on that morning three years ago. Meanwhile, she had filled all the

AT THE SPRING-HOUSE AGAIN.

crocks, and now turned to pass out of the low door when she saw, standing there as he had stood on that other morning, Morton Goodwin. He was more manly, more self-contained, than then. Years of discipline had ripened them both. He stepped back and let her emerge into the light; he handed her that note which Pinkey had dictated to Ann Eliza, and which Patty read :

"REV. MORTON GOODWIN:

"*Dear Sir*—The engagement between us is broken off. It is my fault and not yours.

"ANN E. MEACHAM."

"It must have cost her a great deal," said Patty, in pity. Morton loved her better for her first unselfish thought.

He told her frankly the history of the engagement; and then he and Patty sat and talked in a happiness so great that it made them quiet, until some one came to call her, when Morton walked up to the house to renew his acquaintance with the invalid and mollified Captain Lumsden.

"Faix, Moirton," said Brady, afterward, when he came to understand how matters stood, "you 've got the answer in the book. It 's quare enough. Now, 'one and one is two' is aisy enough, but 'one and one is one' makes the hardest sum iver given to anybody. You 've got it, and I 'm glad of it. May ye niver conjugate the varb 'to love' anyways excipt prisent tinse, indicative mood, first parson, plural number, 'we love.' I don't keer ef ye add the futur' tinse, and say, 'we will love,' nor ef ye put in the parfect and say, 'we have loved,' but may ye always stick fast to first parson, plural number, prisint tinse, indicative mood, active v'ice ! "

Morton returned to Jenkinsville circuit in some

P

trepidation. He feared that the old brethren would blame him more than ever. But this time he found himself the object of much sympathy. Ann Eliza had forestalled all gossip by renewing her engagement with the very willing Bob Holston, who chuckled a great deal to think how he had "cut out" the preacher, after all. And when Brother Magruder came to understand that he had not understood Morton's case at all, and to understand that he never should be able to understand it, he thought to atone for any mistake he might have made by advising the bishop to send Brother Goodwin to the circuit that included Hissawachee. And Morton liked the appointment better than Magruder had expected. Instead of living with his mother, as became a dutiful son, he soon installed himself for the year at the house of Captain Lumsden, in the double capacity of general supervisor of the moribund man's affairs and son-in-law.

There rise before me, as I write these last lines, visions of circuits and stations of which Morton was afterward the preacher-in-charge, and of districts of which he came to be presiding elder. Are not all of these written in the Book of the Minutes of the Conferences? But the silent and unobtrusive heroism of Patty and her brave and life-long sacrifices are recorded nowhere but in the Book of God's Remembrance.

THE END.